Persell

BINDING Law

Sin City Gigolos, Book 3

For all the women whose children grew beneath another woman's heart but found their home in yours.

Your families are beautiful. You are beautiful.

Chapter One

When Ryker Martinez opened the hotel room door after the delicate but deliberate knock, he raised an eyebrow.

A pleasant surprise.

The woman on the other side of the door wore a dress that hugged each curve. Her long hair cascaded down her back. Her eyes were glazed with lust. She was beautiful, and her gaze raking over his body as though she already had plans for it promised paradise.

Just hit the gigolo jackpot. Leaning on the door jamb with a forearm propped at head height—the perfect pose to highlight the flex of his chest beneath his thin button-down—he returned her bold perusal, starting from her sexy peep-toe shoes and ending with eye contact. "Well, hello, *querida.*"

His client met his gaze boldly. "Hello." She only held his eye contact for a moment before devouring his body again. Her gaze traveled slowly down his chest to the front of his slacks. He didn't have to glance down himself to know that his quickly stiffening cock was pushing against his meticulously pressed pants. She nibbled her bottom lip and sighed in a way that made her large breasts press against that dress he'd already fallen in love with. Her gaze met his again. "It's a pleasure to meet you, Ryker."

He grinned. *Oh, I will be enjoying tonight.*

The bold ones always made it worth his while.

He opened the door wider and stepped to the side. "Won't you come in?" He murmured the words, releasing the usually tight hold he kept on his accent now that he was with a client.

The Latin lover experience or the relationship experience—those were what they always paid for when they hired Ryker Martinez.

The first time his agency had billed him as the Latin lover, he'd nearly cracked a molar gnashing his teeth. But pushing back on using his Puerto Rican heritage as a selling point had seemed irrational in light of the fact women paid him for sex. Like, what, was he going to say, *You can forget I'm human and use me for my body, but not because it's brown?*

He couldn't afford to be so particular.

"*Gracias,*" she murmured back, her northeastern accent putting harsh angles to the vowels.

As she walked past him, he purposefully leaned in.

She stopped, her lovely brown eyes dilating as she gazed up into his face. Reaching up slowly, he crooked his pointer finger beneath her chin and brushed the pad of his thumb along her jaw. He drew in a slow breath, allowing his eyes to go hooded; she would assume he was taking in her scent and liking it. As it turned out, she did smell nice—not always the case in his line of work. Dipping his head, he pressed a soft, lingering kiss to her cheek.

She sucked in an audible breath, and he could feel sudden tension enter her body from the slight touch he maintained on her jawline.

A reaction he'd planned on.

He pulled his lips from her skin, nuzzled her hair from her ear, and whispered, "It's a pleasure to meet you, too."

She shivered, and he heard a nearly inaudible moan sound in the back of her throat.

He escorted her with a hand to her lower back the rest of the way into the room. Because he knew she'd like it, he made sure his palm was scandalously low, the beginning curve of her ass pressing against his pinky. Shutting the door behind her, he clasped her hand and pulled her into a slow spin so she was facing him once more.

"Tell me, *corazón*—" He lifted the hand he held to his lips, pressing a kiss across her knuckles. Her gaze was rapt on his mouth. "What is it that you're wanting tonight?"

She licked her lips. At the same time, he noticed she pressed her thighs together beneath the short dress she'd worn.

Already aroused. He'd barely had to touch her.

"I need to come," she whispered in a husky voice. "Hard. Three times."

He wanted to cock an eyebrow again. *Oddly specific.* But who was he to judge? He'd certainly delivered on odder requests. "That will not be a problem." He stepped into her personal space, and her head tipped back as her hazy gaze stayed locked on his lips. "But are you sure we want to stop at three?" He brushed his thumb across her knuckles as he brought them to his mouth again. "We could go for a much, much higher number."

Her own lips parted as the tip of his tongue darted out, dabbing between her fingers. She sucked in a breath and swayed toward him. "Three…might be underestimating things."

His lips curled. "That's my girl."

Her eyes dilated at that. Women always liked it when he got proprietary, no matter how superficial it was.

He paused in the middle of kissing her hand as her fingers tightened, indicating she was getting ready to act. It was his job to make sure whatever she tried was successful. "Something you want to say, *querida?*"

She nibbled her plump bottom lip, and it immediately swelled. "Not quite," she murmured. Changing their grip, she lowered their joined hands. His hint of a smile went full-blown as he realized she was going to put his hand on her body.

He had all the skills he needed to know exactly where this woman—where *any* woman—needed to be touched. But, thank God, this woman seemed more than willing to take all guesswork out of the equation.

She pressed his curled fingers against the front of her dress. Directly at the apex of her thighs.

Her sex sent waves of heat cascading over his hand. She was already so aroused, he'd barely have to touch her to set her off. *Maybe I should get started on the first of those three right now?*

What a pleasant idea.

As soon as she released his hand, he rotated it, cupping her as much as her tight skirt would allow.

She rocked to her toes. "Oh, God, yes." Her eyes closed. "It's been too long."

He *tsk*ed. "Now who would let an angel like you go untended for long?" He began edging her skirt up with small movements of his fingers. "What a shame."

Her eyes opened, and they were already unfocused. "I agree."

He had her skirt bunched before she realized what he'd been doing, just as he'd intended. He heard her gasp as she felt the first waft of air over her sex. Gripping her skirt in his palm, he extended two fingers, finding...

She moaned.

Holy shit. She was completely bare. His fingers slid against her aroused flesh. "Mmm, no panties, *mi corazón?*" He stroked between the lips of her pussy, the tip of his middle finger finding her clitoris. "Perhaps not so much an angel after all, hmmm?"

"No...no." She shook her head, her long hair falling over her shoulders and down her breasts. "Not an angel—Oh, *shit,* I'm not going to last long."

Best client ever. There hadn't been that many good nights lately. This one promised to make up for all of them. "Don't fight it, sweet," he crooned, stroking her with a surer touch. "Let me make you come."

"*Yes.*" She reached out for him, gripping the lapels of his jacket with both hands. "Yes, *please.*"

With his free hand, he reached up, snagging her hand and weaving their fingers together. "Feel it for me, beautiful." He stroked again, and at the same time, he raised her hand to kiss it. His gaze flicked down for just a moment, taking in the slim fingers he prepared to kiss and nibble as he sent her over the edge.

He froze.

A distinct tan line traversed her ring finger. The ring finger of her left hand.

He had to lock up his facial features to keep his lips from curling in disgust. Without preamble, he dropped her hand. He barely kept himself from snatching his fingers from between her legs, instead, easing them away. She gasped as her eyes opened. Her eyes were wide. Confused. Her skirt was still rucked up around her thighs, and he could see her naked, aroused sex.

His gaze flicked from her body to her ring finger again, and his stomach lurched. He gritted his teeth and took a deep, calming breath. "You're married."

The immediate tinge to her cheeks was all the confirmation he needed.

Fuck, sometimes he hated this job.

I always hate this job.

He straightened his spine. Despite how unsavory he found infidelity—it was, after all, his one and only hard limit— he had a reputation to maintain. He couldn't be rude, no matter how much this woman deserved it. He was on thin ice at the agency anyway after the last married client he refused to sleep with complained. He couldn't afford another disgruntled client. Forcing himself to move, he reached out and smoothed her skirt back down her thighs.

She frowned. "What are you—?"

"*Florecita*, I'm afraid we are done here. I do not take married women as clients."

The haze in her eyes vanished. She reached for him. Luckily, he didn't have to sidestep to avoid her touch, because she dropped her hand before it made contact. "No, no," she said, the mildest tint of panic tinging her voice. "It's nothing like that. You don't understand. My husband and I—"

He tensed, knowing what she would say next: *Aren't in love anymore.*

"—aren't in love anymore." Her eyes begged him to understand. Her body language begged him for something else entirely.

He wanted to pinch the bridge of his nose. *Aren't in love anymore.* He bit his tongue to keep from saying *that doesn't matter.* Or *it's your fault for letting feelings dictate your marriage in the first place.* Instead, he smiled. "I'm sorry, *querida*." He could advise her to call the same number she'd used to book him. One of the other guys would not care that she was married, especially since she was so beautiful. Hell, six months ago, Ryker would have texted

Gage, before his buddy met Cassidy. They'd often stepped in for each other.

But besides the fact that he didn't want anyone at the agency knowing he'd turned down another client, he wasn't going to *help* her cheat on her husband, for Christ's sake.

Overreacting again, Ryker?

Oh, he was definitely overreacting. He knew it. But this was a sore spot for him.

The woman in front of him had exactly what Ryker wanted—hell, what thousands of people wanted—and he knew he'd never get it. People didn't marry gigolos and start families. They fucked gigolos and paid them when they were done. And here was this woman discarding what she had like it was nothing.

Okay, granted, Ryker wanted kids more than he wanted marriage—kids were fucking awesome. Marriage, in his experience—experiences like this one right now, as a matter of fact—was not so awesome. But he was damn well going to provide a stable home for his kids one day, and, in his opinion, that required parents who were well and truly committed to each other but who kept their emotions in check. No falling in and out of love like a sap. Marriage was commitment. End of story. That commitment is what kept children from the hellish childhood Ryker himself had endured.

Did this woman have children? He shuddered at the thought. God help them if she did. She seemed fully prepared to ruin their lives for a paid fuck.

Turning his back, he walked to the door and opened it once more. He carefully avoided saying anything else to her, lest one of the things he was holding back with all his might slipped through the leash.

Her lips parted as she gazed at the open door. "You're really going to make me go? Because I'm *married?*"

Again, he said nothing, even though it'd just become apparent that this was going to turn ugly. The woman's flashing eyes screamed *Warning: Insulted! Prepare for lashing out!*

She planted her hands on her hips, those flashing eyes narrowing.

And, here we go.

Her upper lip curled. "You're a hooker, for fuck's sake! You think you have some sort of moral high ground here?"

God damn it, he really hated this job. He may not have the moral high ground, but he certainly had better manners.

He stepped to the table just inside the door and silently collected his keys and billfold. Turning back toward the door, he paused only to say, "The room's all yours. Enjoy your evening."

Her slight blush escalated to rage red as she realized she wasn't going to get a fucking or provoke a fight tonight. Her lips pinched into a tight little line, all color leeching from them. A second later, however, they opened once more. "I'll make you regret this, you fucking—"

He closed the door, cutting off whichever insult had surely been the start of an avalanche of them. Not willing to gamble on whether she was a chaser who would fling open the door and try to continue matters, he beat feet, barely keeping himself from breaking into a jog.

When the elevator delivered him to the lobby and he reached the glass doors without further incident, he allowed himself to exhale.

He smoothed fingers through the curls that had fallen over his forehead, raking them back into place.

Ryker Martinez, he promised himself solemnly as he fit his key into his car door and flipped the lock, *you will not have to do this forever.*

As he buckled himself in and steered his car toward the dump of an apartment he called home, he couldn't help thinking that, surely, forever was how long it had already lasted.

Chapter Two

As Charlotte Moore hung up the phone, she shook her head. "You didn't really expect this one to turn out differently, Mr. Grabow," she muttered to her empty office. "Surely, you didn't."

The man was going to single-handedly pay her salary in the very near future if he did not stop marrying.

Not that I'm complaining.

She pulled Mr. Grabow's file closer—the file she'd started ten years ago when he'd divorced his first wife, continued two years ago when he'd divorced his second, and was now revisiting as he divorced his third.

Third marriages had a seventy-three percent divorce rate. She'd told him as much when he'd contacted her for the prenup. Her admonishments had, apparently, fallen on deaf ears.

Again, not that I'm complaining.

She dotted a period on the yellow legal pad with a bit more force than absolutely necessary and closed the file. For now. Mediation would begin tomorrow, so she would be scouring every inch of the notes she'd just taken as soon as she returned from lunch—something she usually didn't have to do with her steel-trap mind. But as she'd jotted down Mr. Grabow's myriad complaints and heartaches during their phone conversation, she'd been...distracted.

Even now, she blushed at the internal admission. Charlotte Moore, marriage and family attorney and divorce specialist, worked with all her being to make sure she did not get *distracted*. She couldn't afford to be. Not when she was gunning for partner.

And therein lay the source of her distraction.

The entire office had been buzzing when she'd arrived at the firm of Miller, Smith, and Lee promptly at nine o'clock this morning. Smith's receptionist had told Miller's, who had told Lee's, who had passed it on to everyone else that Smith was planning to retire this year.

Charlotte pressed her knees together beneath her desk. *This year!* Much sooner than Charlotte or anyone else had anticipated.

There was going to be a new partner.

It had to be her.

There was a noise at her door, and Charlotte found herself leaping into action, fruitlessly rearranging papers on her desk as though she'd been caught in the middle of some monumental task instead of going down the thought rabbit hole on the job.

After a suitable amount of time had passed wherein she'd appeared busy, Charlotte raised her gaze.

Immediately her spine relaxed. *Just Mark.*

"Heya, Charlotte," he said, swinging into her office and collapsing into the chair in front of her desk as though his skeleton had had a sudden and severe systems failure.

She pressed her lips together as she stared at him over the top of her glasses. Her insubordinate clerk. She tried to frown disapprovingly at him, but he stared at her with his guileless, blue eyes, that dimple of his making an appearance in his chin as he gave her a lopsided grin, and she felt her lips twitch and lose their form. He was just so young. Practically a puppy.

"Sorry," he said, taking the rest of the starch out of her frown. "Good morning, Ms. Moore."

"Good morning, Mr. Williams." She returned to shuffling her papers, but not before she caught his grimace at her use of his surname. For some reason, the man-child resisted formalities with every iota of his young, hipster verve. "Are you off to lunch?" He always checked in before heading out with the other clerks while Charlotte ate her take-out lunch at her desk.

"In a bit." He leaned forward in his chair. "I wanted to talk to you first."

Charlotte's hands paused amid refiling a closed-case folder. *Oh, dear.* This didn't bode well. No one ever voluntarily talked to her. She warily raised her gaze again. Mark was still sitting casually in the chair, but there was a shrewd gleam to his eye that put her on edge.

"To me?" she asked.

He raised both eyebrows. "Have you heard the gossip?"

Despite herself, Charlotte's heart gave an extra hard *thump*. She attempted another frown. "You know I abhor gossip." Mostly because whenever it was about her, it...*hurt*. No one had anything nice to say about Charlotte.

Outside of her work.

Which is all that matters.

"You won't abhor this gossip." Mark waggled his eyebrows.

To encourage him or... She sighed, giving up the fight before it'd really begun. "What have you heard?"

He propped his elbows on his knees, his eyes sparkling. "There's going to be a new partner. Smith is leaving."

She wanted to roll her eyes. She'd compromised her standards for *that*? She reached for a stack of papers to her left. "Of course I know that."

He grinned. "Did you know there's already a list of three potential replacements?"

Her fingers clenched, crumpling the papers she held.

When she looked at Mark again, he'd relaxed everything from his posture to his facial expression, triumph oozing from every pore. "Hadn't heard that yet, huh?"

She cleared her throat. "Oh?" She looked down at her hands in an attempt to appear casual but couldn't hold the pose for long. Her gaze sprang back toward Mark's direction. "A list?" *Please let me be on it. Please, please, please.*

"Rumor mill says Carter," Mark ticked off one finger, "Wesson," another finger, "and…"

She couldn't help it; she closed her eyes.

"You."

Her eyes opened again. Mark was grinning—and not his usual, impish grin. She was terrible at social cues, even after all these years of meticulous study. Was his grin friendly? Or was he laughing at her?

Rabbit hole again. She blinked. The list. Right. Carter, Wesson, and— "Me?"

"You," he confirmed.

An unfamiliar feeling filled her chest and began to rise. What was this? Hope? Before she could school herself to know better, that hope traveled to her lips, which curled into their own smile, making Mark's broaden.

But then his grin disappeared far more suddenly than it had appeared. "There's more, though."

Of course there is. There always was. "Go on."

Mark fidgeted in his seat. "They told me there's some concern over naming you partner."

She braced herself. It didn't help. There was a searing burn in the general region of her heart. She didn't have to ask who *they* were. It'd be almost everybody.

I haven't tried to be liked. She hadn't tried to earn anyone's approval but her parents' since elementary school, when she learned she would be routinely rejected because of her inability to know what was appropriate in any given situation. As an adult, she had something better than being liked. She had the respect of others. That was worth a thousand friendships. She used her work time to *work*, thank you very much.

Speaking of which, it was time to kill this conversation. "Yes, well, thank you very much, Mr. Williams. Enjoy your lunch."

"Oh, no, Charlotte." Mark leaned back in his seat and shook his head. "No dodging. I want you to hear this."

Aghast, she looked his direction, not quite able to meet his gaze, though she'd practiced looking others in the eye since high school when her classmates had made it clear that not doing so made her "odd."

"Excuse me?" she asked.

"Because, I think you're exactly what this firm needs in a partner. You've never lost a case—"

She opened her mouth.

"—and I know you're about to say *nobody wins in a divorce case*," Mark said louder, cutting off her protest before she could voice it. "And you're just proving my point."

She pursed her lips. "Mr. Williams, what I do is not extraordinary. It's merely playing the odds. Knowing the law, knowing the statistics, and studying the judge's decision patterns. It's a simple algorithm. The outcome of any case is never a mystery."

He stared at her for several seconds. "Okay, no one else in this firm thinks that way. This firm needs you, and it'd be tragic if you let a few personality challenges stand between you and what I know is a very important goal of yours."

It wasn't until the tip of her tongue started drying out that she realized her mouth was agape again. This was highly illogical. Subordinates did not talk to their bosses this way. And even she knew it was extremely uncouth to accuse someone of *personality challenges*. Didn't he know that? Unfortunately, her mouth was too dry for her to tell him in case he didn't know. She made an odd, croaking noise in the back of her throat.

"Now," Mark continued, clearly unfazed by how inappropriate he was being, "we both know Carter and Wesson are part of the good ol' boys club that needs to be shaken up around here. Beyond that, though, they're extremely personable." He gave her a pointed look. "You need all the leg up you can get."

Extremely personable. If there were ever a phrase that described the opposite of Charlotte's personality, there it was. As much as she wished it weren't so, Mark had a point. She braced herself. "All right," she said slowly. "What have *they* said?"

Mark narrowed his eyes as though he were trying to determine if she really wanted him to continue. She waved him on impatiently. He sighed. "I believe the term I've heard is *cold fish.*"

She couldn't help it; she winced.

He wasn't done yet. "They think you distance your clients."

Charlotte frowned. "Distance?" That was a good thing! Distance is what made her good at her job. Emotions clouded judgment—and there was plenty of high emotion in divorce court. She needed to be sharp. She opened her mouth to tell him just that.

"No, distance is not a good thing," Mark said.

She closed her mouth again, tempted to glare at the man. How did he always do that? Read people like they were wide-open books? "Why ever not?"

"Because, when you're a partner, relationships are just as important as everything else."

She narrowed her eyes. Drat. She didn't like it when other people had valid points.

He leaned forward. "By the way, what's your secret?"

Her heart stuttered. "Secret?" She forced a laugh.

"Yeah." He waved a hand through the air. "Working so well in a field revolving around relationships without having one of your own."

Now, her palms were sweaty. No relationship of her own. Was that a snag of some kind? Oh, no. Did the partners wonder about her lack of a relationship? Think it was a stumbling block in her ability to relate to her clients? How in the world would she convince them otherwise if they did? She would never marry and have children. For one, relationships were a challenge. She didn't do things she couldn't excel at.

And for two, the idea of having children terrified her. She was too dedicated to her career. What is she was a bad—

"Have I ever told you that my little sister is on the spectrum?" Mark asked as he straightened his wristwatch and looked down at it with singular focus.

Charlotte froze. Mark glanced up at her.

He knows.

She tried to swallow, but it felt like there was a golf ball lodged at the base of her throat.

She wasn't ashamed of herself. Had grown out of that long ago. But her Asperger's was not something she advertised. She wanted to be successful based on actual merit, not "She does so well for someone *like that.*"

When she trusted the wrong people with this information, statements like that always followed. So, she didn't trust people with her diagnosis. Ever.

Mark was a horrible gossip. He would tell everyone. Ruin her here at the firm.

She could feel the golf ball in her throat rising. She placed her fingers over the imaginary bulge.

Deflect. Get him off this subject.

Her mouth opened. "It's a shame, really." *What is this you're saying? Stop yourself right now!* "My fiancé will be so disappointed I'm being passed over for partner due to something so silly."

Her lips parted.

Mark's brow furrowed but then immediately straightened. Then, his own lips parted.

Oh, no. Oh, no! She didn't have a fiancé! She didn't even have a *friend*, much less a lover, committed or otherwise.

"A fiancé?" Mark asked.

The words just kept coming. "That's right. I've already texted him this morning about the open spot for partner, and we're both so excited."

"Wait." Mark leaned forward. "You have a *fiancé?*"

"Mr. Williams, I am becoming offended."

Immediately, his hands shot up, palms out. "No offense intended, I assure you. I've just never heard you talk about him before."

Her brows drew together. "We're at work. Of course you haven't." If she *did* have a fiancé, she wouldn't discuss him when she was on the clock and should be devoting all her energy to her clients.

It was, apparently, such a Charlotte type of response, it seemed to solidify her asinine claim of having a fiancé, if Mark's suddenly wide eyes were any indication. "Wow." He rubbed the back of his neck with one palm. "Congratulations are in order, I guess. Charlotte Moore is getting married." He shook his head and raised his eyebrows. "Wow," he said again.

She glowered. "Go to lunch, Mr. Williams. Now."

He launched to his feet. "Yes, ma'am." He took a not nearly quick enough sideways step toward the door. "And, seriously, congratulations. This is great. For a lot of reasons."

For a lot of reasons. The words hung in the air between them, and she realized what she'd done in her moment of panic. Yes, she'd gotten Mark off of the subject of autism, but she'd made a mess for herself. Not only had she invented a fiancé, but she'd no doubt invented him to make a better impression with Miller and Lee. So that she'd look like a more desirable candidate.

It was incredibly unethical.

It was incredibly un-Charlotte.

Mark's back was to her as he reached the door. She had just enough time to call him back and correct matters—as embarrassing as such an admission would be.

"Mr. Williams!"

He paused. Turned. "Yes?"

She licked her lips. Opened her mouth. Nothing would come out. No *There's been a misunderstanding.* No *When I said* fiancé, *I really meant* friend José.

Nothing.

Mark's eyebrows rose again.

"H-have a good lunch," she said, her voice cracking.

"All right," he said slowly. When he exited the office, she saw him shake his head through the window next to the door, and she cringed.

The cringe took a turn toward shaking hands when she caught sight of Mark snagging one of the other clerks and engaging in a quick, close conversation that entailed several glances at her door, as though they were completely oblivious to the fact that she could see them gossiping about her.

Not oblivious. They just didn't care.

What had she done?

Her stomach roiled, and all thoughts of digging into the salad she'd picked up for lunch vanished.

What had she been thinking, telling Mark she had a fiancé?

Could have been worse. He could have been gossiping about your Asperger's.

But now, she had to figure this out. Truly, what was wrong with her? This was quite the pickle she'd gotten herself into.

She snatched a legal pad toward her and plucked a perfectly sharpened pencil from the holder on her desk. She always thought best this way: writing on a legal pad.

Think, Charlotte, think! What was she going to do to get out of this? Within the next five minutes, the entire office would think she was getting married.

At the top of the legal pad, she scrawled Fiancé Scenarios in flowing script. And then she began doing what she always did when she had a puzzle to solve: she'd write down each and every possibility, no matter how outrageous, and decide on one she could live with.

Right below the centered title, she made a dash and then wrote *Confess the truth to everybody.* Below that, she wrote *Fall in love immediately and get engaged.* Then the list really started rolling, and the items increased in their craziness: *Hire someone to be my fiancé; Tell everyone we broke up; Pretend the fiancé died in a fiery crash.*

When she reached the bottom of the legal pad, she paused and scanned through the list. With a sigh, she leaned back in her chair and tapped the eraser of her pencil against the legal pad.

She could only live with one of the scenarios. She'd tell Mark that she and her fiancé had broken up.

But she wouldn't tell him for a while. She had explicit experience with lies in her line of business. She knew which ones didn't work, like the one wife number three had told Mr. Grabow: *Oh, honey, he's just a friend.* Charlotte also knew which lies did work. *Oh honey, I'll always love you.* If she had any hope of convincing the office she'd truly had a fiancé, she couldn't suddenly invent their split. Everyone would be suspicious.

She pinched the bridge of her nose, disgusted with herself.

There was a cursory knock on her door, and before waiting for her to say *come in*, whoever had knocked opened it.

Her head shot up, a glare already shaping her eyes—no one came into her office without permission.

She sucked in a breath so hard she nearly coughed. "Mr. Lee!" The Lee of Miller, Smith, and Lee. Without thought, she swept the legal pad containing her list off the side of her desk where it would land in the trash can. Unfortunately, her sweeping arm also caught her can of pencils, her letter opener, and her cell phone.

Items went flying everywhere. A pencil even rolled to rest near Mr. Lee's expensive leather loafers. The legal pad did, however, land in the trash can with a cacophonous *thud*.

When the dust settled and she gathered her wits once more, Mr. Lee was looking down at the pencil right in front of his shoe. Slowly, his gaze rose to meet hers. "Is this a bad time, Charlotte?" he asked, the corner of his lips twitching.

She closed her eyes, pulling in a slow breath. She opened her eyes again, forcing a laugh that sounded just as awkward as she could have ever imagined. Like a cross between a hyena and a barn owl.

Mr. Lee's eyes widened.

She cleared her throat. "It's always a good time for you, sir." Much better. "What can I do for you?"

"Well," he said, striding toward the chair in front of her desk, "I'm sure you've heard by now that we're looking for a new partner." He stopped by the chair but did not sit in it, instead resting his hands on the back. He seemed to tower above her, and she had to crane her head back to maintain eye contact. "Smith is retiring."

"Oh, is he?" Should she stand, too? What was the proper protocol here? "How wonderful for him."

Mr. Lee made a noncommittal noise in the back of his throat. "Yes, well. I'm here to inform you that we're considering you for partner."

Despite knowing this was the case, she still felt a thrill so sharp in her chest it nearly hurt. She was going to laugh again, or something equally abhorrent. "That's great!" She shoved the words out of her mouth so quickly that they emerged at a near shout.

Mr. Lee barely stifled a wince. "I'm glad you think so," he said in a smooth voice. "Are you free tonight?"

Of course. She was always free. "Let me check my calendar, but I'm pretty sure it's open."

"Excellent," he said, as though he didn't suspect she was going home to her empty apartment tonight like she did every night. "We're having a little mixer this evening. Carter and Wesson, the other two candidates we're considering for partner, are bringing their wives. Miller and I will be there with our wives as well. Can you bring your fiancé? We'd like to get to know you—and him—a little better."

Her hand spasmed against the desktop, sending her palm scooting across the lacquered surface with an unpleasant squeak. "My f-fiancé?"

"Yes." He smiled. "We just heard the news. Congratulations, by the way."

She laughed again, and it was even worse this time. Mr. Lee, with all his smooth courtroom polish, wasn't even able to school his wince this time.

No! This couldn't be happening to her. What was she supposed to do? Her gaze slid to the barely visible corner of the legal pad as it protruded from the trash can. Her brain quickly scoured through her memories, trying to locate another scenario that would work right now. On such short notice, she could really only think of two: confess and most likely kiss partner goodbye or find a fiancé. Stat.

That first option wasn't really an option at all. This was her dream.

She cleared her throat, but the lump was back, and it didn't budge. "My fiancé. Of course. We'll both be there."

Mr. Lee's face cleared. "Wonderful. I'll have my secretary e-mail you the particulars, but you can go ahead and take off for the afternoon so you can get ready."

Her gaze flicked to the clock on her wall. It was only noon. She needed all afternoon to get ready? Just what kind of mixer was this? And why did anxiety always taste bitter? "Yes, that sounds great. I'll see you this evening."

But he was already walking out the door. He closed it behind him, and she sagged in her chair. "What am I going to do?"

Her cell phone chimed from somewhere on the floor, making her jump. She lurched to the side, spotting it under the corner of her desk. Nearly upending her chair in the process, she leaned over and reclaimed her phone.

She had a new e-mail. As she opened it, she discovered it was from Lee's secretary. "Already?" It contained the address and time for tonight's "mixer." Dress was noted as *black-tie formal.*

Right. So, she needed a fiancé and a gown, all in the next few hours. She found both prospects equally intimidating and impossible.

Look at what you've done to your life in a handful of minutes.

This is why it was so important to divorce oneself from emotion. Chaos and emotion were always bedfellows, and she could not afford chaos.

With a sigh, she straightened the items she'd sent flying all over kingdom come, gathered her laptop bag, and retreated. She'd take a cab to a dress shop so she could do what she did best to help rectify the fiancé issue: research.

Everything could be solved with a little research.

Walking past her Cadillac, she made her way down the block until she saw a cab drive by. With a simple raise of her hand, she secured her ride.

She climbed into the back seat.

"Where to?" the cabby asked.

Charlotte waved a hand in the air. "I need a gown."

The cab driver gave her a look through the rearview mirror, but without another word, he pulled back onto the road and started heading, apparently, somewhere she could purchase black-tie formal attire.

Pulling out her phone, she opened her Google app. Normally, she did voice recognition when she conducted searches, but her question was…delicate. She didn't need any more curious looks from the driver.

Into the search box, she typed *I need a date.*

The first five hits all had the word *escort* in the website name.

An escort? That was perfect! Why hadn't she thought of that? She clicked on the first link that wasn't an ad, and a beautiful website popped up.

Already, she was breathing easier. What a simple solution. She'd hire an escort to pretend to be her fiancé, and after she secured partner, she would tell Mark that she and the fiancé had broken up. He'd spread the word. Done and done.

She scrolled through the website, scanning the escort company's mission statement—because escorts had a mission, apparently—and looking for the company's phone number.

Some text at the bottom caught her attention, however. She slowed down. Re-read.

We serve some of the most prestigious men and women in the world: CEOs, lawyers, educators, and more!

Lawyers. Oh, no. Other lawyers used this escort service? She couldn't have that. Maybe it was a fluke? Maybe only this particular escort service catered to lawyers? She closed the website and clicked on a new one.

Same thing.

Another website: same thing.

Escorts and lawyers apparently went together like carrots and hummus. She never would have guessed that in a thousand years. If she hired an escort, there was a chance that he'd be recognized either tonight at the mixer or in pictures later if they were shared at the office.

She glanced at the clock on her phone. Drat. She'd wasted nearly ten minutes on this! Ten minutes she didn't have. She went back to her Google search, her fingers trembling slightly now. Below the first five hits pertaining to escorts, a different word caught her attention.

Gigolo.

"As in prostitute?" she whispered in the back of the cab.

There was a snort from the driver's seat, and Charlotte felt her cheeks heat. She didn't dignify the sound with a glance. Maybe if they both just pretended she hadn't said the word *prostitute*, it would disappear from real-life occurrences.

Could she hire a gigolo to pretend to be her fiancé? One thing was for certain: there was a better chance her circle wouldn't know him. And if he *was* recognized, who would willingly admit a gigolo looked familiar?

It could work.

Pulling in a slow breath, she wrapped all the courage she could manage around herself and clicked on the link.

Immediately, she winced as techno music filled the back seat, originating from the website, which had video of two men gyrating to the beat in very, very tiny underwear.

She jabbed at the unforgiving glass of her phone so hard, the knuckle of her finger popped. But she managed to exit the website. Bracing herself, she glanced up at the driver. He was smirking at her in the mirror.

"Big night tonight?" he asked.

She narrowed her eyes. She may be embarrassed as hell, but she wasn't going to let him know. "How much farther to the dress shop?"

Her voice was just terse enough to get that smirk to vanish. "About ten more minutes." When she simply stared at him, he added, "Ma'am."

That was more like it.

All right, ten more minutes. She redirected her attention to her phone. This time, however, she made sure to lower her media volume to zero. She clicked on the next website, and when it loaded, she frowned.

The website was…classy. If that wasn't an oxymoron—classy gigolo website—she didn't know what was. It didn't look much different from the escort sites she'd visited. She scrolled through the entire website, and by the time the cab pulled over in front of a dress shop she hadn't known existed, she'd made a decision: she'd call this place.

She paid the driver, tipping him generously but not generously enough to be memorable, and stepped onto the curb, securing her laptop bag over her shoulder.

Before she could lose her courage, she pressed the phone number link. Immediately, it started ringing. Just as quickly, she hung up.

"What am I doing?" She looked around, saw the sidewalk was empty, and repeated the question, louder this time. "What am I doing!"

This was truly the strangest, most ill-advised plan she'd ever devised in one of her moments of panic. Ever. This had bad news written all over it, and even if, by some miracle, she escaped this unscathed, she was still behaving unethically.

She *hated* that.

But do you hate it more than the idea of losing partner?

She stiffened. One moment later, she pressed *redial*.

She fiddled with the top button of her blouse as the phone rang, and rang, and—

"Hello," a smoldering voice said in her ear.

That voice gnashed against her nerves, sending every single one into annoyance mode. Everything from his tone to the implicit promise of paradise dripped with lies. She should have never placed this call.

"Hello?" the voice asked before she could hang up, this time in a more normal tone.

This more honest voice made her hesitate. Before she knew what she'd decided, she was saying, "Yes…um, hi?"

"Oh, hello, sweetheart." The fallacious smolder was back, and Charlotte gripped the phone so hard, it creaked. "What can I do for you?"

Sex oozed from that question. Sex and lies. The reason every relationship was doomed from the start. Charlotte recoiled. "I…made a mistake." She pinched the bridge of her nose. She couldn't go forward with this. But what was she going to do? "I need a fiancé."

"Hold on a second," the voice said.

"No, wait—"

"We got somebody who wants the relationship experience here!" The guy had obviously pulled the phone from his mouth and was shouting this.

Charlotte's lips parted. "*What?* No! I said I made a mistake." She shook her head. The relationship experience? That was directly not what she wanted. "I'm hanging up now—"

"Hello?"

All thought of speaking flew from her lips, leaving her mouth simultaneously parched and producing too much drool. The new voice that crossed the line was nothing like the man's who had first answered. That one simple *hello* felt…genuine. Honest in a way Charlotte had rarely experienced. It put her at ease, but at the same time, goose bumps erupted all over her skin. Her nipples tightened, chafing against her utilitarian bra. Things that had never happened before at the sound of a man's voice.

"Um—"

A husky chuckle filled her ear, and she shivered. Actually *shivered.* "Hello?" he asked again.

"Hello," she blurted breathlessly.

"Ah, there you are, *querida.* I was hoping I hadn't lost you."

Why did her legs feel weak? As though she was going to sink to the sidewalk at any moment. "You didn't lose me."

"I'm grateful. What can I do for you?"

It was the same question the first man had asked, and, like the first time she'd heard it, it was full of innuendo. This time, however, she was not repelled. For one, it wasn't just sex that was dripping from this man's voice; it was promise. Whatever she wanted, he would deliver. With a smile.

Charlotte's brain liquefied. *What are words?* Why was she even calling again? Oh, yeah. "I'm supposed to be married."

There was a sudden silence on the other end of the phone.

Charlotte frowned. "Hello?"

"I don't sleep with married women." The words were clipped.

"No! No, I'm not married. Don't hang up!" She was shocked by the desperation tinging her voice. When a man walking past slowed mid-stride and glanced her direction, she realized she'd yelled. She turned her back to him, hoping he would go on his way. She lowered her voice. "And this is not about sex. Not even close. Please." She closed her eyes. "I need your help. I…messed up."

There was another silence on the other end. This time, however, it was much shorter than the first. "*Querida*, why don't you tell me what's happened. From the top."

He hadn't hung up! She didn't know why that felt like a victory, or why she so desperately wanted him to stay on the line in the first place, but… Charlotte peeked around to make sure no one could overhear her again. She was alone. Releasing a breath, she said, "I'm going to be passed over for a promotion because I'm not like everyone else. So…I told the office gossip I have a fiancé so I would appear more personable." She bit back a groan. Yep, it sounded just as bad out loud as she thought it would.

"Are you—?" There was a scoffing noise on the line. "Passed over because you don't fit inside some sort of box? Jesus, is it 1950?"

Oh, and now I've gone and fallen in love. "Exactly!" She threw her free hand in the air. "It's outrageous!"

"It is. Good for you for sticking it to them."

She nibbled her bottom lip. "Except now, my fiancé and I have been invited to a mixer this evening to see if I'm a good fit socially."

"Ah, that's where I come in. Am I right?"

Thank God, he seemed to understand everything. "Yes!"

"*Florecita,* you said this wasn't about sex. I think you want an escort, not a gigolo."

"No! I certainly do not want an escort. Lawyers use escorts, and there's a chance one would be recognized."

A brief pause. "You're a lawyer? Wow. That's—"

She closed her eyes. Here came the jokes.

"—powerful," he finished. "Again, good for you."

She suddenly needed this to work out with a ferocity that startled her. "I just need one night," she said in a rush. "It will be the easiest job of your career. No sex, but your usual rate. You just have to pretend a little." She swallowed. "P-please."

"Of course," he said immediately, his voice so soothing, all the muscles she hadn't realized she'd clenched relaxed. "Of course, I'll be there for you."

She swayed a bit on the spot and then frowned. *Just relief that my promotion can proceed as planned.*

"What's your name?" he asked.

She'd hired him to be her fiancé, and they hadn't even exchanged names. "Charlotte," she blurted.

"Charlotte," he repeated. His soft accent curved around her name, seeming to embrace it over the line. "I'm Ryker, and it will be my pleasure to serve you tonight."

An ache settled low in her belly, shooting pangs of longing straight to the apex of her thighs. She *had* said no sex, right? *Why did you say no sex!*

"But I'm going to need to know when and where to meet you, and what I should wear."

"Oh!" She flushed. "Yes. It's black tie."

"Does that mean you'll be wearing a gown?" His voice was husky as he asked the question.

"Not that it matters," she forced herself to bite out when she wanted to melt. "But, yes."

"It matters, because I can match you. The color. If you'd like. Pocket square. Tie."

"Oh." Like high school prom? Yuck. "No, black tie will be fine." She quickly rattled off the location and time.

"No problem. I'm looking forward to it."

Not a lie? She licked her lips. She couldn't believe she was going to say this, but if tonight had any hope of success, he needed to know. "I have Asperger's."

A pause. "What was that?"

Oh, drat, she'd whispered. She exhaled. "Asperger's," she said again, louder this time. "It's...uh...I have trouble with knowing what's expected in relationships, and—"

"Oh. Charlotte"—he cleared his throat—"that's not going to be a problem. At all," he said emphatically.

The tight muscle in the back of Charlotte's neck relaxed. "It's not?"

"Of course not. Why would it be?"

The question she asked herself every time someone treated her like a leper. But how...alarming to hear someone else voice it. She was going to shut that internal nonsense down right now. She straightened. "Excellent."

"I'm glad you told me. I'll make sure I respect any of your boundaries."

Her brow furrowed. "Boundaries?"

"Yes. Tell me, where do you stand on touching? Anything I should know before tonight? For example, should I kiss you when I greet you or avoid that?"

"Oh." A man had never asked her that question before. Maybe that's why she'd never enjoyed dating, come to think of it. "I, uh…" A kiss. Something warm settled in her belly. "A kiss is fine."

What would Ryker's kiss be like? Would his lips be as soft on hers as his voice was curling in her ear? He was, no doubt, an excellent kisser. Something she had no experience with. She'd never really enjoyed kissing in the past. Her first boyfriend had always gripped her cheeks between sweaty palms when they kissed.

Even now, her stomach lurched at the thought of that slimy skin on her face. "But I don't like my face touched."

She held her breath. This would be the part where he balked. *Don't touch your face? What kind of freak are you?*

"Okay," he said immediately. "No problem. Anywhere else I should avoid?"

She was tempted to pull the phone from her ear and stare at it. That was it? No tantrum? She swallowed hard. "I…I don't know."

Oh, God, what if he touched her somewhere tonight and she freaked out? She hadn't done that since she was a small child, but she hadn't been touched by many people in the last decade or so, either. She was accidentally, and sometimes purposefully, standoffish enough that most people didn't casually touch her. They especially didn't touch her intimately. "Charlotte?"

"What?" It felt like she was trying to push her voice through a tight straw.

"I promise everything will be okay tonight. No matter what. If I do anything that makes you uncomfortable, just…talk about the weather."

She frowned. "The weather?"

"Yeah. It can be a kind of, I don't know, safe word. You can say anything weather related—Wasn't it cloudy outside?— and I'll stop whatever I'm doing immediately. No one will think anything of it."

"Huh." She licked her lips. "That…could work."

"It will work. We'll make it work."

She felt herself relaxing. "Okay. That sounds…good."

"Anything else you want to discuss?"

"No…no, I think that's sufficient."

"Good. I won't let you down, *querida*. See you tonight."

"Okay. See you tonight." There was a barely audible *click* in her ear. She lowered the phone to find he'd disconnected the call. Without his delectable voice soothing her, her shoulders immediately crept back up toward her ears. What had she just done? Pursing her lips, she blew a strand of hair out of her eyes. "What have I gotten myself into?"

She'd lost all her sensibilities on the phone with that man. Becoming physically aroused and abandoning logic. How was she possibly going to conduct herself professionally tonight with him beside her in the flesh? *Maybe he'll be horribly ugly.* "Yeah, right." She didn't have that kind of luck.

An hour later—an *hour,* for God's sake—she emerged with a gown draped over her arm. She hailed another taxi and nibbled her bottom lip the entire drive back to her car at the office and then the even shorter drive to her apartment just one floor below the penthouse. She may not be partner yet, but she did just fine.

The usual sense of arriving home evaded her as she rode the elevator up. She didn't know how to do her hair in anything other than the usual bun she wore. She certainly didn't know how to do makeup.

But she had her fiancé, her gown, and a tenuous plan. How bad could things be?

Chapter Three

Ryker settled the phone back in its cradle, the corners of his lips tipping up.

Charlotte.

An intelligent lawyer. Who worried she had trouble with relationships. Well, in his line of work, he knew that the vast majority of people had trouble with relationships. For a variety of reasons, most of which stemmed from the selfish nature of humans.

Asperger's wasn't a problem.

At least, it shouldn't be. His smile vanished. Chloe, the girl just a couple years younger than him who had been a foster sister of his at his least favorite foster home—she had seen firsthand how someone could view her autism as a problem. And Ryker, and for that matter Gage as well, had gotten front row seats to the emotional abuse she had suffered at the hands of foster parents who didn't know how to communicate with her the way she needed.

Gage had been a handful at that age, but he had outlasted Chloe in that home.

"Martinez!"

Ryker spun around. His broker, Tom, was hanging out of his office, a glower marring his rugged, aging face.

Ryker blinked several times before he could displace the image of Chloe's pale face gazing through the back seat window of a sleek black car as a social worker had driven her away for good.

Shit. He scrubbed a hand down his face. When he looked at Tom again, the older man's glower had only darkened.

Uh oh. He knew that look.

I'm in trouble. Again. But it was hard to concentrate on that while still rocked from his little unscheduled trip down memory lane.

On his back, he could feel the burning gazes of everyone hanging out in headquarters, hoping for new client phone calls. The living room-like "bull pen" of Stud Finder was extra packed today, as walk-ins had slowed down after the holiday season.

Lovely.

Ryker swallowed and finally succeeded in sending the past back to the past. "Yes?"

Tom didn't say anything, just jabbed a finger toward his office and disappeared inside. Someone behind him snickered as Ryker began trudging down the hallway.

Ha ha. Gossiping old ladies, the whole lot of them.

Tom was already sitting behind his desk, his large arms crossed over his chest and a fierce frown creating extra wrinkles at the sides of his mouth that Tom would flip over if anyone pointed them out.

"Close the door."

So, it was big trouble. Damn it, this could only be about one thing.

"Now, have a seat."

Ryker did so, licking suddenly dry lips. "What's up?"

Tom's glare narrowed. "How did your date go last night?"

Ah, shit. Ryker hated being right. He forced a casual shrug. "Just fine."

Tom rolled his eyes. "Oh, bullshit, Martinez." He leaned forward and planted his elbows on the desk, then jabbed both pointer fingers Ryker's direction. "Damn it, kid, I told you to cut it out with the married vendetta."

Ryker gritted his teeth. Why did no one understand this? It's not like fidelity was a completely foreign idea. "It's not a ven—"

Tom slashed a hand through the air. "Yeah, right. Do you know the identity of the woman you scorned last night?"

Ryker rolled his shoulders, hoping to displace the sudden heavy ache at the top of his spine. "All our clients are the most important woman in the world," he hedged.

"And now you're going to be a smart ass?" Tom shook his head, his eyes widening ominously. "Boy…"

Ryker cleared his throat and folded his hands in his lap, a copper-like taste stinging the back of his tongue. "Who was she?" he asked softly.

Tom seemed to deflate before his eyes. His palms hit the desk with a slap, and his features drooped. "A politician's wife," he said.

His tone sounded like an apology.

Ryker closed his eyes. "Fuck."

"You can say that again."

Stud Finder was a legalized brothel, but a politician could make that status tenuous. Ryker opened his eyes.

Tom smiled sadly. "You're fired, kid." He shook his head. "I did warn you. Several times."

Ryker nodded. "I know." He tried to appear calm on the outside, but his mind was already scrambling through this clusterfuck that had just been dropped into his lap.

He lived client to client. Always had. The only future he really wanted was so far out of reach, he never saw the point in planning for it. He didn't even have a savings account.

He could kiss future legitimate clients goodbye. The gossips outside this office would spread this gaffe with a politician's wife far and wide. He'd be blacklisted at all the other agencies within an hour.

Rent was paid up through the end of the month, but after that—

"I hope your convictions on marriage were worth all this," Tom said, sweeping a hand through the air, seemingly indicating the shitstorm that would be Ryker's life now.

Perspective. Thank God.

Ryker raised his chin. His convictions were worth it. They were worth everything. The only married woman Ryker would ever sleep with would be the one married to him.

Like that will ever happen.

Tom took in Ryker's raised chin and *ts*ked. "You were one of the best I've ever seen," he said softly. "Besides myself, of course, back in my heyday."

Ryker stifled a grimace. Ew. "High praise, indeed."

Tom's face turned into an emotionless mask. "Now, get out."

Ryker sat motionless in the chair for a moment before Tom's words registered.

Right.

He'd been dismissed.

Bracing his hands on the arms of the chair, he pushed to his feet, his body feeling slightly heavier than normal. By the time he got to the door, Tom was already on the phone, his baritone voice rumbling as he no doubt tried to put out the fire Ryker had started.

He avoided everyone's stares as he trudged down the hallway and out the front door of Stud Finder, closing the door behind him and cutting off the curious gazes of everyone who had watched his walk of shame with fascination.

Damn, life could turn on a dime. But, then, Ryker knew that better than anyone. One day you're happy with two loving parents; the next day—

He shook his head. He couldn't afford another trip down memory lane so soon. He had his own damage control to consider.

Settling into the driver's seat of his car, he leaned forward and rested his forehead against the steering wheel.

What was he going to do now?

His cell chimed in his back pocket.

He jerked upright. Charlotte. That was the calendar notification he'd entered into his phone while he'd talked through the details of their date tonight on the landline. He glanced at the clock on his dashboard. It was going to be tight, but he had just enough time to get to his apartment, shave, do some quick research on his client, slip into a tux, and make it to the address she'd given him.

And he'd better make it on time, because he needed money, and she was very likely the last high-paying client he could count on.

Chapter Four

Everything is going to be a disaster!

Charlotte had to fist her hands at her sides to keep them from tugging up her strapless bodice yet again. Why, oh why, had she chosen a strapless gown? It felt as though the bustier the saleswoman had foisted on her was pressing her breasts up against her chin.

She hadn't known a simple undergarment could defy God and science.

Miller and Lee's jaws had practically dropped when she'd arrived minutes ago. Although their wives had greeted her seemingly normally enough, and for a moment, Charlotte had had the asinine thought that everything tonight was going to be okay.

It had been only two minutes, and she had already adjusted that opinion. All five of them—Charlotte had arrived early and Carter and Wesson had yet to show—stood in a loose circle. Silence had descended immediately following the introductions, and she had no idea how to fill it. She was supposed to be wowing them with how well she fit socially.

"Er," Miller said as his wife jabbed him in the side with her elbow. "I thought your fiancé was coming?"

Miller's wife—Charlotte thought she remembered her being introduced as Gloria—rolled her eyes. "What he meant to say, dear, is congratulations on your upcoming wedding. How exciting!"

Charlotte took a glass of champagne from the tray a waiter held before her. "Oh, yes. I'm very excited." She realized belatedly that her tone had sounded anything but excited, so she threw in a smile. "And"—what was his name again?—"Ryker will be here any minute. He had to come straight from work, you see, so we couldn't come together."

Come together. The words immediately made her blush, calling to mind that husky voice that had curled in her ear earlier today. That man would definitely make sure he and whomever he was with would *come together.*

What was wrong with her? She didn't think like this. The blush increased in intensity, and she was mortified to feel it spread to her breasts as well, something this ill-advised gown was no doubt revealing to everyone.

Sure enough, Lee's gaze flicked down to her chest and then just as quickly back to her eyes. She just barely caught her hands in time to keep them from flying up and covering her cleavage. She opted for raising her glass to her lips instead.

"Oh?" Lee asked, taking his own flute of champagne. "What work does he do?"

Charlotte froze with her glass perched against her lips. *Oh, no!* Work? Why had she said that? She hadn't had the time to create a backstory or even discuss a need for one with Ryker in their short phone conversation! She couldn't say, *Well, actually, Mr. Lee, he's a male prostitute.* She took a sip of champagne to give herself more time. It was dry, bordering on bitter. Ugh. She hated alcohol. The sip stayed cradled in the dip of her tongue as she pondered both how to respond to Lee's question and how to get the champagne out of her mouth without having to swallow it.

"Yes," Lee's wife, Patricia, said, "and what does he look like? We're dying to hear all about him!"

Charlotte swallowed her champagne in one bracing gulp. It went down the wrong pipe, setting up residence somewhere above her lungs. Hacking coughs immediately racked her body. At the same time, her mind was screaming. *What does he look like?*

Good question!

She had no clue. None. Zip, nada. *Oh, God.* He was going to show up here, and she was not going to recognize him.

He'd be wearing a black-tie tux. All the waitstaff were wearing black-tie tuxes.

I'm doomed!

Mr. Miller reached out and snagged her flute of champagne, placing it on the tray of a waiter who had rushed over the moment Charlotte's coughs had begun. "My goodness, Charlotte." He gripped her elbow as her coughs continued. "Do you need to sit down?"

She placed a hand over her chest and tried to draw in a deep breath, but her hand only found the firm and gravity-defying mounds of her breasts: an untimely reminder that she was oh-so-out of her element.

Mr. Miller patted her on the back, and she felt a corresponding jiggle in her bodice and wanted to die.

An actual possibility if you don't stop trying to breathe champagne!

Finally, the coughs began to subside. She sucked in a ragged breath. Another. "I'm…sorry," she croaked. "Don't know what's…wrong with me." *On so many levels.*

"No reason to apologize," Mr. Miller said, a sparkle of amusement in his eyes. "I get choked up when I think about my wife all the time. Comes with the territory."

Charlotte's eyes widened. Was Mr. Miller, a divorce attorney, a…*romantic?* How did something like that happen? "Guilty," she said, her voice still a rasp.

God, she couldn't believe she'd hacked up a lung in front of everybody. But maybe it had distracted them from their line of questioning?

"So," Mr. Lee said, "you were about to tell us about your fiancé?"

Drat. "Oh, you know." Charlotte waved her hand in the air in what she hoped was a vague fashion. "He does a bit of this. A bit of that."

Mr. Miller raised his eyebrows.

Charlotte's heart rate accelerated.

At just that moment, Mrs. Miller gasped softly, making Charlotte, with her already tightly strung nerves, jump. The other woman's gaze was locked on something over Charlotte's shoulder. Automatically, she turned to look, too.

She swallowed her own gasp.

The world's most beautiful man stood framed in the open doorway. He wore a black-tie tuxedo, but there was no mistaking him as part of the waitstaff.

Her fiancé had arrived. She gulped.

Oh, no. She tensed.

He was...impossibly gorgeous.

He was tall, his head only inches from the top of the doorframe. He was also slender, but his tux clung to him in a way—hugging his shoulders and thighs—that belied the amount

58

of lean muscle he carried on his athletic frame. Black curls tumbled over his forehead, setting off eyes that, even from across the room, Charlotte could tell were a breathtaking chestnut shade. His lips were full. And inherently wicked.

She startled. *Inherently wicked?* What an absurd thought.

Those gorgeous eyes scanned the small gathering, and she held her breath. She had certainly recognized him, but would he recognize her? And—she swallowed hard—would she be able to bear the disappointment she saw flash in those beautiful eyes as he realized she, with her glasses and tight bun, was his date?

His gaze landed on her and stopped. She braced herself, knowing she couldn't show any reaction to those around her. He tilted his head as he looked at her hair, her glasses. When his gaze dropped to her lips, she thought she saw his own lips part slightly. Surely, she'd imagined the reaction. Yet, when his gaze landed on her prominently displayed breasts, there was no imagining his reaction.

His parted lips curved into a smile. That heated gaze swept down the rest of her form leisurely, and his smile widened. By the time he looked back at her face, their gazes locking, the shade of his eyes had changed.

His pupils had dilated, making his eyes appear darker. She didn't know what that could possibly mean, but it wasn't necessarily disappointment. Her heart chose to latch on to that possibility and start racing.

He licked his bottom lip, then sucked it between his teeth.

Charlotte swayed, catching herself with what she hoped was a barely perceptible stumble-step.

Then, he started walking her way.

***

He straightened his cuffs, tugging first one and then the other into perfect alignment.

It gave him the opportunity to school his reaction as he approached his client. Because Charlotte, the woman who had so formally conducted their conversation over the phone, looked both exactly like he'd expected and nearly knocked him on his ass with the sexpot figure he hadn't anticipated.

Her brown hair was slicked back into an updo, but it wasn't any sort of hairstyle one would expect for a formal occasion. Instead of soft, flowing, and romantic, the style was simple. If he had to guess, though he couldn't see the back of her head, it was an unembellished bun. No doubt the style she chose every day.

Her face was dominated by a truly impressively sized pair of black-frame glasses. They obscured nearly all her features—

her eyebrows, eyes, and cheeks. Everything except her lips, which had almost immediately snagged his attention.

She wore red lipstick. Badly. The red strayed from the outline of her lips and even stretched infinitesimally beyond the corners.

And yet, the sight of those red lips had gotten him right in his gut. The immediate hunch that she was unused to makeup? For some reason, he found it unbearably intimate. As though they shared a secret.

And then—dear God—her breasts. They were... *big*. As soon as he thought the word, he wanted to shake his head. What an inadequate description. Charlotte's breasts were a revelation. A miracle. They were pressed high and oh so full. Plump. They'd be firm beneath his lips. Beneath his chest as he lay atop her—

Stop that! She'd explicitly said no sex. More's the pity now that he'd seen her beautiful, tempting body. It was so sweetly curved. Voluptuous. The thing of fantasies.

Seriously, stop it.

He cleared his throat just as he arrived before the group of five people who had watched him walk across the room with barely disguised fascination. As he stood before Charlotte, he discovered a new thing about his date: she was incredibly petite. The top of her head barely met his chest. He'd known she was shorter when he'd first seen her from across the room, but he hadn't anticipated just how tiny she was.

Visions bombarded him: lifting her with ease, pressing her to an accommodating wall, and directing her legs around his waist as he buried his face in those magnificent breasts.

He peered through her glasses, seeking to meet her eyes. And that was when he lost his breath. Behind those blocky glasses, the woman was hiding the most beautiful blue eyes framed with thick, dark lashes he'd ever seen. He rubbed suddenly sweaty palms against the outside of his thighs—a reaction he hadn't had to a woman since he was a teenager.

Her body—God, her body was a wicked fantasy. But her eyes? Her eyes were the real dream.

Her red lips parted. "H-hello, Ryker." A blush tinged her cheeks. And lower.

He wanted to groan from the effort of keeping his gaze locked in place. "Sorry I'm late, *mi amor*." He nearly coughed as soon as he said the words. Endearments? They flowed from him like honey from a hive. He'd never called a woman *my love* before, however. Never even been tempted.

To cover up his slip, he reached for her. Her eyes widened as she watched his hand move between them. When he snagged her hand and tugged her toward him, she gave the smallest, sexiest little gasp. He leaned down and pressed his lips to hers as they'd planned, swallowing the gasp down. Her taste—champagne and something simultaneously comforting and stimulating—rocketed down to his toes. Before he knew what he was doing, he was lapping her top lip with a tiny flick of his tongue.

She gasped again.

Every cell in his body strained to deepen the kiss. To slide his tongue deeply into her mouth. Wrap his arms around her. Feel those breasts against him.

This is more than what you planned. He didn't know where she stood on a kiss like this.

Mustering every bit of self-control he possessed, he pulled back. His eyelids were heavy as he gazed down at her. Her eyes were enormous. Her mouth was still open, and he noticed with some satisfaction that her red lipstick was a shade lighter than it had been.

She was okay. He exhaled.

Stroking the back of her hand with his thumb, he used his other hand to swipe whatever lipstick he'd managed to collect from his own lips. She watched the movement raptly, and her eyes dilated. "You look beautiful," he whispered as he returned his hand to his side, his voice deeper than he'd been expecting.

"Th-thank you," she whispered back.

"Well," a male voice beside them said. "I certainly hope you're Ryker."

He nearly jumped. Somehow, he'd forgotten they were surrounded by people. *Head in the game, Martinez.* He was on duty tonight. He couldn't afford to forget that.

Dragging his gaze from his alarmingly interesting client, he acknowledged the others. Two men and two women stared at him. The men seemed confused. Their brows were drawn together, and they were looking at him as though he belonged to an as-yet-unidentified species. The women were also looking at him as though he were something they'd never seen before, but their gazes were heated. Something he was very used to, so he took it in stride.

He turned to the man who had spoken. "I'm the lucky guy, yes." He extended his hand. "Pleased to meet you. I'm Ryker Martinez."

The man took his hand, giving it a firm—very firm—shake. "Ben Miller." He gestured to the woman beside him, who was still staring at Ryker with an open mouth. "This is my wife, Gloria."

Ryker shook her hand as well. The woman's fingers trembled in his palm. He smiled warmly at her. "A pleasure to meet you, Gloria."

She made a noise that sounded suspiciously close to a squeak. He bit the inside of his cheek to keep from smiling too broadly.

He turned to the other couple, who introduced themselves as Joseph and Patricia Lee. As soon as the introductions were over, everyone started fidgeting: clasping and re-clasping purses, straightening already straight jackets, clearing throats. Awkward silence had never bothered Ryker, and it wasn't about to start now.

However, the others were staring at Charlotte, then Ryker, and back to Charlotte over and over again, varying degrees of confusion marring their expressions.

As though they don't know why I'd be with her.

An emotion he hadn't allowed himself to feel in years started churning in his gut.

How dare they!

He was being too sensitive. They might not even be thinking what he was guessing. But his juvenile protective instincts—the ones that had done Chloe no good—made a roaring reappearance.

But now, he was no longer a kid. *You could do good this time.*

He reached for Charlotte's hand again, weaving their fingers together. She visibly jumped at the contact, her gaze shooting his direction. Her expression was a mirror image of the confused expressions of her co-workers, and he stifled a wince. They weren't going to be believable if she didn't act like they were in love.

At just that moment, there was a cacophony at the door. All six of them turned toward it, and Ryker saw four new people entering the space. Everyone started shouting greetings in a much more exuberant fashion than any of them had displayed up to this point.

Tugging on Charlotte's hand, he pulled her into his side. Leaning over to whisper in her ear was a greater feat than he'd originally anticipated, given their disparate heights, but he tried to make it appear as sneaky as possible.

"Did you notice the weather outside?" he asked, taking the first opportunity he could to check in with her.

She blinked. "Oh! No. No, I didn't notice any weather." A small, shy smile curved the corners of her lips, and he wanted to daub his tongue in the slight dimple that appeared on the right side.

"Good." He leaned in farther. "But remember," he whispered into her ear, "we're supposed to be in love." He pulled back slightly to see if she'd understood, but immediately, he was caught by the sight of the goose bumps that had broken out all over her shoulders and upper arms. Without thought, he followed their trail where they traveled across the firm peaks of her breasts as well. His fingers tightened around hers before he could school the reaction. "Relax with me, *am*— " He gritted his teeth. *Amor?* Again? "*Bonita*," he corrected. *Yes, fuckwit, stick with* bonita. "They won't believe us if we don't relax."

"You want me to relax?" Her voice was barely audible, but he could hear the strain beneath the surface. "I can barely think around you!"

He began to grin and bit into his bottom lip in an attempt to stop it, but it was no use. "Now, what a lovely compliment, *bonita*." With his free hand, he trailed the backs of his fingers down an arm still peppered with gooseflesh.

She turned her head and pinned him with a glare that was a little unfocused. "That's not helping," she hissed.

His lips still quirking, he dropped his hand. He kept his other wrapped around hers, though. They simultaneously turned to look at the others. With the newcomers, they were now a party of ten.

All eight of the others were staring at them. The opportunistic glint in the eyes of the two new men set Ryker's teeth on edge.

Must be Charlotte's competition.

A muscle in his jaw clenched. He didn't like the way those guys were measuring her up, clearly looking for any area of weakness. They had all the warmth of a cobra coiled to strike.

Charlotte stiffened and stepped closer to him. For fuck's sake, it made him feel ten feet tall. And protective as all get-out.

He squeezed her hand. *I've got you, beautiful.*

"Hello." He extended his hand toward the closest newcomer. "I'm Charlotte's fiancé, Ryker."

The man raised both of his eyebrows as he took Ryker's proffered hand. "Nice to meet you, Ryker." His grip was tight. Forceful. Purposefully intimidating. Jesus, did all lawyers try to intimidate new acquaintances?

Ryker didn't get intimidated. He smiled sanguinely.

His façade flickered for a moment. "I'm Michael Carter."

The other man stepped forward. "And I'm Chip Wesson." They shook hands, and Ryker was pleased to find that Chip, at least, seemed to possess a soul of some kind. "We were so happy to hear Charlotte's news today. Congratulations, you two."

Aaaand, scratch the soul assessment. Chip's statement had been anything but congratulatory. It had been shrewd, with just the right amount of *if you can believe it* in the subtext.

Ryker gritted his teeth. He wasn't misreading this. These people thought he was out of Charlotte's league. *Charlotte's?* The woman standing beside him looking so beautiful he had been constantly fighting a hard-on for the past twelve minutes? The one who, he had discovered through his preparatory research, had never lost a case?

She was out of his league. By miles. He put his arm around her shoulders, tucking her into his side. She fit there like a puzzle piece, her head just reaching his bicep.

"Thank you," he said. "We're pretty excited."

"Oh?" Michael said. "The wedding date must be close then! When is it?" His smile had a hint of cruelty to it.

Ryker had always known how to handle asses. He just usually preferred the warm, firm kind. Not this jackoff.

Ryker lifted his chin. As Charlotte trembled against his side—had to be from nerves—he tightened his arm. "It's two Saturdays from now, actually. Just right around the corner." He smiled down at the crown of Charlotte's head. "Can't wait to make her Mrs. Martinez."

Charlotte gazed up at him in horror.

And that's when he truly realized what he'd just said. *Two weeks from now?* Oh, fuck. Damn it, he had told himself not to be distracted!

His past had been too loud today. Pair that with getting fired, and…

He'd slipped. And now he'd really put his foot in it.

Smiling broadly down at Charlotte, he hoped he was keeping his smile from looking strained. He leaned down and placed a kiss to the crown of her head.

Her hair smelled like apples.

"Two weeks!" Mr. Lee chuckled. "Charlotte, when were you going to tell us?"

She raised her chin. "I've been focused on my work."

"Besides," Ryker jumped in—maybe he could bail her out of the mess he'd placed her in—"it's just a small wedding. But we'll be sure to send you an invitation." He looked down at his fiancée. "Isn't that right, Charlie?" *What?*

"Charlie?" Michael muttered.

Ryker felt a stinging in his hand; Charlotte was digging her blunt little nails into him. She jerked a nod toward her co-workers. "Oh, yes. Of course we will." Her blue eyes practically held chips of ice as she looked at him. "If you'll excuse me for a moment, I think I left my car unlocked. *Darling*"—she bared her teeth at him in what was no doubt supposed to be a smile— "would you walk me out, since it's dark?"

Uh oh. He was so fired. For the second time in one day. And he should be. What the fuck was he thinking, throwing out wedding dates and familiar nicknames?

And why did the fact that she'd called him darling, even in that sarcastic tone, seem to give his chest fits?

He drew her hand through his arm. "I'd be happy to." He nodded toward the group. "We'll be right back." *Though, probably not.*

Her heels clacked an angry, percussive rhythm on the glossy floor as he led her into the hallway. There were dots of pink on each of her cheeks, and it wasn't a blush this time.

When she hauled him into an abandoned alcove down the hallway, he sighed, bracing for the worst.

She jerked her hand from his arm and glared at him. "What were you thinking?" she hissed.

He shook his head. "I know. I know. I'm so sorry." If there was any way to fix this, he would. Unfortunately, he didn't think she'd give him the chance. "And I already know what you're going to say."

She pinched the bridge of her nose and closed her eyes. "We have to get married."

Chapter Five

Silence met her declaration. Which, she had to admit, was better than she'd expected. Slowly, she opened her eyes.

Ryker, who was unfairly handsome even after making her mess even messier, was looking down at her with his brows drawn together. Was he confused? Maybe she hadn't spoken clearly enough?

She lowered her hand. "We have to get—"

He held up a hand. "I heard you." He tilted his head. "I'm trying to figure out if you're serious."

She frowned. "I'm always serious."

He looked over her hair. Her glasses. "I'm beginning to suspect that's true."

Wait, this was going more smoothly than it should. "I...haven't heard a *no*...."

He sighed.

Ah, here it comes.

"Charlie, of course we're not getting married."

Charlie. There it was again. What on earth would possess this man to call her something so ridiculous? "Wait. Why not?"

"*Mujer!* Strangers don't get married!"

She shrugged. "In my experience, being well acquainted with one's spouse does not make the probability of marital success greater."

He paused. "Hmm." He tilted his head. "Not in my experience either, as a matter of fact."

She raised her eyebrows. "See?"

His lips quirked. "You're pretty damn gorgeous when you're making a point." He reached up and brushed his pointer finger against the corner of his own mouth. "You get a dimple. Right here."

She frowned. "That's absurd. I have no dimples."

His gaze met hers. "You have at least one. I'd be happy to explore your no-dimples theory further." His slow grin revealed a dimple of his own in his left cheek.

That dimple distracted her, and she couldn't quite understand what he'd said and why it merited a grin. When her mind finally grasped what he meant, she gasped. "I'm over here trying to talk about marriage, and you're insinuating you'd like to see me naked!"

He tossed his head back, and a deep, rumbling laugh sounded from the region of his belly. After a moment, he looked at her again. "Charlie, if we get married, I'm going to see you naked. Those things are kind of a package deal."

She lifted her chin. "They most certainly are not."

He crossed his arms over his chest, suddenly serious. "They will be in whatever marriage I commit to."

She looked at him from the corners of her eyes. "I think I'm confused. I still haven't heard a no." This was, after all, a quite ludicrous plan. She'd expected him to laugh and run away as soon as she'd proposed it.

He cocked an eyebrow. "If you're serious about a sexless marriage, it is most definitely a no."

"Drat," she muttered. She glared at him again. "You just had to give them a wedding date, didn't you? I was going to tell them my fiancé and I had broken up after I made partner, but now...*Drat.*"

"Charlotte." He reached for her, seemed to reconsider, and returned his hand to his side. "May I ask why you're adamant about us not having sex?"

She wrinkled his nose. "That's extraordinarily personal."

He raised his eyebrows.

Marriage. Right. She sighed. Personal was pretty relevant right now. She shrugged. "Fine. There are a lot of rules to sex. Inherent ones." She looked down at her fingernails. "And I haven't figured them all out. I prefer to excel, and since I can't in that area... Honestly, I can do without it, and I stay more focused when it's not a factor in my life, so—" She shrugged again. "I avoid it." She looked up at him. "Besides, sex is the root of most of my divorce cases. Not enough of it, too much of it with someone else, etcetera."

His head kicked back. "Rules? To sex?"

She pursed her lips. "Yes. Wouldn't someone in your profession know that?"

He shook his head. "*Bonita*, anyone in my profession would tell you that the only rules are the ones you and your partner make yourselves."

Had anyone ever been so wrong? "Not in my experience."

He paused. "Charlie...was someone...mean to you? About how you are in bed?"

She couldn't look him in the eye anymore, no matter how hard she tried. *You're too aggressive. How are you emotionless in everything else but so demanding in this? Why can't you be like everyone else?* "We're off topic here."

"Are we?"

She glared at the spot just over his shoulder. "Yes. Look—" She tucked her chin down and gazed his direction over the top of her glasses. "We can have a marriage in name only." No matter how much just looking at him made her want more.

"I make partner, and then, we divorce." She held a finger in the air. "Twenty percent of marriages end within the first five years. Our divorce will be very plausible."

His lips parted. "You want to get married...and then divorced?" If she had to guess, she would say he looked horrified.

Her brows drew together. "You want to stay in a marriage of convenience?"

He shifted on his feet at that, his gaze redirecting to her feet. Her eyes widened.

Oh, my goodness. He did want that! What in the world—

"Charlotte—" His deviation from *Charlie* made something ping in her chest. "This is a pointless conversation. I can't agree to a sexless marriage. Ever." He met her gaze again. "When I get married, I will be faithful to my wife. Sex is important to me." He held out his hands and shrugged, telegraphing they'd arrived at an impasse.

She felt as though she deflated as she closed her eyes. Was she truly getting ready to say what she was getting ready to say? Was she strong enough to stay focused if she let herself do this? Screwing up her lips, she said, "Fine." She opened her eyes again. "We can negotiate sex."

His head kicked back. "Negotiate sex? That is the saddest statement I've ever heard. Besides, I would never want you to do something you don't want to." He shook his head. His jaw had a firm set to it.

She was losing this. She couldn't seem to catch her breath, and she could hear a hollow whistle between her ears. As black started winking in her vision, she finally sucked down air, and words exploded out of her mouth.

"We'll negotiate sex, and I'll pay you five hundred thousand dollars in our divorce settlement!"

Chapter Six

Five hundred thousand dollars.

The words echoed in the small space, the only way he was able to know for sure he hadn't misunderstood her. And still, he felt the need to clarify. He cleared his throat. "Did you just say—?"

She nodded. "Yes, I did. And I'm serious. We can negotiate whatever you'd like, Ryker, just…" She swallowed hard enough to make her delicate throat bob, and he felt a corresponding bob in his gut. "*Please*," she whispered hoarsely. "I really need this." Her gaze met his for the first time in several minutes, and her blue eyes might as well have shot arrows directly toward his heart. "Partner is my dream."

Five hundred thousand dollars. The solution to all the problems he'd been trying to forget all evening. He could live off that…well, he was no financial planner, that was for sure. But surely he could live off that forever, right?

No more worries about rent or where his next meal would come from.

He bit into his bottom lip as he stared at the top of her head. The truth was, even when she'd first told him they needed to get married, *no* had not been his knee-jerk reaction. Not even close.

The money just made an already tempting offer even more tempting.

Though, if she'd have looked at him with those enormous blue eyes and asked *please* in that broken voice before offering the money, he'd have tripped over himself to give her anything she wanted.

And she was willing to negotiate anything? Maybe even children?

God, it wasn't possible that all his dreams were coming true right here in this small alcove.

He stepped closer to her, even though they'd already been nearly toe-to-toe in the small space. When he moved, she jerked, but she kept her gaze directed downward. "*Bonita*," he whispered. Curling his fingers around hers, he tugged gently at her hand. Though she pulled her hand away, she waited a long moment before raising her gaze to his once more.

Those dreamy, blue eyes. They almost made him lose his focus. He stroked his thumb along the inside of her wrist, and she blinked, her eyes taking slightly longer than normal to open all the way again.

She's affected by me. Maybe there was hope here, after all. "Charlotte, I do not want sex to be a chore you do just to get me to agree to this. That won't work for me at all."

Her gorgeous eyes widened behind her glasses. "B-but, I'll do it! I swear, I will—"

"Shh." He moved his thumb, pressing it over her rapidly fluttering pulse point. "Listen to me, *mujer.*" Unable to stop himself, his gaze drifted to her bottom lip. So lush. Giving. It would take the barest hint of pressure to press the tip of his tongue into her mouth and feel her hot, wet tongue against his.

He drew in a sharp breath and moved his gaze away from the danger zone. "May I kiss you, Charlie? For real?"

She drew in her own sharp breath. "Kiss me? But—" She sounded drugged. Intrigued.

"Let me kiss you, *bonita.* If after the kiss, you don't want to try anything more—" He shrugged with one shoulder. "Then we have our answer. But if you do…well, then we can negotiate. Yes?"

A quick flash of panic passed through her blue eyes. *Desire scares this woman.*

It made sense. From what he'd gathered so far, she loved her control. Was a planner. One who liked to be in charge of herself and those around her.

Which could mean that when she felt desire, she *felt* it. Came completely unhinged. God, if he was right about this theory, and she wanted to marry him...

I may be the luckiest man on this earth.

He licked his lips. She noticed. Her gaze dipped to his mouth, and the fringe of her lashes cast a shadow on her cheeks.

So lovely. "Charlie?" he prodded, hoping against hope she'd let him put his mouth on hers. He wanted to taste her so badly.

She swallowed hard again, parted her lips, and said, "O-okay."

He allowed his eyes to slide closed for a moment as he tried to school his reaction—a reaction that was much more violent than he'd anticipated. His chest felt too full while the emptiness of his arms seemed a crime against humanity. If he didn't know better, he'd say this marriage proposal of hers meant...a lot to him.

He closed the remaining distance between them, and finally—*finally*—those breasts of hers met his body, pressing into his ribcage.

She pulled in a slow, shaky breath, and the effect on her cleavage—her tits plumping so beautifully—nearly sent him to his knees.

"We still okay?" he asked.

She nodded. "Yes." A slow blink. "The weather is…good."

A small smile tugged at his lips. "I love good weather. But, Charlie, if that changes—at all—you pull away. And I immediately stop, no questions asked. Okay?"

She swallowed. "O-okay."

He jerked a quick nod.

Please desire me. Oh, please. He didn't think so much had ever ridden on a kiss before. He was nervous, of all things. "Now, close your eyes," he murmured.

Her gaze met his. "Close my—?"

He cupped her shoulders with both hands as her words petered out. "Just do it, *bonita*." She raised one eyebrow, but when he curved his fingers and began massaging the tight muscles above her shoulder blades, her eyelids fluttered closed.

Without her scrutiny, he could breathe a little. Still, his nerves thrummed in the background.

Her lashes were so thick and dark. Those lush lips were parted, and he was close enough that when she exhaled, her breath coasted over his neck.

He took his time; anticipation was one of the best aphrodisiacs he had in his arsenal. He stretched his thumbs, with one stroking the hollow of her throat. With the other, he pressed gently against her jaw, being sure to avoid her face and scrutinizing her expression for the slightest hint that his thumb so close to her no-touch zone was acceptable. Like he'd intended, she tipped her face up more, her expression still serene.

He gritted his teeth, nearly undone by the sight. Dragging his thumb along the underside of her jaw, he tilted her face just a bit more and bent down.

He paused just before contact, and, even with her eyes closed, there was no way she could miss how close he was to sealing his lips over hers. Her breathing hitched. Beneath his hands, her delicate throat tensed.

He pressed his mouth to hers.

Warmth spread through him. A warmth that harkened to home and belonging, which was absolutely absurd since he had no experience with either.

She melted against his chest, drawing him quickly from his tumultuous thoughts as her firm breasts pressed even more fully against him. He dropped one hand, winding his arm around her. Splaying his hand between her shoulder blades, he pressed. As she followed his guiding like a dream, he parted his lips and gave a slow, sensuous lick to the sensitive inner curve of her upper lip.

She gasped.

She didn't pull away.

Perfect.

Tilting his head, he deepened the kiss, this time, pressing the tip of his tongue to hers, then farther into her warm, welcoming mouth.

A harsh moan sounded between them. A thrill of victory shot through him, but...*he* had moaned—not her.

As it turned out, that didn't matter. His moan seemed to electrify her. With a soft cry, her hands, which had been hanging at her sides, suddenly fisted in his jacket. There was a yank as she pulled herself up to her tiptoes, which, endearingly, only gave her an inch or so more in height.

All thoughts of *endearing* vanished, however, when, with a growl, she sucked on his tongue. Hard.

His eyes slammed shut. Eyebrows drawing together, he tightened his arm around her back, returning her now frenzied kiss stroke for stroke.

As he nipped her bottom lip, she rocked her hips against him, and all thought, all finesse, vanished.

Fuck. With his arm about her, he lifted. Her toes left the floor, and, rather than protest, she wrapped her arms around his neck and kissed him harder. He strode forward, and her back met the wall of the alcove with much more force than he'd intended.

With a momentary flare of panic, he prepared to withdraw from the kiss. To apologize and make sure she was okay.

But she made that growling sound again—soft, husky, and sexy as hell. Her fingernails bit into the back of his neck, and she undulated her hips once more.

With a groan, he cradled the back of her head, his fingers doing irreparable damage to her bun, but keeping her head from smacking into the wall. He trailed the fingers of his other hand down the soft skin of her neck, down her shoulder and arm— carefully avoiding her breasts. If he touched them, this would turn wild.

Well, more wild.

He hesitated with his hand fitted into the curve of her waist. Was he really going to do this? Ravage this woman in a public place?

Wouldn't be the first time. But it would be the first time he'd wanted to do something this badly.

Decided, he skated his palm over the curve of her hip to her ass. His client was deliciously curvy. Her ass filled his hand to capacity, and he couldn't prevent a definitive squeeze.

She broke from the kiss with a gasp—had he found one of her boundaries? But just as quickly as she'd broken the kiss, she kissed the corner of his mouth. His cheek. Nipped his jaw. Opened her lips over his pulse point and sucked.

"Jesus," he bit out. His forehead met the wall above her head with a *thunk*. He was harder than he'd been in memory. Had gone as hard as steel as soon as she'd given him permission to kiss her. Her soft stomach was cradling him, and he longed to rock his hips as she'd been doing since he'd gotten her in this position.

He squeezed her ass again and gave in, allowing himself one small thrust.

Stars lit behind his closed eyelids, the tip of his cock rubbing against her at the most perfect angle.

He was just about to do it again—control be damned—when the very clear sound of someone clearing his throat sounded from the edge of the alcove.

With a gasp, Charlotte jerked her lips from Ryker's skin. Ryker, however, didn't budge except to tighten his fingers in her hair. "*Bonita*," he whispered in a voice so soft he knew no one else would hear. "Shh. Everything's okay. It's good we've been caught."

He gave her a moment to absorb that, then, with regret so deep it physically pained him, relinquished his grip on her ass.

With a quick tug of his jacket, he made sure his outrageous erection was covered, then quickly perused his date.

Her hair was mussed, and her cheeks were rosy from both a blush and—he winced—a pretty impressive case of whisker burn. There was nothing he could do to help make her more presentable, but he took a moment to tuck a strand of particularly wayward hair behind her ear before turning to greet their interrupter—and his current least favorite person, whoever he may be.

Mr. Miller—wait, was it Mr. Lee? *No, Mr. Miller has the gray hair.* The gray-haired bastard stood several feet away, staring at them with ill-concealed surprise. Ryker tugged on his jacket again, made sure he was protecting Charlotte from the worst of the man's scrutiny, and then raised his eyebrows.

Mr. Miller cleared his throat again. "I'm sorry to interrupt."

He heard Charlotte groan softly behind him, and Ryker had to bite his lip to keep from smiling.

"Mr. Lee was called away on a legal emergency for one of his clients, and it looks as though the evening has been cut short." Mr. Miller said this quickly, as though he was dying to get it out so he could walk away and try to forget what he'd seen.

"Oh," Ryker said, his voice so husky even *he* was a little taken aback. He cleared his throat. "What a shame. I hope everything is all right."

"Er, yes," Mr. Miller said. His gaze flicked quickly over Ryker's shoulder. He felt Charlotte stiffen against his back, and as Mr. Miller glanced just as quickly to the floor, Ryker wrapped his arm backward, his hand finding Charlotte's hip and giving what he hoped was a reassuring squeeze.

"Anyway," Mr. Miller said to the floor, "it was extremely…nice to meet you." He looked at them again. "Charlotte, thank you for making time for us tonight."

"Of course," she squeaked from behind him.

"Yes." Mr. Miller stared at them for a moment longer. "Well, enjoy your evening." As soon as the words left his mouth, the man winced, as though he realized just how they were going to enjoy the rest of the evening. Then he turned and walked away, his loafers clacking against the marble floor.

As the sound of his footsteps faded, he felt her forehead meet his back, and she sagged against him. "I can't believe that just happened. I'm ruined!"

If she hadn't sounded so forlorn, he would have chuckled. "Charlie." He looked over his shoulder, saw her raise her head, and then turned around. Her pupils were still blown as she looked up at him, and he nearly lost his concentration. He reached out and snagged both of her hands in his, stroking his thumbs across the delicate bones of her wrists.

She glanced down at their joined hands for a moment, seemingly fascinated by his thumbs' movement across her skin. When she looked back up at him, he continued, "For some reason, they were skeptical that we are a couple."

She snorted—a sound he wouldn't have thought was in her sophisticated repertoire. "For some reason? Are you blind?"

His brows crashed together. "Don't say that."

She rolled her eyes—another surprise. "Ryker—"

"I'm serious," he said, cutting her off. "Don't say shit like that."

She pursed her lips and gave him a look that spoke volumes, but she didn't say anything out loud.

"What I was trying to say," he said pointedly, "is that there is no question in Mr. Miller's mind right now that we're together. And soon, there won't be a question in anyone else's mind either, because that man will tell all."

Her pursed lips relaxed. Parted. "Oh, my goodness." She smiled, and as it was the first smile of hers he'd ever witnessed, he wasn't prepared for the effect it had on him.

Her plump, red lips revealed perfectly straight and white teeth. He caught a glimpse of the tip of her tongue, so pink in contrast to her now-smeared lipstick.

But the clincher was, behind her glasses, her eyes crinkled at the corners, making her blue eyes reach new depths of color and expression.

He nearly took a stumbling step.

"I might *not* be ruined!" She bit into her bottom lip as she smiled.

He blinked several times. *What did she say?* She was happy, so it had to have been something good.

Holy God, her smile.

Her smile faded.

No!

"Are you okay?" she asked, her brows drawing together.

He relaxed. Smiled himself as he stroked her hands again. "I'm doing great, actually."

A comfortable but laden silence descended. He continued to brush his thumbs. She looked up at him.

"So, would you still consider getting——?"

"Do you still want to get——?" he said at the same time.

They stopped, the word neither of them had said sounding as loudly in the small alcove as if they had shouted it.

Married.

He licked his lips. Took the plunge. "Take me home with you, Charlotte."

She drew in a sharp breath. "To talk, or——?"

He shrugged with one shoulder. "We can talk. There's a lot to talk about, yes?"

She swallowed hard. "But that's not what you meant."

With a tug of their hands, he brought their bodies flush again. He was still hard, and when his dick met her stomach, pleasure much stronger than the mere contact merited rocketed through him.

If her gasp was any indication, she was suffering a similar phenomenon. Her gaze dipped to his lips, so she was already watching his mouth as he said, "I want us to have sex. All night. We can talk in the morning."

She swayed forward, pressing her breasts into him and making him grit his teeth as he fought not to react and wait patiently.

Say yes. Say yes!

"All night?" she asked in a whisper. She nibbled her bottom lip and then released it. "Do you promise?"

Hallelujah! Dropping one of her hands, he tucked the one he still held more firmly in his, intertwining their fingers. Without another word, he pulled her from the alcove and started hoofing it toward the exit.

She wordlessly kept pace with him, but her breaths quickened, and he hoped he wasn't imagining the increase in her pulse as he felt it fluttering at the base of her hand.

The cool night air of the desert greeted them as soon as they walked outside, but it didn't cool his lust one bit. "Which car is yours, *bonita?*"

Silence greeted him.

He turned to look at her over his shoulder, but her gaze was directed downward.

Is she—? She was! She was staring straight at his ass.

With a groan, he squeezed her fingers, which got her to jerk her gaze back to his. "I'm sorry, did you ask me something?" she asked.

He licked his lips. *"Mujer, voy a manchar ese lápiz de labios por todo tu hermosa cuerpo."*

Her eyes widened. "Smear my lipstick all over my body, huh?"

And, she spoke Spanish. "I said your *beautiful* body," he growled. "Tell me where your car is, Charlie. Now." Because if she didn't get in it soon, he was going to take her right here in the parking lot.

She blinked several times. "I took a cab."

He jerked a nod and was off again. Wishing he had something better than an early '90s, forest-green Honda to take her home in wasn't going to keep him from bundling her up in his passenger seat in record time. Ryker tugged her around the back of his car and unlocked the passenger door. Holding it open with his hip, he brought the hand he held up to his lips, cradling it between both of his palms. He pressed a soft kiss to her knuckles, then lowered her hand. "In you go," he said softly.

As soon as she was settled, he closed the door and made his way to his side. Surreptitiously, he tried to rearrange his erection in the midst of his strides, but it was still pinched as hell in his tailored slacks. He gave up as the time came to get into his own seat.

He cranked over the car, then placed his palm over her thigh. "Where to, Charlie?" The question was quiet. Husky.

She watched his mouth as she rambled off her address. While they drove through the streets of Las Vegas, Ryker kept his hand right where he'd placed it, allowing himself only the pleasure of stroking her thigh with his thumb when he wanted to ruck up her gown and finger her between her legs.

His painfully hard cock kicked in the confines of his pants, and he tried to keep his mind distracted.

Tried in vain.

Though the drive seemed interminable, they actually arrived at Charlotte's building much quicker than normal, thanks to a lack of traffic. They hadn't spoken a word to each other throughout the entire drive, but it hadn't been awkward.

The heavy silence had only stoked Ryker's desire to get her behind closed doors at last. She directed him to her second parking spot, and he pulled his clunker alongside a slick Cadillac, feeling his first niggling of anxiety.

Five hundred thousand dollars. A Cadillac. A building that houses the wealthiest people in the city.

Ryker was far out of his element.

As soon as he parked, Charlotte reached for the door. He *tsk*ed and hauled ass out of the car, skirting around the trunk and making it to her door just in time to hold it open for her and offer his hand.

She blinked at it in apparent surprise. How often had someone treated this woman like a lady?

Her fingers trembled when she placed them in his. When she rose to her full, diminutive height and gazed up at him through her glasses, Ryker had to swallow hard before he could speak. "Elevator?"

She nodded to a point over his shoulder. They were silent as they walked that direction and stepped inside. Before he could ask which floor to press, she pushed the button herself.

One floor below the top.

Jesus, he was out of his element.

The doors closed them in. For the first time since he'd kissed her, the silence between them was not natural.

She knotted her fingers together in front of her and stared at the numbers changing over the door.

He placed his palm in the small of her back—just a light touch that both reminded her why he was here and how good it felt when they touched at all.

She looked over her shoulder and gave him a strained smile. He rubbed his hand in a small circle, leaned down and brushed his lips against her hair.

She closed her eyes, and beneath the palm he held to her back, he felt her relax.

Then the elevator dinged. As the doors opened, she tensed all over again. When Ryker looked out of the elevator, he involuntarily tensed as well. The lobby was opulent. Marble floors, lush plants, and area rugs. A massive chandelier held prominence in the center.

Only two doors were visible from inside the elevator. Which meant Charlotte's apartment took up half the floor.

He gulped, called on reserves of courage he didn't currently feel, and ushered her from the elevator with his hand still in place right above her bottom. As they walked beneath the chandelier, the crystals cast beautiful designs of light all over Charlotte. Her hair, her shoulders, her gown.

Those breasts.

"Which—" he coughed. "Which apartment is yours, *bonita*?"

She nodded toward the door on the right. He realized she hadn't said anything since they'd gotten into the car, and the worry that she was having doubts, or worse, second thoughts, set up shop in his chest.

She dug a key from her small clutch and unlocked her door.

As Charlotte closed the door behind them, he knew he should survey her space. Learn what he could of her from it.

But her silence was a more pressing matter.

"Come here, Charlie," he whispered.

Her shoulders sagged a bit, and she turned toward him, a resigned look flitting through her eyes. But she walked toward him, stopping a few inches away.

He wanted to touch her, but wanted even more for her to have a chance to make an unclouded decision. He ducked his head, trying to capture her gaze. It proved elusive. "Charlotte, do you want me to go?"

Her gaze jerked to his at that. Her eyes widened. "No!"

Is she horrified at the thought of me leaving because she'll not have a fiancé, or because she wants me as desperately as I want her?

"I...want you to stay the night." Her gaze couldn't quite hold his as she confessed this.

Something uncurled low in his gut and seemed to stretch. Now, he allowed himself to touch her.

Sliding his hand into the curve of her waist, he pulled her toward him. She shifted toward him more than willingly, their bodies coming flush. With his other hand, he crooked a finger beneath her chin and raised her face to his. When she met his gaze, he asked, "Is this nerves, then?"

The corners of her eyes relaxed a bit, as though he'd put her at ease. It was a completely fortunate accident that he'd done so.

She nodded. "It's been a while."

That wasn't unusual in his line of work. "How long?" he asked, brushing his fingers along her jaw.

She swallowed. "Law school?"

His fingers stilled.

She closed her eyes behind those thick glasses. He quickly forced his fingers to resume their stroking. He was dying to know why a woman like Charlotte would forego sex for what had to be ten to fifteen years. Of course, he didn't want to make the same mistakes some slob, probably drunk on Pabst Blue Ribbon, had made. Mostly, though, he wanted to find out if he needed to hunt anybody down. Have a little *chat*.

He trailed his fingers along her jaw until he could swirl one around the shell of her delicate ear. She shivered. "I'll make sure this was worth the wait then, yes?" he said quietly.

Her eyes opened again. "Yes," she breathed.

"Anything you need to tell me before I take your lips again, *bonita?*"

She frowned.

"Anything I shouldn't do? Any other place you don't want me to touch?"

That enchanting blush from earlier erupted over her chest. His gaze dipped despite his best efforts.

Dying to see those breasts!

"I-I...can't imagine...not liking anything you'd do." Her gaze lowered. "To me."

Oh, hell, he was going to spontaneously orgasm right here in the entranceway to her apartment.

He swallowed hard. "Well, if something comes up, you let me know. I'll ask no questions."

She nodded, the blush now moving up her neck and to her cheeks.

He couldn't wait any longer. Leaning in, he pressed a kiss to the crown of her head. "I'm going to take this beautiful gown off," he murmured against her hair.

She stiffened a bit. "N-now?" Her words brushed across his Adam's apple in an exhalation of breath.

"If I'd had my way, I would have taken it off you in that hallway, Charlie." He wrapped his arm more securely around her waist, his fingertips finding the hidden zipper in the middle of her back. "I've been impressively patient."

Her breath this time carried a husky chuckle. "Okay, then." Her voice trembled slightly, but she sounded sure.

Her zipper came undone with barely a sound except the thunderous pounding of his heart. His fingertips brushed along boning, and he realized she was wearing something beneath this gown that had the potential to be miraculous. When the zipper was all the way down, he stepped back, anticipating the vision that would await him.

She clutched her loosened gown to her breasts, her blush in full force.

He allowed his gaze to leisurely move over the body he'd been dying to ogle.

Tonight, this body was his. Maybe even for longer. His cock surged within his pants.

The barest hint of a bustier peeked out from the top of her bodice. He brought his gaze back to her face. "Drop the dress, Charlie." His voice was so low, he nearly didn't recognize it.

Her fingers tightened in their hold, her knuckles and nails blanching white. But just as he wondered if he was pushing her too hard too quickly, she lifted her chin and—

The gown cascaded to the floor around her in a rush of silk.

He sucked in an audible breath. "Jesus God, *mujer*."

She stood before him in a black satin bustier, a black lace panty so fine it was nearly transparent, and—he took a stumbling step forward—a garter belt and stockings.

Shit. Shit! He pressed the heel of his palm firmly over his cock, pressing down as hard as he dared. The move just barely kept him in check, but his balls protested with all their might.

Turning from her before he could take in any more details in the dim light, he scanned the area quickly, locating a sofa several feet to his right. He strode that direction, drawing a few slow, measured breaths to try to tamp down his arousal. Unbuttoning his tuxedo jacket, he spread the lapels and sank into the sofa. Forcing his gaze to hers, he crooked a finger. "*Ven aquí, bonita.*"

With absolutely no hesitation this time, she stepped out of her dress and walked toward him. He clamped his teeth together to keep from panting. The way her thighs and breasts moved as she walked in those heels. God, she was a revelation.

That her breasts were at all contained in her bustier was a miracle. They were thrust so high, he could see a hint of her areolas, a dusky rose that made his mouth water.

He knew he should be keeping his gaze locked with hers, gauging her reaction and adjusting his moves accordingly so she was highly aroused at all times. But he couldn't drag himself away from that rosy color, hoping against hope for a glimpse of nipple as those breasts bounced dangerously with her every step.

When they stopped jiggling, he frowned and looked up at her face again. She stood a good foot away from him, framed between his sprawled knees, her hands twisted in front of her at her waist as though she were pondering covering her breasts or the apex of her thighs and unable to decide which.

He relaxed into the back of the sofa and spread his arms across the back. Her gaze traveled over his torso, the blue of her eyes heating in response. Her fingers loosened their death grip on each other, and her elbows slackened into her side.

Good.

"Are you good at following directions, *bonita*?"

Her chin lifted, seemingly without her knowledge. He knew the question had burned her sensibilities, and he waited for her to protest. Which, honestly, would be more than fine by him. He was here to pleasure her, not himself. It was just, his instincts kept telling him she wanted him to take control. To lead and demand.

He hoped his instincts were right, because the mere suggestion that he might be able to command her was sending him into a lather.

"It depends on what's in it for me," she said, her voice husky.

He cocked an eyebrow. *Good girl.* "Oh, I'll definitely make it worth your while."

She licked her lips. "Then…try me."

He examined her for one more long moment, gauging her level of honesty. He swallowed hard. "Strip for me, Charlie."

Her face blanched. "S-strip?"

He lowered his gaze to her breasts again. "Take off everything you're wearing. Starting with that bustier that insists on hiding your nipples from me. I want it off. All of it."

"Get naked…*alone?*"

He looked at her face again, for a moment worrying that he'd misread the situation and she was horrified.

She was definitely nervous, but that wasn't the dominant expression she wore on her lovely features.

She was titillated.

Instead of answering, he simply relaxed further into the cushions and continued to hold her gaze.

With a hard swallow, her trembling fingers traveled to the top of her bustier. He nearly leaned forward as her fingertips brushed against the mounds of her breasts, but, with a firm grip to the top of the couch, he was able to keep himself in place.

She looked down as she worked to undo the first hook and eyelet, and after a moment of struggle, she licked her lips.

Something lurched in his stomach as he realized how unpracticed she was with this form of lingerie. How lucky he was that he got to see her in it.

And soon to be out of it.

When the top fastening sprang open, she gasped.

He nearly did, too, because, *finally*, he caught the barest glimpse of her nipples before they disappeared behind the cups again. Surrounded by that delicious color, her nipples were two tiny points, so hard they looked painful. They'd be firm against his tongue. Between his teeth—

She released another fastening, and another. He forced himself to exhale. Which only proved to be a bad idea, because once his lungs were empty, she'd reached the bottom of the long line of hooks and eyelets. Her bustier sagged open, and, with a raise of her chin, she spread it wide and let it fall to the floor.

His empty lungs clamored for air, and he sucked in a harsh breath that nearly caused him to choke. He played it off with a small cough, but the burning in his chest remained.

They were full. Heavy. Perfect. God, she was a double D at the least. His fingers tightened on the back of the sofa again as he longed to lift those breasts in his hands. Weigh them. Bring them to his lips. Chafe them with his stubble.

As she reached for her garters, her breasts bobbed and a whimper escaped his lips.

She paused, her fingers on one garter fastening. Her gaze shot his direction.

He didn't bother hiding what he was thinking, just kept his focus rapt on those breasts.
Would she be one of those women he could bring to orgasm simply through sucking her nipples? He was more than game to test that theory.

"Keep going, *bonita*." His voice was barely recognizable, and, when he chanced a quick glance down to his groin after she looked there and then away quickly, he saw that he was shamelessly tenting his tuxedo slacks. There was even the smallest wet spot right over where the crown of his dick pressed against them. He was weeping for her.

She quickly released one stocking and then the other and began rolling both down her full legs simultaneously. As she leaned forward, her breasts swayed, and he couldn't keep himself in check any longer.

Keeping one arm stretched across the back of the couch, he reached out for her with the other, cupping her right breast in his palm. He hefted it, fitting her hard nipple between his pointer and middle finger and pinching it with a contraction of his fingers.

She gasped.

He groaned.

They were so heavy. So hot. With a harsh swallow, he released her and fisted his hand next to his thigh. "Quickly, Charlie." He clenched his teeth as he took a deep breath. "The rest off. Now."

She straightened; her nipples were surrounded by a smattering of goose bumps that traveled all across her breasts and chest. He'd given her those with one simple touch.

Nothing simple about that touch.

She unfastened her empty garter belt and let it fall to the floor, then hooked her thumbs in her panties and began sliding them down her thighs.

The first thing he noticed as they trailed down her legs was that she'd been wearing not panties but a thong. There was a quick pang of regret that he hadn't seen her from behind while she'd worn them, but then his gaze found what she was revealing to him, and he suddenly didn't care about anything else.

Her sex was covered by a tiny, maintained patch of short curls that were a shade darker than her dark hair. His fingers longed to discover how soft those curls would be. Just beneath the curls, the lips of her sex were swollen and slick. With a final shimmy and a kick of her leg, she sent her thong flying to join the pile of her lingerie. And that little kick revealed just how swollen her clitoris had become.

He was done waiting.

His gaze locked on the apex of her thighs, he demanded, "Come here. Straddle me."

His tone brooked no negotiation, and she stumbled forward, more than eager to follow. But, between his spread knees, she hesitated.

If she straddles me, she be completely exposed. There would be no hiding anything from him. She'd be vulnerable.

"Show me heaven, *bonita*," he whispered, letting his control slip for a moment and putting all his longing in his words.

Her gaze snapped to his face. She scanned his features and seemed shocked to realize how badly he wanted this. Wanted her.

Hesitantly, she placed one knee on the sofa beside his thigh.

Her pussy flowered for him. He gritted his teeth as he caught his first glimpse of the dark shadow of her opening. Her thigh trembled as she shifted, putting her weight on it. As she reached out for his shoulder with one hand, he caught the harried sound of her breathing.

His was just as broken.

Her fingers made contact with his shoulder, and he curled his arm, placing his own hand over hers and holding her steady as she slid her other knee onto the sofa.

Her knees hugged his thighs tightly. What would it feel like for them to be hugging his ribs as he pinned her beneath him?

His gaze was riveted to her bared sex as she settled her bottom over his knees. He found himself licking his lips, wanting a taste of the treasure she'd been hiding between her thighs.

He squeezed the fingers he held secure against his shoulder, brought them to his lips, and kissed her fingertips before directing her hand toward her own body. Snagging her other hand from her thigh as well, he placed her palms over her straining nipples, being sure to keep his own fingers from her breasts.

Once he touched them, this was over.

"Cup these," he demanded. "Bring them to my mouth."

He was more than ready to put his nipple-orgasm theory to the test.

"Y-you want that?" she asked breathlessly.

He met her gaze. "More than you could possibly know."

Licking her lips, she adjusted her hands, skimming them down her breasts. Her flesh plumped around her fingers, and Ryker bit back another groan. Slipping her hands beneath her breasts, she lifted them, and the sight made him clench his fingers.

Though she seemed to be doing fine balance-wise on her own as she leaned forward, he slid his fingers into the nip of her waist. She was surprisingly soft, and he found himself flexing his fingers as he held her steady.

Her eyes went heavy lidded as she obeyed him, bringing her magnificent breasts closer to his lips. He tried to be patient—he truly did. But as soon as her nipples were within reach, he strained forward. His first instinct was to suck one of her turgid nipples between his lips. But he wanted to immerse himself in her. To be surrounded by her scent and her heat. So, instead, he buried his face between her uplifted breasts, drawing in a long, slow breath as he did so.

She held the faintest hint of perfume in the valley of her cleavage. And, Jesus, they were so firm against his cheeks.

She sucked in a breath as he raked his stubble against first one swell and then the next. Despite his grip on her waist, he found his hands raising of their own accord. They covered hers. Lifted her breasts even farther.

He flexed his fingers. He pressed a soft kiss to the inside swell of one of her tits. "Do you know how beautiful you are here, Charlie? What a fantasy you are?"

He felt her tremble in his lap, and beneath his fingers, hers tightened as well.

"R-Ryker?"

"Yes, *bonita*?" He rasped his cheeks against her again, cradling her breasts in his palms like the rarest treasures.

"Suck me," she breathed. "Please."

He paused for only a moment; there was no mistaking it: it had been a demand.

Gaining confidence, sweet Charlie? Initiative would always be rewarded in their bed.

Raising his gaze to lock with hers, he moved to the right. He allowed his hot breaths to caress her first, and as they did, she squirmed in his lap. While he watched her eyes, her gaze was rapt on his parted lips. And still, he made her wait. Rather than sucking her, he brushed his lips over the very tip of her nipple.

She sucked in a breath. "Ryker," she moaned. "No teasing."

He cocked a brow. "You sure about that?"

She wiggled her fingers beneath his, extracting both of her hands. With absolutely no sign of the hesitation she'd been showing mere minutes before, she curled her fingers over his shoulders and drew him in.

Her nipple slipped between his lips. Helpless to resist her, he closed the seal and sucked with gentle tugs.

Fuck. It was even better than he'd been anticipating. He drew her deep, savoring the slight hint of salt on her skin. The way her nipple rubbed the roof of his mouth.

"*Yes*," she breathed, her fingers moving from his shoulders to his head. They slid through his hair, her nails scraping gently against his scalp and sending shivers throughout his entire body.

He covered her neglected nipple with his other hand, palming her and massaging as he began to suck with stronger pulls. With his free hand, he skimmed his fingers down her ribs. She arched into the light touch like a dream, thrusting her breast against his lips.

He widened them and sucked more of her into his mouth. At the same time, his hand kept moving. Down her abdomen. Over the curve of her hip. Across the top of her ass. Finally, it rested in the small of her back.

He leaned back against the sofa cushions, bringing her with him with that hand firmly nestled just above her bottom.

She gasped as her stomach met his. He relaxed into the couch, more than content to just feast on her as long as she would let him.

He moved his mouth to her other nipple, bringing his hand from her back to cradle her wet, swollen peak.

She'd begun subtly rocking her hips as she straddled his lap. She was craving him between her legs. Had no doubt grown unbearably wet for him.

He had to feel for himself. Confirm.

He sucked her deeply as he eased his fingers between their bodies. When his fingertips brushed through her curls, she jumped. He petted her softly. Soothingly. Within a few heartbeats, she relaxed.

God bless her, she even spread her knees a bit.

"My good girl," he whispered against her wet nipple before drawing her into his mouth again.

His fingers dipped lower, and as he got his first feel of her slick skin, she whimpered and trembled against him.

He pressed the tip of his middle finger at the top of her cleft and slid it down. "Fuck," he rasped against her breast.

She was wetter even than he had imagined.

"Oh," she breathed. "Keep going."

Spreading her lips with his ring and pointer fingers, he obeyed. She soaked his fingers as he sought out her clit. When he found it, she gasped.

He pulled from her nipple with a *pop*. He needed to watch her as he touched her for the first time.

Her lips were parted. A flush stained her cheeks. Her glasses were slightly askew.

Something tightened in his gut. Shoving that aside, he stroked her clit in a firm, tight circle.

She rocked on her knees to his touch.

"Feel good, *bonita*?"

She bit into her bottom lip, seemingly too lost to answer. He stroked deeper, pressing his thumb against her clit and seeking her opening with his other fingertips. When he found it, he eased his middle finger inside her.

She moaned softly. Her hands tugged fitfully at his hair as she rose up on her knees, simultaneously seeming to try to rock to and away from his touch.

She was so tight. Here, clamped around his finger, was the evidence of how long she'd gone without sex.

"Easy, Charlie," he murmured, stroking her clit with his thumb again. "Easy." He leaned up and pressed soft, closed-mouth kisses to her breasts, scattering them across both mounds.

He wanted to stroke her. To bring her off as easily as he suspected he could.

She needed more.

Reaching up with his free hand, he crooked a finger beneath her chin. "Give me that beautiful mouth again."

With a jerky nod and a nearly inaudible moan, she curled her fingers in his hair and lowered her lips to his.

As soon as their mouths met, she licked at his lips.

That's it, Charlie.

He opened for her, sucking her tongue into his mouth just as he had her nipples. She melted into him, wrapping her arms around his neck and lowering back down to his lap.

Which he took as his cue.

With her firmly settled over his knees again, he leisurely withdrew and then thrust his middle finger.

She moaned around his tongue, and when he next thrust with his finger, she canted her hips in time with him, taking him deeper.

He slid a second finger inside her, widening them on each thrust. By the time he eased a third in with the others, she was moaning helplessly into their kiss. Her nails bit at his scalp, and she was rocking her hips faster and faster, her beautiful bottom rolling over his thighs in a way that was going to drive him crazy.

With a cry that hinted she was on the edge of orgasm, she pulled from the kiss. Her eyes were squeezed shut behind her glasses, her eyebrows drawn together so tightly she looked as though she were in pain. Her teeth clamped her bottom lip until the plump flesh was bleached white.

His fingers were slick with her arousal, the sounds of him thrusting them inside her filling the air between them. Her thighs started to tremble in earnest now, and he felt the telltale fluttering of her pussy against his fingers.

"Come for me, *bonita*." He leaned in and lollypop licked her nipple.

She tensed and tossed her head back. A low, constant moan began deep within her chest and soon escalated.

She undulated in his lap, driving his fingers in and out of her sex so quickly he had to speed his own rhythm to keep up. By the time she shattered, her cries echoed through her apartment.

Laving her nipple, he gazed up at her. He didn't want to miss a moment of this sight. Her rosy cheeks, parted lips, and tightly shut eyes were the most arousing things he'd ever seen.

Her slickness dripped down his fingers. Leaning back, he glanced down beneath their bodies.

She'd absolutely destroyed his tuxedo slacks. Her arousal marked his pants, glistening where she'd been grinding against him. His fingers picked up reflected light as he thrust them in and out of her pussy. He stared, mesmerized by the sight until she placed a shaky hand over his.

Ah, too sensitive for now.

He eased his fingers from her body, wiping them on his pants. *The cleaners will wonder what I've been up to.* The thought brought a smile to his face.

She sagged in his lap with a dazed expression, her arms still wrapped around his neck.

Her glasses were the slightest bit foggy.

He bit back a grin.

"Where's your bedroom, Charlie?"

Her head rolled on her shoulders as she met his gaze. "Hmm?"

"Your bedroom?"

"Oh." She shook her head as though to clear it. "Down that way." She pointed to the hallway at the right of the entrance.

He nodded, and in one smooth movement, stood and cradled her against his chest.

She gasped, tightening her arms around his neck as he started striding toward her bed. Gazing up at what was probably a fierce expression on his face, she asked, "We're not done yet, are we?"

He shook his head. "Not even close."

Fuck, walking with a raging erection in tailored slacks was a new form of torture. The sensitive crown of his dick chafed against the fabric, making him grit his teeth.

He needed out of these pants. Now.

And inside her sweet body.

He needed a distraction…uh, the walls were dotted with expensive-looking pieces of art, each highlighted by pot lighting in the ceiling. They looked like originals. Not that he had any real fucking experience with original artwork. They had little resemblance to the flat reproductions he decorated his own dismal apartment with, however.

"Next door on your right," she whispered, leaning in and nuzzling his ear.

His arms tightened around her just as his groin tightened even further.

His ears were his favorite erogenous zone, and, *God*, having her touch them was life-changing.

He toed her bedroom door open and fumbled for a switch, making contact and flooding the room with light.

Her room was decorated with rich grays that ranged from soft and lavender to deep, nearly dark slate. A massive king-sized bed dominated the far wall, and he made his way over, adjusting Charlotte's weight in his arms.

Carefully, he set her bottom down and nestled her against the pillows. As he withdrew his arms from beneath her, he valiantly kept himself from giving her ass another squeeze. He was truly an American hero.

He straightened and shamelessly gazed down at her spread out for him in the full light. Damn but he was a lucky man.

Her gaze skittered away from his, as though she were suddenly shy now that they were in a well-lit room. *Perhaps better not to tell her right away that I have excellent vision in the dark.*

He reached into his pocket and withdrew one of the condoms he'd brought with him just in case—even though she'd insisted she didn't want sex.

A gigolo always had to be prepared. Sex tended to happen.

His movement caught her attention, and she stared at the condom as he placed it within reach on the bedside table.

Slowly she brought her gaze back to his. He raised his eyebrows in question.

Still on board?

Her gaze dipped, caressing his neck, his chest, his stomach. Finally, it stopped at his groin, where she seemed to grow transfixed by his obvious erection. As she followed its rigid outline, she caught a glimpse of the state of his slacks.

She gasped. "Oh, no, I've ruined these!" she whispered, horrified. She stretched out her hand as though she would scrub away the stains.

He caught her fingers and squeezed them. "Improved them is more likely."

She groaned, the sound filled with embarrassment, and covered her eyes with one hand, knocking her glasses askew again.

He squeezed her fingers once more, this time to get her attention. "Watch me, Charlie."

She peeped at him through a crack in her fingers, and he nearly grinned all over again.

Releasing her hand, he grabbed his lapels and shrugged his jacket from his shoulders.

That got her attention. Her hand slid down to cover her lips as he folded his jacket and placed it neatly on a nearby chair. Then his fingers came to his bowtie, and, though she was obviously unaware she did so, she straightened a bit, propping herself up on her elbows for a better view.

And he'd give it to her. A better view or whatever else she wanted, both in and out of the bedroom. Because there was nothing he wouldn't do to make sure this agreement of theirs worked out.

Chapter Seven

She stared raptly as he pulled his bowtie free with a flick of his wrist. Her mouth went dry as he laid it on the bedside table and then began undoing his shirt one slow, torturous button at a time.

The ache between her legs redoubled, making her feel hollow.

One thing was for certain: she had never wanted to see anything in her life as much as she wanted to see this man naked.

All her previous sexual encounters had been accomplished in the dark. Beneath covers. Within five minutes.

This experience already surpassed them all combined, and as she caught her first glimpse of Ryker's chest, she wondered if she'd ever have anything this good again.

Yes, I will. Because I'm marrying this guy.

The thought jolted her. She'd never thought to be married. *And you won't really be now.* A marriage in name only wasn't really a marriage, so she would be fine.

Safe and focused.

You're anything but focused right now. She shoved the wayward dose of reality aside.

His fingers paused on his fourth button with only a scant inch of his chest showing. Not nearly enough.

Her gaze flew to his.

His lips were curled at the edges. "Everything okay, Charlie?"

She cocked an eyebrow. "Not if you're going to stop undressing."

He chuckled. "You just looked...distracted. Wanted to make sure we are on the same page."

She licked her lips. "We're on the same page." She nodded toward his still fingers. "Keep going."

Those lips curled even more, but he kept unbuttoning his shirt, and she found herself exhaling a breath. When he popped the next button, all her relief disappeared only to be replaced with an urgent kind of lust that made her restless enough to want to reach for him, yank off the rest of his clothes, and explore his entire body. With her tongue.

He was muscled. Not heavily—not by any means. But he was lean and defined, a line appearing down the center of his pecs. When he loosened another button, she saw that the line continued down to his abdomen.

She made a soft noise and sat upright. Her breasts felt heavy. Needful of his touch. As though he'd heard their call, his gaze dipped to them as he pulled his shirt free from his pants and undid the last two buttons.

His dark eyes unmistakably heated as he stared at her breasts, as they'd done each and every time he'd looked at or touched them.

Ryker made her feel...*sexy*. It was a completely foreign feeling.

Grabbing both sides of his shirt, he shrugged it off. In the light of the room, his muscles flexed and released in a breathtaking display as the shirt made its way to the ground.

Charlotte gasped as she caught sight of him half naked for the first time. He had a six——no, eight——pack.

Oh, dear God.

She looked frantically around the bed, trying to find something—anything—to cover herself with. A whimper escaped her.

"Charlie?" There was an odd tone to his voice, but she couldn't stop her search now.

She snatched a pillow from the other side of the bed and hugged it to her breasts and belly.

The bed dipped beside her. She felt the heat of him near her side, which meant that his perfect, naked body was oh-so-close to her not-even-close-to-perfect naked body.

"Charlie, talk to me." His tone bordered on stern, something she hadn't heard from him yet. It was just unexpected enough to get her full attention.

"That's what you look like naked?" She sounded hysterical; she could hear it. Unfortunately, there didn't seem to be anything she could do about that.

"I'm not naked yet."

Was he amused? She groaned and clenched her pillow tighter with both hands.

The heat of his palm covering the back of one of her hands made her jump. "*Bonita*, what's going on here?"

She gestured vaguely in his direction. "That's what you look like naked, and this—" She waved at herself, unable to even finish the thought.

Her inability to continue didn't matter, as he didn't give her the chance to finish anyway. "Oh, *hell* no."

Suddenly the pillow was gone.

She grasped at it blindly, her gasp ragged. "Give it back!" Out of necessity, she looked his way again. Just in time to see him toss the pillow across the room. "Ryker!" She immediately reached for another pillow.

He captured both of her hands, pulled them over her head, and covered her body with his.

It all happened so quickly that she had to blink up at him several times to orient herself. Moments ago, she'd been sitting. Now she was sprawled beneath him. He was heavy. It felt delicious. His smooth, hairless chest met her breasts, pressing them flat and stroking her nipples with the softest touch. Her jaw nearly dropped. "What are you doing?"

Though his grip on her wrists was firm, it was gentle, and he brushed over her pulse points with his thumbs. "Proving a point."

She squirmed beneath him, and his gaze dipped to down to her body once more. "Don't look at me!"

His gaze shot up to hers again, and she thought she read a warning in his eyes. "Hate to break it to you, Charlie, but I've already memorized what you look like naked. It's currently one of my favorite mental images. If you keep trash talking it, I'm going to get angry."

She scowled.

He shook his head. "You're only more beautiful when you glare at me, *bonita*."

Against her will, she sneaked a peek at his pecs again. He was...too pretty. She squeezed her eyes shut.

He made a *tsk*ing noise, and she felt his finger curl beneath her chin. "You open those eyes, gorgeous. Right now."

Reluctantly, she did.

"You think I look good naked?" He shoved his hips forward, something hard and wicked grinding against her sex. "Well, this is what my body thinks about *your* naked body."

She felt her scowl return. "Don't mock me."

His eyes widened. "Jesus. I don't know what your previous lovers have done exactly, but I know each and every one of them needs to be punched in the face. Preferably by me."

She sniffed. "One of them was already punched in the face." Her gaze skated away. "By me."

Ryker was silent for a moment, and she was so tempted to look at him again, but she kept her gaze focused on the painting beside her bedroom door. She couldn't believe she'd just confessed that. It remained one of her most regretted moments. A complete lack of control that had culminated a long list of losses of control and heralded in a long list of consequences.

Ryker gave a husky groan. "Well, if you hadn't proposed already, I'd be on my knees right now."

Her gaze shot back to his, and she was shocked to see he looked...serious. It was written all over his face, from his heated gaze to the flush on his chiseled cheeks. He didn't seem aghast at her confession in any way. In fact, if she were more knowledgeable about these things, she'd say her confession had even turned him on.

His eyebrow quirked. "It's not too late for me to get on my knees, by the way. For a different purpose."

She pressed her lips together, but within moments she understood what he was hinting at, and they parted. No one had ever done that to her. For her. Would she even like it? Too much to think about right now. "Maybe later," she muttered.

Another groan. "You can count on it." He rocked his hips again. "Now, can I please finish getting naked?" He leaned down, nuzzling her jaw and brushing a kiss against her neck. "If I'm not inside you in the next minute," he whispered against her ear, "I may convince you I'm not a professional when these breasts—" He pressed his chest more firmly against hers and broke off with another husky groan of his. "When these breasts," he continued, his voice more ragged than a moment before, "make me come right in my pants."

She bit her bottom lip and tried to focus. Oddly enough, it was that repeated husky groan that grounded her.

She'd never heard a sexier sound in her life. It seemed that might be the noise he made when he was losing control. She wanted to hear it more. Wanted to know if she could make it come more deeply. Or more desperately. Even more softly, as though he were helpless against what she was making him feel.

She lifted her chin. "Take off your pants."

His eyes flashed, and for a moment, she worried he'd say something she'd heard before in a situation like this. That women weren't supposed to be bossy in bed. That she couldn't expect him to give her what she wanted in the bedroom when she couldn't do the same outside of it. If he said something like that, it would confirm that sex just wasn't for her.

But, in the next second, he was lifting his hips from hers. Shuffling her wrists until they were gathered in only one of his hands, he reached between their bodies. She felt him tugging at his belt; the sound of his belt buckle clicking in the quiet room ratcheted up her nerves while simultaneously making her melt between her legs a little bit more.

As he kicked his pants down his legs, she was bombarded with a flurry of sensation: his grip around her wrists was still incredibly gentle; his torso was completely smooth; the hair on his thighs tickled the insides of her own thighs, making her want to clasp him with them in a hug; his hot breaths skated over her neck and collarbone.

She wanted him more than she was afraid of what would happen between them. Of what would occur immediately following and what the consequences would be.

It was terrifying and freeing at the same time.

I'll deal with that later. Get my head on straight again.

Now, though, she was going to have sex with this beautiful, considerate man. And she was going to enjoy it, she had no doubt. He wouldn't stand for anything less.

His pants fell off the end of the bed with a telltale clatter of belt buckle. Immediately, however, there was another sound. A crinkle.

Ryker placed a square packet between his teeth and ripped it open. He squeezed free the condom, flicked the foil aside, and his hand disappeared between their bodies again.

The sight banished another dose of her nerves. When his lush eyelashes fluttered as he rolled the condom down his length, every emotion but lust beat a hasty retreat.

She licked dry lips and found herself rotating her hands in his grasp, reaching for his fingers.

His gaze met hers as she twined the fingers of both her hands with his one. He tilted his head. "You're with me," he whispered, the sound of his words so slight, she wondered if he'd meant to say them out loud at all. His tone was blatantly relieved.

She squeezed his fingers. "I'm with you."

When he leaned down and rested his forehead against hers, he swallowed audibly, and then she felt a nudge against her entrance. A nudge by something large. Something stroked over her swollen, throbbing clitoris.

His thumb.

Another stroke. With his crown wedged against the opening of her sex, the brush of his skin against her clit made her wild. She found herself raising her knees on each side of his hips, desperately wanting a bit more pressure.

And getting it.

Her eyes slid closed as the broad tip of his erection entered her just slightly. And all the while, his thumb kept stroking.

His forehead still pressed against hers, he whispered. "Look at me, *bonita*."

It took Herculean effort, but she opened her eyes and met his gaze.

"I can't hurt you, Charlie."

The edge to his voice took her by surprise. She frowned. "Hurt me?"

"With it being so long since you—" He broke off, swallowing hard enough to make his Adam's apple bob. "If it's uncomfortable, you have to tell me. Promise?"

"P-promise." This could never hurt. The things he was doing to her body—

He eased forward, timing the shallow pump of his hips with another stroke of her clitoris.

She moaned, her eyes fluttering, but her promise making her force them wide again. "Keep going," she gasped, rocking her own hips.

He produced a harsher, shorter version of his signature groan; she was going to explode. She wiggled her hips at the same time that he withdrew just a bit, and when he next thrust, she met him, canting and raising her hips.

He slid in deep.

She gasped, going rigid beneath him.

Okay, that does *hurt.*

He bit out a curse. "Charlie." His hand cupped her shoulder, and she realized he wasn't holding her wrists anymore. Her fingers were curled like claws in each of his arms. "*Charlie.* You have to look at me, *bonita.* Please."

My eyes are closed? She blinked several times and tried to focus on Ryker's face. It appeared her eyes were swimming with tears, but she could see his clear distress.

"Okay, we're done," he said firmly. He began to pull out so slowly it was obvious he was afraid of hurting her more.

But the smooth, long drag of his erection inside her lit off thousands of sensations. All of them...good.

She clutched his shoulders and tightened her thighs around his hips. "Wait," she gasped. "Just, wait a second."

He froze. "Shit. I hurt you again. Charlie, I'm so, so sorry."

"No…I think…" She looked down at his body, his bulging muscles straining as he held himself above her. Her heart quickened, the sight of his gorgeous body making her go wetter between her legs. Immediately, the rest of the discomfort vanished. She gazed back into his eyes, feeling her own widen in wonder. "I think I *like* it."

His brows crashed together. "Charlie…"

She tightened her thighs again, thought better of it, and wrapped them around him instead to make sure he wouldn't persist in this ridiculous withdrawing business. Her calves trailed across the firm globes of his backside and brought his pelvis more firmly against hers. It was at that point, as their bodies came into closer contact, that she realized his thumb was still pressed against her clitoris.

"Mmm." She moaned. "I need to you stroke me again. While you move." She curled her fingers into his shoulders when he still looked hesitant. "Ryker, please."

He closed his eyes on a groan.

But it was his *husky* groan. The sound brought goose bumps to her chest. She'd won!

Then the world rotated. Quicker than she could realize, he'd flipped them, his strong hands wrapping around her knees and prying her death grip off his waist just in time to keep him from crushing her legs beneath him.

Next thing she knew, he was wiggling beneath her, finding a comfortable spot in the location she'd just vacated. She was perched atop him in an approximation of what they'd done on the couch earlier. Except this time, he was inside her with more than just his fingers.

His fingers squeezed her knees. "If we do this, you drive, *bonita*. I won't hurt you again."

I drive? Oh, no. They were doomed. She didn't know what she was doing! Didn't he know that? She braced her weight with her palms to his chest. How she was going to do this? Only one thing was for sure—she *was* going to do this. Stopping was not an option.

"*Damn*, these breasts." His hands left her knees, and he filled his palms. She noticed for the first time that the skin of his hands was rough and abraded her nipples in the most tantalizing fashion. He squeezed and pressed her breasts high, and the heat in his eyes as he stared raptly at her chest made her writhe.

Immediately, his gaze snapped to hers. "Oh, yeah, *bonita*." He rotated his hips beneath her. "More of that."

131

She felt heat fill her cheeks, but the look in his eye emboldened her and she squirmed.

A husky groan.

Planting her palms against his chest more firmly, she bore down on him with more confidence, swishing her hips back then forth.

He bit out a curse. His palms smoothed down to her ribs. "Lean down, Charlie. Bring these pretty breasts to my mouth."

He didn't wait for her to follow instruction, just tightened his arms around her, hugging her close and raising himself at the same time. He buried his face between her breasts, licking and nipping them; she gasped as she found the new position pressed her clit against his pelvic bone in the best way imaginable.

With a moan, she wriggled anew, amazed to discover the press against her clit felt better than she could have even dreamed.

"That's it," he murmured between kisses to her left nipple. With a lick, he drew it into his mouth, bit down gently, and began to suck. One of his hands skated down her back and palmed her bottom. With firm pressure, he guided her into a slow, steady roll with her hips.

Her eyes widened as he filled her to capacity before slowly withdrawing. Like a genius, he timed the tugs of his mouth on her nipple to each gentle thrust. Her head lolled forward, and she whimpered as that tight coil that had led to paradise earlier tonight began tightening once again.

"Ryker," she gasped.

In answer, he gave her nipple one final kiss and then switched to her other, covering the one he'd abandoned with his rough palm. He plumped her left breast as he began the same torturous sucking of her right nipple.

"Oh!" she cried as she rolled right to the edge of orgasm. She knew her nails were biting into his chest, but she couldn't seem to stop herself as she struggled to press her clit against his pelvis as hard as she needed to in order to coast over the edge.

She rolled and rolled against him, hovered right on the precipice, and she…*can't get there.*

She whimpered again. This time, even she could tell the whimper carried desperation. "Ryker," she said, his name a plea. "I can't—"

He released her nipple. "Easy, *bonita,*" he breathed against her wet flesh. "I've got you." Squeezing her bottom and cradling her back, he moved them again, rolling them over.

She moaned as he filled her with one, firm stroke. Her head thrashed on the pillow. *So close!* "Please, Ryker—"

His thumb pressed against her clitoris again, and she cried out, bucking her hips into his touch.

"Just need it harder here, yeah?" He stroked her again, his touch bordering on rough.

"Yes!" she cried. She writhed against him, uncaring how embarrassing she most likely looked in this moment as she chased pleasure with abandon.

"Fuck, you're hot." He timed a husky groan perfectly with another stroke of her clit and searing thrust inside her sex.

"Ryker!" She split apart at the seams. Her sex milked him. She ground her clit against his thumb, clawing his back as she arched her own.

He made a broken sound in his throat. "Charlie," he breathed. Burying his face against her neck, he thrust hard. And fast.

Her eyes rolled back as she clutched him close and her orgasm ratcheted up. Sounds tore from her throat with a violence that would surely shock her in a few moments. With no clue what she was saying, she gave herself up to all the pleasure.

Dimly, she heard his desperate groan—a sound that carried a hint of pain this time. He went rigid over her, burying himself as deeply as he could within her.

Moments later he shuddered in her arms. Biting down on her collarbone, he began a slow languid roll of his hips as heat flooded her sex. She could feel him coming, even through the condom.

Her head canted back as her own pleasure made her shake just as badly as he was shaking.

He collapsed atop her, his weight at once vital and so heavy she had trouble breathing. As she was gasping for air already, that proved troublesome. With a sigh that couldn't possibly sound more sated, Ryker rolled off her, solving the problem without her having to ask.

Their ragged breathing filled the room. Between her legs, she ached. Tingled. Throbbed.

Want to do that again. Soon.

She rolled her head to the side, gazing at him as he struggled to catch his breath beside her. He mirrored her movement, meeting her gaze.

He grinned.

She felt herself returning it.

"I'm definitely marrying you," he said, his voice a hoarse rumble.

Elation unlike anything she'd ever felt filled her.

And that brought terror down over her as quickly as if a bucket of ice water had been poured over her head.

Elation? Really? As though she'd forgotten everything life had taught her?

She looked back up at the ceiling, suddenly breathless for an entirely different reason. "That's good," she said in her best impression of a calm, rational person. "Very good."

His fingers wrapped around hers, and she barely resisted the urge to snatch her hand away before she could feel anything else. "Hey, you okay, Charlie?"

She forced a smile and looked at him again. "Of course. Just tired." She squeezed his fingers and then released them, crossing her arms over her chest. "We'll talk particulars in the morning, okay?"

His brows drew together, and he looked as though he were going to protest, but after a long moment, he nodded. "Sure, *bonita*."

With a nod of her own, she rolled onto her side, presenting him with her back. Behind her, she heard the sheets rustle as he got out of bed and then water running in the bathroom.

What she needed was a plan. A well-executed, legal plan. With all the logistics neatly spelled out, she would be protected. So would he, for that matter. It was best for both of them. This marriage in name needed only to be set up explicitly and with plenty of boundaries.

She immediately felt better, until Ryker crawled back into bed. She worried for a moment that he would try to put an arm around her. Cuddle her in some way.

When he stuck to his side of the bed, she breathed a sigh and finally relaxed into her pillow. In no time, her eyelids started drooping. Just around the time she heard him softly snore, she slipped into sleep as well, a plan already formulating.

Chapter Eight

He caught himself reaching for her for about the tenth time and pulled his hand back to his side.

Damn, but he wasn't used to sleeping with other people. Finding out he was a snuggler was a little disquieting, especially knowing how ill-received his cuddles would be. He turned toward the window yet again, giving her his back. This time, however, his eyelids lit up pink.

He blinked them open and squinted into the sun streaming through the window. He frowned. He'd swear the curtains had been drawn the last time he'd looked at them.

Glancing over his shoulder, he discovered that not only was Charlotte's side of the bed empty, but she'd also made it.

Meticulously.

Her pillows were propped up against the headboard, the duvet neatly drawn up.

Before this moment, Ryker hadn't known it was possible to make a bed with someone still in it. He found his lips curling as he imagined her staring down at his sleeping form, frustrated that he was thwarting her attempts to set her bed to order.

Charlie was one of a kind, that was for sure.

Where was she?

He stretched, arching his back and grinning as the movement made Charlie's scent waft up from the sheets. His clients overwhelmingly came to him reeking of some scent or other. If he had to live with her no-nonsense soap smell mixed with the mint of her toothpaste for the rest of his life, it was more than fine by him.

He tossed back the duvet, biting his lip to contain a grin as he inadvertently sent her carefully placed pillows flying. Maybe he'd pick them up after he hit the john.

Maybe not.

He had a feeling a little chaos would be good for Miss Charlotte.

Not "miss" for much longer.

Unable to bite back his grin this time, he crossed to the bathroom. A few minutes later, he emerged with fresh breath and hair that had been tamed with a quick, wet-fingered comb through.

As he left her bedroom, he followed the soft sounds he heard coming from the end of the hall. He couldn't stop staring at the artwork again as he passed.

He bet just one of these paintings would pay his rent for a year.

In the living room and foyer area, his gaze automatically traveled to the couch.

He was a big fan of that couch.

His lips curling, he surveyed his surroundings with a little more leisure than he had allowed himself last night.

Her penthouse was opulent yet understated. She'd decorated in varying shades of white that ranged from pristine to what someone more discerning might call *cream*. The effect was at once welcoming while also making him want to wash his hands before touching anything.

Not unlike the lady of the house herself.

There was a sound to the right. A massive dining table stood several yards away beneath an impressive chandelier. Through an open doorway, bright light streamed. More sounds echoed.

He'd found Charlie.

Running his fingertips along the smooth wood of the table as he passed, Ryker walked through the door. His gaze found her right away. She sat at a large island in the middle of her kitchen—a space that was just as white as the living and dining rooms. She'd propped her elbows on the white marble surface. Papers were spread all around her.

Her brow furrowed as she perused them, a pencil in one hand and a mug in the other.

Her hair was back in a bun, and—he blinked several times to be sure—she was wearing a business suit. On a Saturday morning in her own kitchen, at—he glanced at the clock on the microwave—8:30 a.m.

Oh, she definitely needs some chaos in her life.

"Good morning, *bonita.*"

Her head snapped up so quickly, Ryker nearly winced. That had to hurt. He certainly hadn't been quiet as he'd approached. Whatever was on the papers in front of her was consuming.

Charlotte pushed her glasses up her nose with the hand that still clutched a pencil. "Good morn—" She broke off. Behind her glasses, her eyes got as wide as saucers.

She stared at his chest, then his groin. Her lips parted.

He bit the inside of his cheeks just in time to keep a smile in check. *Oh, did I forget to put on clothes, Charlie?*

And the sight of those lips paired with her bun, glasses, and careful appearance was having a very pronounced effect on his dick. As he hardened beneath her gaze, her tongue darted out and across her top lip.

Something in his gut clenched.

He took a step forward; maybe it'd be a good idea to mess up that hair now rather than later.

With a gasp, she jerked her gaze away and up toward the ceiling. "Where are your clothes?" she asked in a breathless but stern voice.

He spied a coffeemaker to his left and started making his way toward it. "Right where I left them on the floor of your bedroom."

She was quiet for a couple moments after that, and he found himself holding his breath in anticipation of what she'd say in return—something he'd never done around a woman in his life.

"I folded them actually. Everything is on the dresser. You know, if you want to go put something on."

Of course, she folded everything. He began filling his coffee mug. "I'm good." Just to fuck with her, he shifted his weight, flexing his ass.

She made a soft noise that closely resembled a squeak. When he spun around again with no warning, her gaze was focused just where he'd known it would be. And now it was on his cock.

Her cheeks flushed, but she didn't look away.

Progress.

He began walking her way, blowing on his coffee as he did so, his erection bobbing with each step.

Watching her eyes bounce up and down as she followed its movement made something light fill his chest. There was a 50/50 chance that lightness was a laugh. The other possibility was unidentifiable.

When he stood right beside her, he leaned down, aiming for her lips.

At the last second, she turned her face, and his lips met the softness of her cheek. He frowned.

"I'm glad you're up," she said to the countertop. She tapped her pencil against one of the papers. "I have some paperwork to go over."

When she looked up at him again, it was as though shields had come down over her eyes, all hints of lust carefully locked away. "Why don't you have a seat?" she asked, nodding toward the stool right next to her.

He narrowed his eyes. "What kind of paperwork?"

She blinked. "The prenup. Of course."

Ryker's coffee turned sour in his stomach. He smacked his lips and placed his coffee mug on the island. "On second thought, I think I will go get those pants."

She frowned, seeming to pick up on his sudden change in mood but not why or how it had changed. Before she could say anything, however, he turned and walked from the kitchen.

Well, the word *prenup* had certainly taken care of his erection in a hurry.

He shoved his fingers through his still-damp hair. Rationally, this was a good thing. A prenup protected them both, though, God knew—he cast another glance at the artwork lining the hall—she needed more protecting than he did.

But he certainly had no plans to divorce Charlotte. Ever. Marriage was for keeps, no matter the circumstances under which it began.

True to her word, Charlotte had placed his folded tuxedo pants on the dresser. She'd moved his jacket, shirt, and bowtie—which perched atop the pile akin to a cherry on a sundae—to the dresser as well. How he'd missed it when he'd gotten out of bed was a mystery to him.

Not true. You know exactly how distracted you were by the idea of seeing her again. Touching her again.

And she wanted to talk prenup.

With a sigh, he jerked his pants from the bottom of the pile, taking sick pleasure in the way the rest of his neatly folded clothing went flying to the floor. Some of that pleasure abated, however, when he had to bend over and retrieve his shirt. Made him feel like he'd thrown a temper tantrum. A mild one, but, still.

He shrugged his shirt on, buttoned most of the buttons, and rolled up the sleeves. Charlotte had even attacked the stains she'd left on the front of his pants. They were nowhere to be seen, more's the pity. He looked passable. Just in case, though, he undid another button over his chest. Couldn't hurt.

He bent down and retrieved his jacket and bowtie, straightening them and laying them over the back of a nearby chair. But when he started eyeing the throw pillows he'd displaced earlier…yeah, he was shamelessly stalling and made his way back to the kitchen.

He found Charlotte just as he'd left her, except now she was shuffling the papers into some kind of order. His jaw began to hurt. Great, he was clenching his teeth now. Rolling his shoulders, he cleared his throat to let her know he was back.

Her head jerked up. There was an immediate flare of relief on her features, but then her gaze narrowed in on his forearms and the narrow vee of skin his partially unbuttoned shirt revealed.

So, it had been a good idea to forego that extra button. Straightening his posture, he walked back to the stool she'd wanted him to take earlier.

As he sat, he noticed his coffee still steamed within his mug. He wrapped both hands around it for something to do, then smiled at his future wife, hoping against hope the smile wasn't as strained as it felt. "So," he said. "A prenup?"

She nodded emphatically. "And a little bit more, too. Written agreements. I figured it was best to spell everything out from the start so both of us know what to expect."

"Hmm." He took a sip of coffee. "In that vein of thought, you should know that I don't expect to divorce you."

She blinked up at him. "W-what?"

He took a deep breath. "I don't agree with divorce."

Her brows met in the middle, and her lips parted. "Don't agree with divorce?" she asked the same way she might ask, *You don't agree with global warming?* She spluttered for a moment. "So, you just…thought we'd…" She drifted off, seemingly at a loss.

"Stay married," he supplied after an awkward moment. "For the long haul."

She looked aghast. "But that's absurd!"

He raised his eyebrows. "Is it?"

More spluttering. "Yes!"

He turned his body toward her. "Charlotte, we met last night because you hired me to be your fiancé. Then, within an hour of meeting, you proposed for real." He smiled gently. "*Absurd* seems a bit relative at this point, don't you think?"

Her lips pursed together, and she shuffled her papers, tapping them against the countertop. "Yes, well." She cleared her throat. "You may have a point."

He placed his hand over her wrist, and she stilled, her gaze landing on his fingers with singular focus. "*Bonita*, I understand that, for you, a prenup is non-negotiable. All I'm asking in return is the consideration that, just maybe, a prenup does not have to point toward divorce for us."

She pulled in a slow breath and released it just as slowly. "Ryker," she said, her gaze still locked on his hand, "I cannot make any promises like that. I won't make any promises like that."

He pressed his lips together and retrieved his hand, the stabbing disappointment in his chest completely out of proportion with her logical words. He sighed. "All right, let's hear this paperwork."

She straightened, her breathing immediately returning to regular speed. She pulled a paper from the top of her stack and slid it his direction. "Here are the arrangements for our engagement."

He braced himself for impact as he placed his sprawled fingertips on the paper and pulled it in front of him. He scanned the beginning, but it was so full of legalese, he had no chance of understanding it. He pushed it back toward her and met her gaze. "Why don't you give me the SparkNotes version?"

She nodded readily, as though she were used to this request from her clients. He did a double take. *I'm not her client.*

She pointed at a part toward the top. "You'll move in here today." Her finger moved down. "The guest room will be yours to make up however you'd like." Her finger landed on the final point. "You'll be given a weekly stipend in an amount of your choice. Within reason."

His eyes widened. "Stipend?"

She glanced his direction. "Well, you won't be taking any more clients while we're engaged and married. I assume that's your only source of income?"

Dear God. Was she trying to turn him into a kept man? He nodded cautiously.

"Then it's only fair you're compensated for your time while you're off the job."

He didn't like it. He didn't like any of it. The guest room? That was a big *hell no*. He took another sip of coffee. "Go on," he said.

She seemed encouraged, as though his *go on* was permissive instead of akin to *ha ha, nope*. "Right." She set down the engagement clause and pulled the next paper from the stack. "The marriage."

He propped his elbow on the island and settled his chin in his palm, drumming his fingers along his jaw.

"It must—of course—" A blush bloomed over her cheeks. He straightened, suddenly interested in what she was about to say. She gazed studiously at the paper she held. "Be...consummated." She spoke so softly he had trouble hearing her, but there was no mistaking that word.

He grinned. "Agreed."

At that, she seemed to snap out of whatever embarrassment she was feeling. She rolled her eyes and pinned him with a no-nonsense glare. "To be legal, the marriage must be consummated," she stated emphatically.

"Oh, yes. To be legal." He winked.

Her lips twitched even though the furrow between her brows deepened. "And because monogamy is a must," she thumbed through the papers, "I've notated we will have intercourse once a week." She cleared her throat again. "To meet your sexual needs."

His mouth slackened. "*Bonita*, once wouldn't meet my sexual needs for one day."

She took a moment to absorb his words, and then she gasped. "Once a *day*?"

"Wouldn't be enough. Right. Like I said."

"I mean—" She shook her head. "Don't you"—she waved a hand in the general direction of his dick, which perked up at being noticed—"rub raw?" She winced as soon as the words left her mouth, but that didn't stop the laugh that immediately bubbled up from his chest.

He swallowed it down before it could manifest itself in any sound louder than a cough. "Charlie, lubrication has never been a problem for any of my partners."

The blush, which had never truly dissipated since the word *consummated*, deepened. She tapped the papers on the island again, straightening them when they were already meticulously straight. "We seem to have veered off topic."

He raised his eyebrows. "Have we? This topic is very important to me. And any marriage I commit to."

She stiffened for a moment but then sagged. She reached for her pencil, but instead of writing anything with it, she used it to tap on the countertop and avoided meeting his gaze. She cleared her throat. "Fifty percent of relationships in which one partner has autism are sexless relationships. I…" She cleared her throat again. "I don't know which side of that statistic I'll fall on."

She stared at the marble in front of her.

Oh, Charlie. He reached out and placed his hand over her furiously tapping one, silencing the pencil abruptly. "*Bonita*, I'm really not worried about that. Not in the slightest. Because, do you know what I heard? Fifty percent of those relationships are filled with sex. Hot, dirty, tuxedo pants-staining sex."

A faint smile tipped her lips but was quickly banished. "I know we had sex last night, but, what if that was an anomaly?"

He squeezed her hand. "Hey, I'm willing to test that theory right now."

"Ryker." She looked his direction but still didn't meet his gaze. "I'm serious."

Not the time for jokes, Martinez. "I know you are, Charlie." He squeezed her hand again. "I know you are. Look, forget everything I said about sex. If you were writing this agreement without me in mind, what would you put in it sex-wise?"

She blinked. "I wouldn't put anything sex-wise in it. I think I would want to just take that part of my life as it comes."

He stroked her knuckles with his thumb. "Then that's what we do."

"But, you said—"

"I know what I said." And he could kick his own ass over it. "I take it back. All of it. If we end up in the fifty percent who have sex, that's great. And if we end up in the other fifty…" He shrugged and tried to look casual about it. "Then, we'll figure it out."

She narrowed her eyes and finally met his gaze. "You said sex is important to you."

"*Consensual* sex is important to me." He reached for the pencil and eased it from her grip, then slid the paper she'd been reading from toward him. Finding the clause about sex, he firmly crossed it out, then slid the paper back over and dropped the pencil atop it.

"What's next?" he asked.

She sniffed. God only knew if he'd convinced her he meant what he'd said. But she scanned the paper, then pointed to a line. "I put this here, as it needs to remain private and not part of a legal document that may get out. We must be married for a minimum of twelve months."

He swallowed hard. "The word *minimum* is there?" he clarified.

She met his gaze, drawing her brows together. "Yes, it is."

He nodded again. "I agree to a minimum of twelve months."

Her lips pursed, and he thought for sure she was going to spout another dooming statistic, but then she pulled out a thick stack of papers without further comment. "Now for the prenuptial agreement."

He glanced at the document and saw the word *whereas* about twenty times. With a grunt, he reached for more coffee.

"In the event of a divorce after at least one year of marriage, you are entitled to a one-time amount of five hundred thousand dollars but nothing else. I will be entitled to none of your money or property."

He swallowed hard, and the coffee burned all the way down. "Wait, that's pretty one- sided."

She blinked at him. "Of course it is."

He tilted his head. "What if we veer off plan, and the divorce is my fault? Won't you want some form of compensation?"

She frowned. "Nevada is a no-fault divorce state."

He pressed his lips together for a moment. "That's not the point."

"The law is always entirely the point."

He pointed in her direction. "If I screw this up, you deserve something."

She sighed, obviously humoring him. "Do you have anything to give?"

He opened his mouth. Closed it. "Damn, *mujer*. Go for the jugular."

She frowned. "It was not my intention to hurt your feelings. I'm just trying to be rational."

Rational, he was beginning to see, was her most dominant character trait. He sipped his coffee. "Fine. But I'm putting my foot down. In the event of infidelity or other unforgiveable things—you can decide what yours are—I will not be entitled to anything."

She sighed again. "Of course, I included that. For your knowledge, those lifestyle clauses are infidelity, abuse, or fraud."

"Jesus." He set his mug down. "Fraud?" He didn't even know what that meant. "Wait...abuse?" He waved a hand between them, suddenly lightheaded. "If you're worried about that, that's a big deal."

Like, agreement-ending deal. Fuck, was she scared of him? He tasted bile in the back of his throat.

She placed a hand over his forearm. It was the first time she'd voluntarily touched him today, and it immediately calmed him. He raised his gaze from her fingers to her eyes.

"Ryker," she said softly, "if I was worried about any of those things, you wouldn't be here right now." Her gaze dropped, and his nerves returned. "There is one thing I need to disclose, however." She pulled her hand away and placed it in her lap. "Before this goes any further. It will show up on my health record, which you'll have a copy of by this afternoon."

Well, fuck, that's ominous.

She fiddled with the corner of her stack of papers. "About ten years ago, I had an STI." She sucked in a breath. "It was gone with one round of meds," she said in a rush, "and I've never had another one. But I wanted you to hear it from me before you saw it on paper."

The wheels in Ryker's head were spinning so fast, he thought he smelled burnt rubber. One of those genius-in-the-sack shitheads she'd been with all those years ago had given her an STI?

"Oh, Charlie." He reached for her.

She sniffed and stacked her papers once more. "Anyway…"

His hand fell back to the countertop.

"I'd appreciate a copy of your record as well," she said, still not looking at him.

He regularly updated his, had done so just last weekend. "You'll have it by this afternoon."

She nodded. "Great. Thanks." Her words were clipped. She handed him the stack of papers. "You'll want to get your lawyer to look over these. I'd love to sign the final copy this afternoon. Two weeks before the wedding date is pushing it, so we want the ink dry as soon as possible."

He took the papers but didn't look at them. "There's one thing we didn't discuss."

She straightened, her gaze shooting to his. "There is?"

He took a big breath and went for it. "Children."

Her lips parted. "*Children?*"

"You know, miniature humans? Cute? Get into everything?" He bit back a smile.

Her lips clamped shut. "Yes, I know what children are, thank you." She spread her palms out, seemingly at a loss. "We're only going to be married a year!"

"At minimum," he interjected, raising his eyebrows. "And a baby takes nine months, *bonita*."

She was quiet for a moment, and he could practically see her thoughts racing. "I just want to clarify. It sounds like you want children."

He didn't even try to deny it. "Very badly."

Her eyes widened. "Wha—?" She shook her head. "Why?"

He tilted his head. "Did you not hear the *cute* part earlier?"

"Plenty of things are cute. That's irrelevant." Her brow furrowed.

"Not really."

"I just didn't expect a gigolo to want children," she said so softly it made him think she was talking to herself.

A muscle flexed in his jaw. "You sure you want to bring up stereotypes and who, between the two of us, should want children?"

"Valid point." She sighed. She pinched the bridge of her nose. "I don't *not* want children."

He reached for her again, this time making contact and placing his hand over the back of hers where it lay on the countertop. "That's your prerogative, no matter what. We just need to talk about it first."

At that, she met his gaze again. "I'm sorry. I don't know what to say. I just…wasn't expecting this," she said again with a small shrug.

He drew in a slow, deep breath. "I get that," he said finally. Hopefully, he had enough courage for what he planned to do next. "Look, I've already told you I'm all-in on this, so I'm just going to"—Jesus, was he really going to do this?—" put it all out here, okay? Maybe if you know where I'm coming from, this will make more sense."

He didn't know what he expected, but it wasn't the faint flash of anxiety he saw pass through her eyes. If anything, women were always pressing him to reveal too much of himself. Now, he wanted to and she didn't seem receptive.

"Okay," she said.

He sat still for a moment before the word registered. "Okay?" he repeated.

She straightened as though she were bracing herself. "Yes. Okay. Let's hear it."

He was quiet for a moment as he waited for an extra kick of bravery. "So this"—he gestured between them—"a marriage of convenience, with the addition of kids—Charlie, that would be my dream come true."

"Your dream is a loveless marriage and children?"

Great, he was already messing this up. "I know it sounds weird."

"It doesn't sound weird. It sounds very typical. Of the people I see in my office every day getting a divorce."

He winced. "Hear me out."

She leaned back in her stool and gave him a *go ahead* wave of her hand.

He couldn't look at her now. "I grew up in the foster system."

He perceived her stiffening beside him, and he waited for her to say something. When she didn't, he continued. "Got put there when my parents' marriage dissolved, and then their new marriages dissolved, and then we moved all over, and I got shuffled to the sidelines, and suddenly no one wanted to take care of me." He laughed humorlessly. "I mean, I was in this home with tons of kids who were there for horrible reasons—parents hooked on drugs, abuse—stuff that would give you nightmares. And the question I hated worst from them was 'Why are you here?' Because my reason was my folks just couldn't get over their fucking feelings enough to do what they were supposed to."

He saw her move in his peripheral vision. "Ryker—"

He held out a hand, a wordless plea of *not yet*. If he didn't get it all out now, he doubted he would later. "To me, marriage is a vow. The whole point of a vow is you keep it, no matter what. No matter what you feel from day to day, which is always changing. No matter what you feel for someone else in any fleeting moment. *Nothing* is more important than a vow. And the best thing parents can give their kids is stability."

He was finally able to force himself to meet Charlotte's gaze. The concern he saw there set him back a moment, but he forged ahead. "Charlie, look at this place." He gestured to her apartment. "Can you imagine the home we could give kids? They wouldn't want for anything, and you and I—we'd be partners. Neither of us would let emotion get in the way. We'd be in it for the right reasons. We could do this thing *right*."

Something flickered in her gaze. "Ryker—" She licked her lips. "I feel it necessary to point out that, after our agreed upon settlement, you could provide just fine for children with someone else or even by yourself."

I don't want this later, I want it now. Later was never guaranteed. What, like an amazing catch was going to agree to marry him twice in his life? He nearly snorted. Not likely.

He cleared his throat. "I'll concede that point," he said carefully, "if you'll concede that my plan has merit, too."

She raised an eyebrow. "Your concession is contingent on my concession?"

He raised a mimicking brow. "You've already conceded that twelve months is the minimum. If this marriage sticks…"

She gave him a look that clearly said this marriage had no hope of sticking, so he wisely chose not to say anything further.

"We've discussed children," she said firmly. "Can we agree that we're at an amiable impasse?"

He narrowed his eyes. "By *amiable impasse*, do you mean we've neither committed to having nor committed to *not* having children?"

She hesitated. "Yes. That's what I mean," she said finally.

It's not a no. He still felt a stab of disappointment, and the very real possibility that he was growing attached to the idea of Charlotte as his children's mother concerned him. He needed that necessary distance. "Then, yes, we can agree to that."

After all, Charlie was right. If they did part ways after a year, he'd be more than financially equipped to undergo becoming a father in some other way. She was not the only egg in his basket.

She sagged with obvious relief. "This is great. So, you'll have your lawyer look at the papers this afternoon? Maybe while you're out packing up your place?"

Oh, yeah, he was moving in today. "I can do that." Like he had a lawyer. Or a bunch of stuff to pack up at his place. "Be back around dinner time?"

She was already reaching for the briefcase beside the island. "Oh," she said in a faraway tone, already moving onto the next item on her no-doubt extensive to-do list, "yes, that will be fine."

He nodded. Right. He'd been dismissed. He tried to hold his head up high as he walked back to the bedroom to finish getting dressed—after all, it seemed he was coming out ahead in all this paperwork. But, for some reason, he felt defeated.

He already missed Charlie. Oh, not the version of her that had just litigated him into a coma, but the Charlie he'd glimpsed at the party and in the bedroom last night.

Business Charlie was going to take some getting used to. And he *would* get used to her. Would appreciate and respect her. He had to: that was part of being committed to marriage.

He'd always known commitment took work.

Guess the work is already starting.

Chapter Nine

As soon as Ryker had walked out of the kitchen, Charlotte had sagged forward, closing her eyes.

Distance yourself. Distance yourself!

But the haunted look in his eyes as he'd talked about growing up in foster care kept flitting through her mind until the dull ache in her chest grew so acute, she reached for the bottle of Tums she kept in her briefcase at all times.

Then she'd heard the front door close, and distance had been easier to come by. She'd pulled out Mr. Grabow's third divorce file and had been working steadily since. That's why, when her landline rang, she jumped, then immediately glanced at the clock over her microwave.

Five forty-five? When had eight hours passed by?

Her phone rang again, and she launched herself from the stool. Her landline never rang. Hadn't since she'd lived here. As it was all the way in the foyer by the door, she had to hoof it through her apartment to get to it before whoever was on the other end gave up.

"Hello?" she asked breathlessly after the fifth ring.

"Ms. Moore, this is Roger."

She frowned. "Roger?"

"The building's doorman, ma'am."

Her cheeks heated. "Oh! Yes, of course."

"I have a gentleman down here by the name of Ryker Martinez. He says he's your fiancé." The weight of doubt hung heavily on that final word.

Charlotte straightened her back. "And you detained him instead of letting him come right up?" she asked, infusing her tone with her best courtroom you're-an-idiot fire.

There was a pause on the other end. Finally, "He doesn't have a key, ma'am."

Drat. This was definitely her fault. She forced a laugh. "Oh, he forgot it again. He's so funny." Another laugh. "Send him up immediately, please," she said in a way that negated the *please.*

"Of course, ma'am." *Click.*

Ryker was back. A foreign lightness filled her chest, and she found herself smoothing a palm over her hair. Every strand seemed to be in place, and it still felt insufficient. She heard the elevator ding faintly out in the lobby, and she opened the door immediately.

Ryker stepped off the elevator looking even more impossibly handsome than when he'd left this morning. His hair curled over his forehead, and he shook it back as he drew the strap of a duffle bag over his shoulder. His expression seemed carefully blank as he walked toward her.

"I'm sorry," she blurted.

His stride hitched, but other than that, he gave no indication of a reaction. "For what, *bonita*?"

"I can't believe I didn't give you a key. Or tell the doorman to expect my fiancé. I…I wasn't thinking." She swallowed hard. When his lips curled, the most intense relief fluttered through her.

"You're always thinking, *mujer*."

She felt a jolt of pure happiness— he was teasing her. She cursed herself a fool. "I wasn't this morning. I'm truly sorry."

His careful expression vanished and a grin spread his lips. "Well, I think we scandalized poor Roger, so it might have all been worth it."

She felt her own lips curling. "Good." She stood aside so he could enter her apartment—their apartment. As he passed her, his delicious scent curled around her, and she found herself leaning into the space he'd abandoned as he set his duffle bag down inside the door.

He spun around to see her leaning there in midair, and she immediately straightened. "I have a spare key in the office. I'll get it right away." As she took a step toward the hallway, her stomach growled. She cast a surreptitious glance his direction, hoping he hadn't heard.

His eyes twinkled. "Been a long time since lunch?"

A soft shake of her head. "I think I skipped lunch, actually."

"Charlie," he admonished.

She tilted her head. Granted, she was not a good judge of what other people were feeling, but he looked genuinely...concerned for her. "It happens all the time." She waved her hand over her shoulder as she started down the hallway once more. "I'm perfectly fine."

She was pretty sure she heard him grumble behind her as she approached the office. It might have been her stomach again, however.

Closing the door behind her, she allowed herself to sag against its cool surface for a second. For some reason, her heart had started thundering the moment she'd seen Ryker again. And she'd been weirdly obsessed with his lips as he'd talked and smiled. There was the slightest dip in the middle of his bottom lip; would it cradle her tongue as perfectly as she was imagining?

"Gah," she said to the quiet room, pushing away from the door. "Stop thinking like this!" She would get nothing done if she couldn't focus on the important things in life.

Speaking of which…

There was a spare key in here somewhere, but she hadn't seen or thought of it since she'd moved in. Despite that fact, she knew exactly where it would be, thanks to her meticulous organization. She crossed the room to her desk, located the miscellaneous file in the bottom drawer, and found the spare key and elevator card clipped to the inside cover.

She smiled as she retrieved them, closed her desk again, and made her way down the hallway. Her smile faded, however, when she saw Ryker's bag but no sign of Ryker.

There was the sound of a cabinet closing in the kitchen, and Charlotte redirected her path. When she walked in the kitchen, Ryker was closing another cabinet.

"Found the keys." She held them out as he turned around.

"Are you aware," he said, completely ignoring the keys she held in her hand, "that there is nothing to eat in this apartment?"

She lowered her hand. "Untrue." She nodded toward the cabinet he'd just closed. "There is a box of Raisin Bran in that cabinet."

He narrowed his eyes at her.

She was confused. "Are you hungry?"

He made an odd noise in the back of his throat. "*You're* hungry!"

Oh, yeah. And Raisin Bran did not sound appetizing. Come to think of it, she couldn't remember when she'd purchased that box of cereal. It may be past its expiration date. Usually, she ate at the office, picking up whatever ready-made meals she needed along the way. She couldn't remember the last time she hadn't had all daily meals there, weekends included.

She rolled her shoulders, not liking the feeling that she was failing at something, which was obviously Ryker's current opinion about her kitchen. "We can go to the store after the rest of your belongings arrive."

Now, it was Ryker who rolled his shoulders. "I just have the one bag."

The one bag? She bit the words back just in time, realizing drawing attention to such a fact would be a faux pas. She cleared her throat. "Then, we can go now if you want." She paused. "Do you…um…cook?"

His lips twitched. "Not even a little."

She sighed. "Me neither. The store seems a lost cause then, wouldn't you say?"

He pressed his lips together, then, "Pizza?"

She hesitated. Even though she bought ready-made meals, she tried to keep them healthy. "I haven't had pizza in…years. I think."

"You *think*?" He looked horrified. "You don't even know for sure?"

Her lips parted, but she didn't know what to say. *Well, you have one bag of personal items* was immature and off topic. They might both be messes.

Shaking his head, he pulled his cell phone from his back pocket. "Do you have a preference when it comes to the restaurant, or…" He raised his eyebrows.

"I'll leave it to your expertise."

He grinned. "You won't be sorry."

As he placed a call, she became distracted by the way he moved his free hand while he talked. She had never thought fingers particularly attractive before, but she liked everything about his.

He pulled his phone from his ear and pressed the screen with his thumb. "Done. Pizza will be here in thirty minutes."

She hadn't even paid attention to what he'd ordered. She swallowed, trying to displace the image of his fingers deep inside her body with something more practical and coming up blank. "I'll notify Roger." Best to avoid a repeat of what happened earlier.

She should really turn around now and head toward the phone, but she was hungry—*really* hungry—and Ryker looked so appetizing standing there in the center of her kitchen.

Say something and leave! She cleared her throat. "I can show you to the guest room, if you'd like."

It wasn't until that moment that she realized his gaze had been heated, because her words cooled his warm brown eyes as if she'd thrown a glass of water on embers. The loss of heat gave her a similar physical reaction. She wrapped her arms over her stomach. "Everything okay?"

He gave her a tight smile. "Are we sure we want to sleep in separate rooms? We cohabited pretty well last night."

Her brows drew together. "Share a room?" She hadn't even considered the possibility. As she did so now, she got some of that warm feeling back. "Is that what you want?"

Her question seemed to make him tired. "I want what you want, Charlie." He sighed. "Lead the way to the guest room."

Well, now she wasn't sure she wanted him in the guest room. Drat! How could he possibly have her thoughts in constant flux! Precisely why she avoided relationships like the plague.

She sighed herself—if he could do it, so could she—and nodded toward the kitchen door. "This way."

He wordlessly followed in her wake. They paused a moment for him to collect his duffel from the foyer, which only raised her questions concerning *one duffel bag* all over again. How did one get to be an adult and accumulate so little?

Did this tell her about his personality: Ryker was someone who put little value on material possessions? Or—the possibility that made her stomach turn—did this tell her about his quality of life?

Did Ryker live in poverty?

She didn't like that possibility. She didn't like it at all.

She was so distracted that she nearly walked past the guest room. Luckily, she caught herself before she had to backtrack. It had always been laughable that she even had a guest room—who would visit her? She had no living family that she would claim.

No friends.

She corralled her rebellious thoughts and pushed the door open. "Here you are," she said softly.

The fresh scent of lemon cleaning products wafted out. It made sense: the only person who ever entered this room was Erin, the woman who cleaned every other week for her.

Ryker walked into the room, gazing around as he did so. She tried to look where he looked with fresh eyes, seeing it for the first time.

With a sinking feeling, she saw how Spartan it was. She hadn't bothered with artwork for a room no one would ever see. The sheets and duvet were white, as were the walls.

The thought of him staying in this room made her want to wrap her arms around him and whisper, *stay with me instead*.

She hadn't even realized she'd taken a step in his direction until he dropped his duffel to the carpet with a dull *thud*. The sound was enough to jolt her still.

He turned to her, a smile on his lips. "Charlie, this is great," he said. *Genuinely*.

She blinked several times. "Oh. I'm…glad." She looked around again, but she didn't see whatever he was seeing. "We can redecorate it however you'd like."

He shook his head. "It's already perfect."

And this, for some reason, made her stomach sink even lower. It seemed to all-but-confirm that he'd come from an unseemly situation. If he found this *perfect*, just what was he used to?

She swallowed and nodded. "I'll leave you to it, then." She backed out of the room, keeping him in her sights until the last possible moment as he turned back to his duffel and unzipped it, eyeing the dresser across from the bed with purpose.

Walking back to the foyer to notify Roger of their impending pizza delivery, she felt irrationally lonely. Somehow, distance had cropped up between Ryker and her since last night.

Somehow? She'd thrust three legal documents in his face over breakfast, made him go through a mortifying encounter with her doorman, and consigned him to the most depressing place of residence in the history of bedrooms.

She had put the distance between them. Just as she'd intended. Just as she needed.

So why did she hate it?

She went through the motions of calling down to the lobby, then sat in the fading light of the living room, watching the sun set through the picture windows that occupied the entire outer wall of her apartment. The vivid colors of the Strip took on new definitions as millions of tiny lightbulbs lit the night.

"Charlie?"

Though his voice had been quiet, Charlotte still jumped. Her head turned toward the sound, and she found him standing at the end of the couch, shocked to see him so close. She hadn't heard him approach.

She rubbed a palm down her face, then smiled at him. "All done?"

He ignored the question. "Are you okay?"

She nodded so vigorously, she felt like a bobblehead. "Of course!"

His lips quirked. As he walked around the arm of the couch, she saw he'd changed into some sweat pants and a T-shirt. Her mouth went dry as she spotted his hard nipples pressing against the thin cotton. He sank down onto the cushion next to her, and her body automatically leaned toward his in the shift of the center of gravity.

She didn't fight it.

"Been a big day, huh?" He placed his hand down on the couch cushions between their bodies. His pinky pressed against her outer thigh, and she wondered if it was a coincidence until he just barely stroked her with it.

She nodded, her gaze rapt on his slowly moving pinky. "Big day," she repeated dumbly.

"You know," he said, continuing to stroke her, "even good changes are stressful."

Another nod. "Tell my clients that all the time."

He breathed a laugh. "Of course you do." His finger continued to stroke. She felt mesmerized by it. "Charlie? *Bonita*, look at me."

She wanted to shake her head. To keep staring at his fingers. With Herculean effort, she raised her gaze. Hers clashed with his, and with a surge in her chest, she realized that the embers were back in his eyes. "Yes?" she asked breathlessly.

He slowly raised his other hand, as though he were giving her ample opportunity to dodge it if she wished. She was too fascinated by all the possibilities of where it could be headed to even dream of dodging.

He tucked a strand of hair behind her ear. "Charlie," he said softly, "we need to give ourselves some grace here."

"Grace?" Seriously, what were words?

A husky chuckle. "The adjustment to being together…no matter how much we both want it, the adjustment is going to be hard. We just need to accept that. I promise you, I'm not going anywhere. Okay?"

"I'm not going anywhere either," she said automatically.

He stroked the shell of her ear now. "That's good."

She licked her lip, and she thought she heard his breathing hitch. "I…didn't like today," she confessed in a small voice.

His thumb paused, and she almost protested, but before she could, he resumed stroking her ear. "It wasn't my favorite either."

Though her gaze wanted to sink to his lips, she forced it to stay in place, locked on his eyes. "But we're okay?"

He made a sound deep in his throat, then leaned toward her. "We're more than okay, *bonita*." His mouth was close enough to hers that his breath caressed her skin as he spoke. "We both want emotional distance. That doesn't mean it's going to be easy to come by or maintain." He shrugged. "We'll figure it out along the way."

Just like that, all the weight disappeared from her gut. "Exactly," she breathed. "You're exactly right." Finally, she allowed her gaze to dip to his mouth. It was so close. So lush. She'd be able to press hers to it with the smallest movement—

He chuckled again. "I like hearing those words out of your mouth. Feel free to use them during our marriage whenever you'd like."

Her lips curled. "Then be right a lot."

"Deal," he whispered. And his thumb stroked her ear again.

She bit back a moan and leaned in to close the distance between their mouths, needing to taste him.

The shrill ringing of the phone rent the air.

They both jumped, jerking back from each other. The hand he'd been touching her with dropped to the couch between them. In the sudden silence, it became apparent how loudly and quickly they were both breathing.

Ryker muttered something beneath his breath that sounded like a curse, and right on its heels, the phone rang again.

Charlotte tried to push to her feet but quickly found her knees were weak.

He placed a hand on her thigh. "I'll get it," he said softly. Pulling in a deep breath, he stood.

An impressive erection strained the front of his pants. The fabric was soft enough that it clung to every ridge.

Charlotte gasped softly, unable to take her eyes from it.

He curled a finger beneath her chin and tilted her head back until her eyes met his. "That's not helping, gorgeous."

The phone rang again.

With another curse, Ryker dipped his hand inside the front of his pants, rearranging himself so that he pointed upward. Charlotte caught the barest glimpse of the swollen head of his shaft before he tugged his T-shirt back into place and stalked toward the still-ringing phone.

She blinked at the spot he'd just vacated, seeing that tantalizing glimpse on the back of her eyelids with every rapid flutter of her eyes.

He picked up the phone mid-ring. "Hello," he said amiably, though the tension in his shoulders was visible through his cotton shirt.

She wouldn't have managed so cordial a greeting.

He nodded. "That's great. Have a good night." He hung up, turned toward her, and opened his mouth.

Someone knocked on the door.

Ryker closed his mouth and smiled, the curl to his lips slightly sheepish this time. "Pizza's here."

She was swollen and achy between her legs, her head was humming so loudly she was surprised he couldn't hear it, and, all together with everything that had happened in the last twenty-four hours, she found everything suddenly and severely hilarious.

She placed trembling fingers over her lips. Ryker's brows shot together, and he took a step toward her, but when she snorted—the very thing she'd been afraid of—he stopped in his tracks.

"Did you just—"

She snorted again.

He grinned. She wanted to bury her face in her hands, but he jabbed a finger her direction. "Hold on to that thought." He spun back to the door and practically threw it open.

The pizza delivery girl on the other side gasped and shrank back, but Charlotte's mirth disappeared as the gorgeous young adult's eyes widened. She blatantly raked her gaze over Charlotte's future husband.

Charlotte's mouth gaped open, feelings she was positive she didn't covet filling her with hot anger.

Ryker reached for the pizza she held, plucking it from her hands. "Thanks, kid. The tip was sent electronically."

He shut the door right as the *kid* was opening her mouth—no doubt to proposition him.

Charlotte straightened in her seat. Ryker hadn't even spared her a glance. Had called her *kid*.

She blinked to find Ryker standing suddenly before her, the pizza balanced on one open palm. "So, that's how you laugh, huh?"

Drat. He hadn't forgotten the snorting. She shrugged with one shoulder. "When I find something truly funny, yes. Fortunately, it doesn't happen often."

He raised his eyebrows. "Fortunately?" He shook his head. "What a shame." With a nod toward the kitchen, he took off, pizza in tow.

"Not a shame," she grumbled beneath her breath, hefting herself from the couch. She'd had that horrific laugh her whole life.

By the time she entered the kitchen, Ryker had already placed the pizza on the island and was digging in the cabinets.

Silently, Charlotte walked to the fridge to get them drinks, returning to the island with coconut waters at the same time he set two plates and a roll of paper towels down.

He smiled at her. "Nice teamwork."

She smiled back. "You, too."

He flipped open the lid, and the slight aromatic scent that had been wafting through the kitchen emerged full force. The pizza was covered with tiny pepperonis, each one about the size of a nickel.

She tilted her head. "Never seen pepperoni that small before."

"Prepare to be amazed." He slid a slice onto one of the plates and set it before her.

Her stomach promptly growled again.

With a chuckle, he said, "Eat up, Charlie."

The tiny pepperoni had an extra crunch, and the cheese was so gooey, the bite practically slid down her throat. She moaned. "Oh, man. This is good." She took another, bigger bite.

Ryker made a soft, affirmative noise, giving her a close-lipped smile as he chewed.

They ate in companionable silence, and over the course of the next fifteen minutes, Charlotte put away three entire slices of pizza. She hadn't eaten that much that quickly in memory.

As she pushed back her empty plate with a contented sigh, she realized that Ryker had his elbows propped on the countertop, watching her. His plate was pushed to the side and empty as well.

She felt her cheeks heat. "How long have you been finished?"

He shrugged. "Does it matter?"

That burn deepened. "I was...hungry."

His lips tipped up at the corners. "And you're not anymore?"

She shook her head.

"Good." Like a shot, he was on his feet.

Her neck craned back as she struggled to maintain eye contact and not stare at the body that not even delicious pepperoni pizza had been able to displace from priority thought processes. As it turned out, the effort was unnecessary. He gripped the edge of her stool and spun her, wedging himself between her thighs.

She sucked in a breath as he pressed against her stomach. He was hard. Her hands flew to his hips, her fingers digging in before she could school the reaction. She looked down. Sure enough, the very clear outline of his erection showed through his pants. She nibbled her bottom lip and kept staring. "When did that happen?" she asked in a breathless voice she hardly recognized.

He gave a short, strained laugh. "Never went away."

Her gaze shot up to his. The lines around his eyes were deeper than normal, as though he were struggling for control. "You mean, this whole time…"

With gentle fingers, he tucked a strand of her hair that must have escaped the bun again behind her ear. "If you're imagining what it was like to watch you devour something with your mouth while my cock was trying to burst out of my pants, well, it was just about as intense as your mind can possibly picture."

Her eyes widened. "My mouth?"

He swore beneath his breath. "Are you aware"—he trailed those fingers down the column of her neck—"that you make sex noises when you eat?"

She gasped. "What? That is patently untrue!" She didn't know if she was outraged or not.

"If I promise not to touch your face, may I touch your lips, Charlie?"

Her brows drew together. It was difficult to place this sudden switch in conversation. "Technically, lips are part of the face."

"Yes." He raised his eyebrows.

It was several seconds of silence before she realized he was waiting for a reply of some kind from her. "I...suppose we could...try?"

"You tell me no the second you don't like it."

"Well, yeah."

His lips quirked. "Good."

So slowly she could barely track the movement, his fingertips approached her lips. She waited for the panic to flash, but it didn't, and her shoulders dropped imperceptibly. She knew exactly what he was going to do, unlike her college boyfriend who had helped her discover the face-touch aversion. Completely accidentally. Also, she knew deep in her gut that telling Ryker to stop would result in nothing more than him stopping. No fits. No walking out the door.

His fingers reached the corner of her mouth, and, with a touch so light she barely felt it, he stroked the tip of one finger along her bottom lip.

"Okay?" he whispered, his voice husky.

Tingles spread in the wake of his simple stroke. "Yes," she whispered back.

He swallowed, making his throat bob, and then stroked her upper lip. For some reason, she felt compelled to part her lips for him. "That's my girl," he whispered. He promptly trailed the tip of his pointer finger along the top of her bottom lip.

Would he let her lick it?

His finger paused. "You did it again!"

"Did what?"

"The sex noises. I swear, you're doing it on purpose."

She tried to shake her head, but she really didn't want to displace his finger.

But then his finger moved. She moaned a protest, only to discover that he'd simply transferred his attention back to her upper lip. "You like that?" he asked, his voice deeper than it had been even moments before.

She leaned into the touch, her grip on his hips tightening. She used her hands to ease him closer to her, hoping she was moving subtly enough without him noticing. If the pressure between their legs increased just the slightest bit—

There. Her eyes nearly rolled back. The base of his erection was pressed deliciously against her clitoris, which gave a wholehearted throb at the contact.

"Okay," he muttered, "I can't take any more of this."

Before she could ask what *this* was, his finger vanished and his lips descended. He pressed a soft kiss to her mouth, then pulled back just a fraction. "You keep making those noises into my mouth all you want, *bonita.*"

And she must have, because he groaned and flicked his tongue against her upper lip before sliding it into her mouth.

Her fingers flexed into his hips, and though her thoughts scattered as his talented tongue stroked hers, one persisted:

She wanted her hands on his rear end. Badly.

They'd been naked together just the night before. Had woken up that way in fact, much to Charlotte's dawning horror when she realized the sun was illuminating the room brighter than the lights had the prior evening. She'd never gotten dressed that quickly in her life.

Yet despite all they'd done together, she was hesitant now, which frustrated her. In the courtroom, she was a shark.

"I can feel you thinking." Ryker's lips brushed hers as he talked. "Right here." His palms flattened over her tense upper back. Before she could respond, he dug his thumbs into a muscle she hadn't even realized was clenched.

She moaned. Loudly. Dear God, if those were the sex noises she made when she ate, she could never eat around anyone again!

"You okay?" he asked in a murmur, continuing to sooth that muscle. "Anything we should talk about?"

She shook her head. "Definitely not." Even the idea of him knowing her past failures in the bedroom—more than he already did with her necessary STI divulgence—made her want to hide and never emerge.

She needed to distract him. And herself, honestly. She drew in a sharp breath and went for it. Her hands shot from his hips to his bottom with absolutely no finesse. In fact, she'd moved so fast and hard, she practically ended up smacking him. On his rear.

She slammed her eyes shut as that ever-ready blush heated her cheeks again. Why couldn't she do anything right in this area of her life? With a feeling of dread, she pried one eye open and peeked up at him.

His expression revealed nothing, and his eyes were still heated.

Much better than a laugh.

She'd worked this hard to get her hands on him, she might as well enjoy it. She flexed her fingers, filling her palms with his firm, curved muscles.

The color of his eyes darkened. "Well, you can do that all damn day, Charlie."

So, she did it again. The way his breathing quickened empowered her.

The next time she squeezed his bottom, he rocked his hips. His erection pressed against her even more firmly, making her gasp. Before she could close her mouth again, his was there. His tongue thrust into her mouth much more insistently than it had before. Almost as though he were losing some of his careful control.

She pulled him tighter, allowing herself to lose a little control, too. Digging her fingertips into his muscles, she met him the next time he thrust against her.

As their sexes ground together, he groaned harshly. Next she knew, his fingers were in her hair. Tugging.

She felt the heavy fall of her hair as it cascaded over her shoulders and down to the middle of her back. She pulled from the kiss just as he did. "What are you—?"

His gaze roamed over her hair, and the look in his eyes was enough to cut her words off. If she weren't mistaken, he looked…worshipful.

With a slow-moving hand, he reached out and wrapped one lock around his finger. "It's curly," he said with something akin to wonder in his voice. "Really curly."

She knew this. Why did he think she kept such a tight rein on it, pulling it back into that compact bun every day?

"And—" He held the curl up and seemed to be looking at it in the light. "Is this red?"

She shrugged, tempted to pull the curl out of his grip.

His gaze met hers, and he shook his head. "Charlie, why would you ever pull this gorgeous hair back?"

"My hair is…difficult," she said with another shrug.

He tilted his head. "To explain?"

She felt her lips curve at that. "No, to control."

She saw comprehension dawn on his face as clearly as if a spotlight had illuminated his incredible good looks.

"Control is important," he said softly.

It hadn't been a question, but she nodded anyway. Control was the most important.

He released the curl he held only to wind another around his finger. "I can understand that. Respect it." He tugged on her curl, and she leaned forward, which seemed to be just what he had been intending, because he closed the distance between them as well. "But you don't need control around me, *bonita*. Let's see if I can make us both lose it, hmm?"

Didn't need control? With the way he made her feel?

Oh, I definitely need control around you, Ryker Martinez. And she couldn't ever afford to forget it. Would never allow what had happened in the past to repeat.

But, the idea of him losing control…now, that had some merit.

If only she could be bold enough to make sure that happened.

"I can tell you're holding back," he whispered.

Her gaze snapped to his. Their breathing had increased so much that, with their mouths as close as they were, they seemed to be trading breaths. "What?" she asked breathlessly.

"I don't know why you are, but, *bonita*, we're about to be married." He stroked her cheek with the curl he held. Her eyelids fluttered, but she resolutely kept her gaze locked on his. "There's no room for caution between us. Or even embarrassment."

Her eyes widened. Was that what she was feeling? Caution was one thing, but…she didn't want to let any embarrassment hold her back. Not with Ryker. The lack of a need for artifice between them was this relationship's biggest benefit.

"Fair enough," she whispered back. Right. So, no embarrassment. It wasn't going to be easy, but she would do it.

She squeezed his bottom one more time and then released him. With her thighs, she nudged him back.

The slight smile on his face faded. "Hey, where are you going?"

She nibbled her lip for a second before she caught herself and forced her shoulders straight instead. "Not going far." She nodded toward the island behind her. "Would you…hop up here?"

He quirked an eyebrow but thankfully didn't question her at all. He turned around, braced his hands on the marble, and hefted himself up in a breathtakingly fluid motion that set the muscles of his arms rippling.

Her mouth went dry, and she forgot for a second why she'd had him get up there in the first place. But when he looked patiently down at her, she shook her head and focused again.

Clearing her throat, she slid from the stool, gripped the seat, and slid it over to the space between Ryker's spread knees.

It screeched against the tile floor every inch of the way.

Drat!

Just a fraction of suave would be nice! Was that too much to ask? She gritted her teeth and took her seat, unable to meet his gaze.

"Charlie," he murmured. His finger curled beneath her chin, and he raised her face. "*Bonita*, it's okay."

Reluctantly, and only because she knew he wanted her to, she raised her gaze to his.

He released a shaky breath. "If this is headed where I think it's headed... Trust me when I say it's okay." His thumb stroked across her bottom lip. "But, you need to know you don't have to do this. Not unless you really, really like it and need it in a relationship."

She swallowed hard and decided to give him another confession. "I don't know if I like it," she whispered. "Never wanted to try it before."

His breathing hitched and then resumed with renewed vigor. "And…you want to try it now?"

She nodded.

He swore beneath his breath, then leaned back on the hand he still had braced against the marble. Beneath his T-shirt, the muscles of his shoulder rolled and bunched. With one final stroke to her lip, his other hand moved to brace himself on the countertop as well. "Remember, we make our own rules here. You can do whatever you want to me, *bonita*."

Whatever I want? Her fingers trembled as they moved toward the drawstring of his sweat pants, but when the very obvious ridge of his penis moved beneath the fabric, a good portion of the embarrassment that had made a reappearance vanished.

She just wanted this too much to focus on anything else. If his body's reaction was to be believed, he did, too.

Her fingertips brushed the cool, smooth skin of his stomach. The firm muscles beneath flexed under her touch, making his stomach dip.

She darted a glance up at his face to find his lips were pressed together, his normally lush mouth pale. He seemed to be focusing with extraordinary mental power on her fingers where they rested against his waistband.

"Go ahead, sweet girl." He licked his lips. "Take a peek."

It was precisely what she wanted to do. She'd seen him last night, but she'd been so horrified at the disparate nature of their bodies that she hadn't had time to really enjoy him for long. She trailed the tips of her fingers across the expanse of his stomach one more time.

Again, his stomach muscles clenched. With her gaze still focused on his face, she caught him briefly squeeze his eyes shut before they jerked open again, as though he didn't want to miss one moment of what her fingers were up to.

Her fingers loved the feel of him. Turning her hand, she brushed her knuckles along the ridges of his abdominals. At the same time, she gathered his T-shirt in a loose fist, bunching up the fabric slowly. Just as slowly, she trailed her gaze downward. She looked first at his lips, which were now parted instead of pressed together. The barest flash of his white teeth and a glimpse of his tongue were visible. His Adam's apple bobbed beneath a swallow, and her gaze rested for a moment in the dip at the hollow of his throat.

What would it taste like if he let her daub her tongue in it?

Let her? Hadn't he just said she could do whatever she wanted to him?

Gripping his shirt, she planted her toes against the bar of the stool and pushed up, pulling him forward by her grip at the same time.

Their chests collided, her gaze focused on her prize the entire time. He groaned softly as she felt her breasts flatten beneath the pressure of his body, and, finally, she pressed her lips to that tantalizing hollow.

Then, she parted them and licked his skin.

His groan this time was harsh and short, and she heard herself mirror it. She felt a tug at her hair again, and then his fingers were against her scalp. He pressed her closer. "Do it again, *bonita*. Take my taste into your mouth." He leaned his head back, giving her better access to his throat. "Feels…so good."

She stretched onto her tiptoes to get closer, pressing her breasts firmly against him. Now she understood his earlier groan. The feel of his chest against hers was…amazing. Was that his heart beating against hers? The swell of his chest as he breathed was undeniable.

She licked the hollow of his throat again, then opened her mouth and sucked gently.

His palm flattened against the back of her head. "Charlie."

His voice was so deep that his words reverberated against her lips. In response, she sucked him harder, adding a bite.

"Going to mark me, then?" His fingers curled against her scalp. "Go ahead, *mujer*. Give me another bite."

She realized as she sank her teeth into his skin that she was undulating against his body, bowing her back and canting her hips rhythmically, as though she couldn't get close enough to him. She was also releasing a low moan at the end of every breath.

And her breathing was fast, her moans nearly constant.

"God, your sounds," he breathed. "Driving me crazy."

Her eyes slid closed. Beneath her hand, his stomach surged and dipped with his own breathing, his skin kissing her knuckles over and over again.

She wanted her mouth on other places. Releasing his skin, she drew back. Or at least, she tried to. His palm to the back of her head didn't budge at first. But the pressure disappeared so quickly, his hand trailing through her riotous curls, that she wondered if she'd imagined that brief resistance.

She gazed down at her handiwork, her eyelids feeling heavier than normal. A bright red mark the size of a quarter lay in the dip of his throat. It glistened from her mouth. She made a deep, contented noise in her chest.

His fingers twisted in the ends of her hair. "Like the look of it?"

She nodded.

His fingers began to wind her curls. "Good. Don't feel like you have to stop there."

"Oh, I don't plan on it." A smooth, confident voice escaped her lips. A voice that surely belonged to a different woman.

"Fucking luckiest man alive," he murmured.

Goodness, this was powerful. Sexy. She tightened her fist in his T-shirt and began tugging it up. Without a word, he shifted his weight forward and held up both arms, allowing her to pull the shirt up and over his head.

As he lowered his arms once more, bracing his weight back on his palms, her mouth dried out at the sight of his torso. Not for a second was she embarrassed. There was no comparing his body to hers.

There was only lust.

Her gaze caressed first one and then the other of his flat, dark brown nipples. They were hard, and the skin of his chest was peppered with gooseflesh. Sleek slabs of muscle covered him from shoulder to hip, and she couldn't decide what to look at next, so she just kept darting her gaze around, trying to see everything at once. "I can't believe this is all mine," she breathed. Then, a moment later, she realized what she'd just said. What if he didn't want her being proprietary? It would be understandable given their arrangement. "I mean—"

"No, you're right." Reaching down, he wrapped his fingers around one of her wrists, then brought her hand to his chest. He placed her palm across one of his hot little nipples. "It's all yours." His grip on her wrist loosened, and he dragged his palm along her arm, his touch sending a wave of her own goose bumps scattering across her skin. "So, what are you going to do with it next?"

I'm going to put my mouth all over you. Starting with those tight nubs of his. She moved her palm, savoring the smooth glide of his skin beneath it. Leaning in, she parted her lips and exhaled over his nipple. Her sex throbbed as his nipple tightened, and his breathing hitched.

The tip of her tongue darted out and lapped at the tip. He seemed to freeze, his breathing suddenly halting at a point that made his chest swell. Waiting to see what she'd do? Not even she knew.

She licked him again. He made a soft noise. So she placed her parted lips over his nipple and sucked ever so softly.

Would it feel as good for him as it had for her last night?

With a hiss, he bowed up to her mouth.

Apparently so. She sucked harder. Beneath her, his weight shifted. His fingers thrust into the hair over her ear, and his thumb stroked the shell of her ear as she continued to suck him.

"That's my girl," he grated with another stroke of his thumb.

His fingers tightened in her hair, and he seemed to be tugging her downward. She allowed it, releasing his nipple and nipping the curve of his pectoral with her teeth, making him grunt softly.

As she made her way down, she made sure to lick or nip every curve of muscle. By the time she reached his belly button, his breaths were audibly billowing and he'd begun to squirm. When she reached up and flicked his wet nipple with a fingernail, she thought he was going to arch right off the island.

Neither of her other lovers had ever been this responsive. If they had been, maybe she'd have had some sort of clue what to do with them. Other than cringe and wait for it to end.

Right below his belly button trailed the slightest smattering of hair. She nuzzled it with her lips and gazed up at him through hooded eyes.

He still cradled her head so gently, but the muscles of his arm were tense and flexed. His opposite shoulder bulged with his body weight as his hand braced against the island. His head lolled back, his throat in stark relief and bobbing with a hard swallow. His curls tumbled over his forehead, and a fine sheet of sweat dotted his chest.

She'd never seen a more beautiful man in her life. And, by his own admission, he was hers.

A heavy ache settled deep in her belly, and between her legs she grew even more impossibly swollen and wet. She pressed her knees together, hoping to relieve the throbbing. It didn't work, but she couldn't tear her gaze away from his body even as every second she looked at him drove her body to new, uncomfortable heights.

She dragged her palm down his stomach, trailing her fingers in the valleys between his muscles until she reached the drawstring of his pants. She paused. "I can take these off?"

His head raised oh so slowly, and when his gaze met hers, she almost startled. He looked as though he'd been caught halfway between heaven and torture. As though he couldn't stand one more second of her mouth and hands on his body, but he'd die if she stopped what she was doing.

No one had ever looked at her like that before.

"Take them off," he said in a voice heavy with gravel. "Leave them on." He shook his head as though trying to clear it. "You're going to blow my mind no matter what you do."

She wanted to grin. Slowly, she pulled the bow of his drawstring loose. Fisting her hands in the waistband, she whispered, "Lift your hips."

The words had barely left her lips before he was raising his bottom. What the move did to his abdominal muscles nearly sent her to the grave. The already cut muscles flexed, creating deep, deep shadows she wanted to explore.

But she gave herself a mental shake and started dragging his pants down his hips. As his goody trail widened, so did her eyes. Where his torso met his legs, a thick cut of muscle flexed.

The V. He has the V! She'd heard about it, mostly from a few of her more sex-crazed clients who lacked discretion. She'd never seen one in real life, though.

No wonder it was such a big deal. Just the sight of it made her want to sink her teeth into it.

As the pants dropped lower and lower, she found herself holding her breath, unable to do otherwise even though her lungs felt as though they were going to explode. Was it possible to perish from sensory overload? As she revealed more and more of his body, her brain was overrun with ideas of things she wanted to do to it. There was not possibly enough time in the world to accommodate it all.

But she had at least a year.

The pants met resistance, and she gave a little tug, which resulted in a hissed breath from Ryker. Immediately, she let go of the pants. "Sorry!" She wasn't quite sure what had happened, but something had.

"Don't be sorry, *bonita*." He braced himself on one arm, sending more rippling displays across the muscles of his torso. "Not your fault." Reaching into the front of his pants with his free hand, he adjusted himself until the head of his penis emerged from the waistband.

Her lips parted.

"Well, it's kind of your fault, but it's definitely no reason to be sorry."

She could hear the smile in his voice, but nothing could make her gaze turn away from this breathtaking sight.

He was enormous, and she was only looking at about three-fourths of him, the base and root of his penis still hidden behind the fabric of his pants.

That had been inside her last night? And she could walk today? Miracles did exist.

The skin was darker than the rest of him by at least two shades, except for the broad head which gleamed a deep, almost-purple in the harsh overhead lights. The sight of that taut head made her lick her lips.

He let loose a harsh groan. "Charlie…"

"Hmm?" she asked, her eyes still riveted to her prize.

Another groan. "You've got to…touch me or something." His hips rolled, punctuating his words and thrusting that head over the ridges of his abdomen. "I can't…take much more."

As though to prove his point, his erection kicked, and before her eyes, a bead of moisture wept from the tip.

She gasped. She couldn't help it. Her womb seemed to clench, making her belly ache almost more than she could stand. Again, she pressed her knees together to no avail.

Touch him? Yes, please.

Reaching out with trembling fingers, she hesitated only a moment before brushing her fingertips against the very tip of him.

His abdominals flexed again, forcing him to exhale audibly. Her eyes widened as soon as her fingertips registered how hot he was. And the skin was so taut. No wonder he claimed he couldn't take anymore. That had to be painful.

Swallowing harshly, she thumbed his slit, spreading the bead of moisture he'd given her. The muscles of his arms trembled in her peripheral vision as she turned her thumb over and examined the gleaming drop.

She brought her thumb to her lips. At the last second, she raised her gaze to his. His cheeks were ruddy; his eyes were glassy as they focused raptly on her mouth.

She darted out the tip of her tongue and lapped the drop from her thumb.

His breath left him in a whoosh.

The spicy taste of him was a mere glimpse of what she could have, and as she swallowed down the sample, she immediately knew she wanted more.

"Okay?" he asked huskily.

She nodded. "Okay." More than okay. In fact, how quickly she could acceptably devour him?

Raising her eyebrows in question, she reached for his waistband again.

"Yes," he nearly groaned in answer to her unvoiced question.

Grasping his pants, she gave a gentle tug this time and pulled them down his thighs. Studiously keeping her gaze from his groin to avoid losing her focus, she knelt and worked the pants down his calves, ankles, and finally over his feet—even those managed to be wildly attractive.

She dropped the pants somewhere behind her, realizing even as she did so that not taking the time to meticulously fold them was more telling than anything else with regard to how lost she was right now. Balancing on the balls of her feet, she leaned forward and pressed a soft kiss to his left calf, then to his knee, before rising.

When she stood once more between his sprawled knees, he was gazing at her softly. Unable to hold the weight of that soft stare, she finally allowed her gaze to sink to where it wanted to be.

Even better than I could have imagined.

His erection jutted proudly toward her. His heavy sac captured her attention—would he like her tongue there as well?

His hips undulated again as she stared; her eyes on him seemed to drive him wild. If she could drive him crazy without even touching him, what could she do when she *did*?

Placing both palms on his knees, she leaned in ever so slowly, parting her lips.

His breathing accelerated, and beneath her palms she thought she felt the finest tremor in his knees. When she was just an inch away from tasting him, he groaned softly and another bead gathered on the tip of his penis.

Invitation accepted. She captured the bead, this time with the tip of her tongue.

A stream of Spanish passed through the air above her head so quickly, she couldn't place the words. The tone of Ryker's voice, however, was desperate. Pleading.

His salty, spicy flavor filled her mouth, and she chased more of his taste, dipping her tongue into his slit and then closing her lips around the tip of his erection. Softly, she sucked.

"Yes." His fingers tightened in her hair. "That's it, *mi bonita*. Oh, God…" He devolved into more rapid Spanish.

His constant chatter grounded her, reminded her that he was here with her every second. That she was, somehow, managing to drive him crazy with the unpracticed things she was doing to his body.

She swirled her tongue around the head, and gazed up to see if he liked it. Every muscle in his torso was flexed in stark relief, but he wasn't looking at her. His neck was arched back, his chest billowing with his harried breathing. His thick throat worked furiously around all the words he muttered.

Doing something right.

Keeping her gaze locked on his torso, she sucked him farther into her mouth, moving slowly down his impressive length. When his tip met the back of her throat, she stopped.

What do I do now?

Thank God he wasn't looking at her. She placed a palm of each of his thighs, the soft hair covering his legs tickling her. Her mouth began to fill with saliva.

So she swallowed.

He froze. Beneath her hands, his thighs flexed. Then, he began to lower his head.

Oh, God. Was she doing it wrong?

Chapter Ten

The sight that met him would have put him on his knees if he hadn't already been seated.

Charlie clenched his thighs in her tiny hands, her blunt nails digging into his muscles. He could feel himself bumping up against the back of her throat, and still she only had about half of him in her mouth. Her cheeks were hollowed; her blue eyes were wide behind her glasses.

"*Mujer*," he began, his voice hoarse. "Did you just—?"

She swallowed again. Her throat undulated around his cock. His eyes nearly rolled back in his head.

How could this possibly feel so good?

Sure, he didn't get head very frequently in his line of work, but he'd never really missed it. If a client deigned to give it to him, it was always a stepping stone to the big finish. Her finish, not his.

But Charlie's mouth around him? God, he was going to want this all the time.

And I can have it.

This woman in front of him was his for the foreseeable future. "Damn, Charlie." He leaned forward, taking his weight from his hand and reaching for her with it. His fingers trembled as he wove them into her hair in a mirror image of what his other hand was doing.

This hair of hers was going to be the end of him. Soft as silk between his fingers, it rioted around her face and shoulders. Tumbled down her back. It would cloak them if she rode him again. Tickle his thighs as she tossed her head back.

He cradled her head in his palms. Again, Spanish tumbled from his lips. He wasn't even quite sure what he was saying, which should alarm him since she seemed to be fluent in the language. But he was helpless to stop the babbling.

Her blue eyes flashed, and he realized her delicate swallows around his length had not been calculated on her part. They were happy accidents.

She was languishing here, her uncertainty clear.

"You beautiful, beautiful girl," he murmured. "Come now." He used his hold on her to guide her back. She didn't relinquish her suction as she drew to the tip again, and he had to fight his spine to keep it from arching.

"Now," he loosened his hold on her hair, the temptation to thrust into her mouth almost more than he could handle, "suck me down again, gorgeous."

Her gaze locked with his, she obeyed. And when he was lodged at the back of her throat once more, she swallowed in that same, earthshattering way she had earlier. "Yes, *bonita*," he said as she started to draw back, this time on her own. "God, fuck me with that mouth of yours."

She moaned and set about doing just what he'd said, as though she'd prefer to do nothing else, sucking him deep and pulling back so fast, he had to release her hair or risk pulling it.

His gut was already starting to tighten when one of her palms started skating up his thigh. He watched with rapt focus as her fingertips tickled over his inner thigh and then upward.

Helpless to do anything else, his thighs spread even more, anticipating where she was going with this.

When she cupped his sac and gave it a gentle tug, he tensed.

For the first time in my life, I'm going to come before a woman.

"Charlie." Her name tripped from his lips several times in a row as he reached for her.

With her mouth still around his dick, she looked up. Whatever she must have seen on his face drew her brows together. She withdrew, her lips letting go of the crown of his cock just as his hands wrapped around her upper arms. "Ryker, are you—?"

She cut off with a squeak as he lifted her against him.

Falling back with absolutely no finesse, his head cracked against the marble of the island. Luckily, Charlotte, with her diminutive height, landed on his chest as the lightest weight.

"Ryker!"

Raising his head, he silenced her with a hasty kiss. He caught the barest hint of his precum on her lips, and he nearly lost his mind.

She moaned into his mouth, and then her hands were in his hair, weaving through the strands and clutching him close as she deepened the kiss, taking it from hasty to the best kind of nasty in the span of a second.

Ryker sank back against the island, wrapping an arm around Charlotte and going for all of his favorite places at the same time: one hand clutching her generous, perfect ass; another hand cupping one of the breasts that would be in his dreams for the rest of his life.

His aching cock was pressed between their bellies, and, like he was fourteen, he was rocking his hips, thrusting it against her in the only way afforded to him.

The pressure was not nearly enough, which was the perfect point, since he'd been moments away from losing it.

But, I swear, I had a purpose in picking her up. What was it?

Oh, fuck yes.

He relinquished his prized handfuls with the barest hint of regret. Nipping at her lips, he pulled from the kiss only enough to whisper, "Clothes off, gorgeous."

She stared down at him with glazed eyes. "Clothes?"

God, she was so cute.

"Off, yes." He pulled her silky blouse from her slacks, his fingertips brushing against the exquisitely soft skin of her lower back. He daubed his thumb momentarily in the dip at the base of her spine before shaking off enough lust to get focused. Reaching between their bodies, he fumbled with one of the tiny buttons keeping him from seeing her naked from the waist up.

She pushed upright with hands braced on his pecs.

She was sitting astride him now, her bottom on his thighs, her knees on either side of his hips, and her hands on his chest. Beneath the thin layer of her blouse, her gorgeous breasts heaved. Glorious red, curly hair tumbled all around them.

His fingers froze on the button they held. "Fuck, you're beautiful."

She stared down at his body. The hands against his pecs turned gentle, sweeping across his nipples and down his abdomen. "I was just thinking the same thing."

When she brushed against the crown of his erection where it lay against his belly, he sucked in a breath. "I really need your clothes off," he murmured. He resumed working on her buttons with renewed fervor.

With a slight color to her cheeks, she joined him, starting from the top. Their hands met in the middle, right above her gently sloped belly. With an audible swallow, she lowered her hands and let Ryker have the honor.

And what an honor it was. He spread her blouse reverently. While her lingerie last night had been decadent, her bra today was utilitarian: a nude color that blended into her skin and covered more than anything had a right to cover when it came to Charlie's breasts. Despite that, her generous curves seemed barely contained by the garment.

He hated the bra on sight for the traitor it was to this family. Her silk blouse whispered against her skin as he pushed it from her shoulders. It fell against his thighs in a mound of cool fabric, and he wasted no time reaching around her tiny frame, his fingers seeking the clasp.

When he released it, she took a deep breath. *Poor baby.* A bra so restrictive she couldn't even breathe deeply? Drawing the straps down her arms, he was tempted to throw the thing toward the garbage disposal a few feet away, but the sight of her tight nipples distracted him.

The bra disappeared; he didn't really register where he'd put it. All that mattered was he get a taste of those nipples as soon as possible.

Pushing up on his elbow, he cupped a breast with his free hand and brought it to his mouth. She leaned forward with a sigh, helping him close the distance, and when his lips closed around her nipple, she sagged against him.

Her palms met the marble with a slap, her tiny arms trembling as they held her up. God, he loved her taste. He laved her nipple, added the slightest bite. *Need to taste more of her.*

Continuing to suck her, he reached between their bodies once more, this time aiming for her slacks. His usually nimble fingers faltered, but he still managed to unfasten and unzip her in record time. Smoothing his fingers along her hips, he eased her pants down, but he could only get them so far before he needed her cooperation.

Her nipple between his teeth, she seemed lost to his mouth. Drawing back, he looked up at her. Her eyes were squeezed shut; her hips moved restlessly against his hands. "*Bonita.*" Her eyes opened, stared into space for a second, then seemed to focus on him. "Help me, Charlie." He tugged on her pants again, but they wouldn't ease past her spread thighs. "If I don't get my tongue in your pussy in the next minute, I might actually die."

Her blue eyes widened.

Went too far? He held his breath, but she lifted her lower body, her hands joining his, and she began shoving her pants and panties down her thighs.

His breath left him in a whoosh. *God, yes.* This was a dream. Together, they kicked at her pants. Her shoes hit the tile floor with two distinct thuds, and then she was naked.

Smooth, warm skin met his. *Hallelujah.* Gripping her waist, he spun her. He narrowly dodged a knee to the face, but would have gladly suffered a smashed nose for the sight that met him once she was kneeling over him, a knee pressing into the tops of each of his shoulders.

"Jesus Christ," he bit out.

"Ryker...I don't know about this." She squirmed, and that was when he realized her breasts cradled his erection.

He closed his eyes and gritted his teeth. This woman was going to kill him. When she squirmed again, his eyes popped open, her words finally penetrating the fog of lust taking over his consciousness. "Easy, *bonita.*" He wrapped his arms around the small of her back and gave her a gentle squeeze. "Stay with me."

She rocked forward on her knees, taking her sweet sex farther from his face, where he wanted it. "But—" Another rock.

Her breasts were squeezing his cock. Hugging it. Stroking it with her every movement. He tightened his arms and palmed her ass in a firm grip. If she kept moving like this...

Tipping his head up, he pressed a kiss high on the inside of her thigh.

She stopped moving.

Again: hallelujah.

He flicked his tongue out, licking higher, but not yet reaching his prize. Her body stiffened in his arms.

Two things became apparent at once. The first was that she'd never had this done to her before. And the second?

She's not going to like this.

For some reason, his chest felt heavy. As though he'd lost some great opportunity when this act had never been his favorite to start with.

He squeezed her bottom, hoping the gesture was comforting. Reassuring. He pressed one last soft kiss to the crease where her ass met her thigh, *it's okay* perched on the tip of his tongue and his hands preparing to lift her off him.

But then, she sagged atop him, her back arching slightly beneath his arms.

"Oh," she breathed, pressing back into his mouth. "That's..." She pressed her cheek into his upraised thigh. "Do it again."

"Fuck yes." He obeyed as though she'd whipped him into action.

As soon as his lips brushed her skin, she arched even more. Her breasts pressed into his groin, and he flexed involuntarily, sending his cock up into her warm, tight cleavage. Before he could stop himself, he thrust.

As his dick met sweet, stroking resistance, stars lit behind his eyelids. *Oh, Jesus.* He thrust again.

Feels so good. Another thrust. *I'm going to—*

He froze. What, was he going to come from this?

His eyes popped open. He was!

With a new surge of desperation, he dove down with the hand covering her ass. With his thumb and forefinger, he gently spread her lips, revealing pink, glistening skin. She was so wet, she coated his fingers in two of his rapid heartbeats.

Mine. Leaning up, he claimed her with his mouth, pressing parted lips right over her opening.

She jolted.

He licked his way into her body, his eyes rolling back at her flavor.

"Oh, God." Again, she pressed her face into his thigh.

He felt the slightest stinging bite and realized she was digging her blunt little nails into his ass.

She rocked back, pressing into his mouth, and he growled, licking deeper. His chin rasped against her clit, and he jutted his jaw even more, pressing right where he knew she'd need him.

"Ryker," she moaned. Widening her knees, she lowered herself, all but sitting on his face.

Lord have mercy. He grunted. Just as he was about to go wild on her, she jerked away with a gasp. "So sorry! I didn't mean to—"

With a nearly violent growl, he jerked his arms tight, sending her crashing back down. She settled on his face more fully than before, nearly sprawling across his tightly strung body.

Perfection. He set back in with a vengeance, and the moment he felt all resistance leave her body and she began undulating to his mouth, his tongue, he knew he would never be the same.

Her nails curled into his ass. "Oh, no," she moaned. Her lush, wet mouth parted against his thigh. "Going to be so fast. Ryker—"

Yes, baby. Let go.

She began rocking atop him with her entire body. The effect on her breasts against his cock was earth-shattering.

With one final admonishing push to make sure she stayed right where she was, he unwound his arms. Skating his palms up the curves of her side, he made his way toward those breasts that were rocking his world.

She began to moan constantly, using his chin to its best advantage. Fuck, the way she moved.

He palmed her breasts, pressing them together around his dick. The pressure was rapturous. His hips started to buck with absolutely no finesse.

She gasped, then smashed her breasts into his groin, increasing his pleasure tenfold. "God, yes," she uttered into his thigh, her harried breaths stirring the fine hair there. "Don't stop...Ryker." She gave a small cry. "I'm going to—"

She cut off abruptly. Every one of her muscles stiffened. Then, pressing her face hard against his leg, she...

Fuck.

She screamed.

Oh, God. Oh, Jesus.

He lapped her like mad as she ground against his face. Between her breasts, he thrust with all his power.

His orgasm took him over in a moment. With a heavy groan that was lost against her pussy, her breasts robbed him of shot after shot of come. His mind whirled as his body shuddered.

Never felt this good before.

It went on and on. The sweet heat between her breasts grew slick with his semen. He was making an absolute mess on her, and he couldn't seem to stop.

He was dimly aware of her slowing undulations against his mouth, and just when he thought he couldn't take a second more of the intense pleasure and live, his own orgasm began to abate. His thrusts lost their desperation until they tapered off.

She lay panting atop him, every muscle in her body lax. With her pressed so firmly against his face, he couldn't quite breathe as much as his taxed lungs seemed to be demanding, but he wasn't ready for her to move yet.

He gentled his hold on her breasts and began to slowly stroke the sides with his thumbs.

My most favorite breasts in the entire world. God, he had plans for these beauties.

When his lungs' demands grew too great, he nuzzled her, pressing one final kiss against her sex before wrapping his arms around her waist and gently easing her down his body.

She seemed to snap out of her stupor. "Oh my gosh, you can't breathe!" She scrambled away, and he caught just the barest glimpse of her pussy—no longer pink but a well-used, swollen red—before she was bounding off the island, her cheeks stained just as red as her sex.

"Hey," he protested, reaching for her.

Her glazed eyes raked his body, which was still spread atop her island. The hungry look in her eyes made him feel as though he were some kind of man buffet. And for the first time in his life, that look didn't make him feel hollow inside.

He was hers. That she wanted him this blatantly was—

His thoughts tapered off as she switched from looking at his body to gazing down at her chest. Her breasts were covered with his orgasm. The sight wrung a low, possessive growl from his own chest.

Slowly, she raised a hand, daubed her fingertips in it, and spread it across her pale, smooth skin. Her gaze met his, and her lips tipped up at the corners. "I mark you, you mark me?"

Was it possible for a man to spontaneously orgasm moments after coming his brains out? He raised fingertips to brush over the mark she'd left him at the base of his throat. "That's right, *mujer.*"

"I can live with that arrangement."

He sat up slowly, reaching for her. She placed her tiny hand in his palm and let him draw her forward. When she stood between his spread knees, he said, "Me, too." With his gaze still held captive by hers, he slid down from the island and began to lead her toward her room. His heart pounded in his ears as she followed silently behind him.

He walked her straight into the grand bathroom off the master, turned on the spray for the shower, and ushered her beneath it once it was warm.

She was astonishingly quieter than normal. For that matter, so was he, which was why her quietness didn't alarm him.

He was content. Happy. Feeling warm from the inside out. He recognized a kindred expression on her face as she melted beneath the warm water while he tenderly cleaned her chest and stomach. When she sagged against him as he massaged shampoo into her scalp, he thought that he could quite possibly do this very same thing every evening for the rest of his life and be perfectly content.

When the shower ended, he quickly toweled himself off, then wrapped a towel around his fiancée, rubbing his palms over her upper arms several times before reminding himself that she wasn't cold and he didn't have to warm her.

That gorgeous hair of hers tumbled down her back, and he gently toweled as much water from it as he could. "Let's get you in bed, hmm?"

She nodded, the movement logy. Which was only natural, given she'd put in a full day of work on a Saturday and gone through the glut of emotion tied to any big life change. Ryker himself was exhausted, the bed calling his name. He wasn't, however, looking forward to sleeping down the hall alone.

When he pulled back the duvet, Charlie slid between the covers, her wet auburn hair fanning out over the pillow. She opened her arms to him. "Come here."

"God, yes." She didn't have to ask twice. He slid in next to her, and she curled into his side, spreading her leg over the tops of his thighs, as though it were the most natural move she had ever made.

Her palm rested over his heart. She nuzzled his shoulder as he wound his arm around her and held her close.

It felt so right.

It felt so dangerous.

He needed to get them back on safe footing. "Why don't you want to get married for love, Charlie?"

Against his side, she stiffened, then sighed. In the sound, he fancied he heard the same realization that he'd had: they were a little too close right now. He tightened his arm before she could pull away. They may need some mental distance, but he sure as hell didn't need any physical distance.

"Lots of people don't want to get married."

Hedging. "I told you my reasons. Didn't that help you with…well, all of this?" He gestured to them both.

Another sigh. "Yes, it did," she said, resignation in her voice. She looked up at him for a moment, then glanced across the room. "I'm a divorce lawyer. Isn't that reason enough to want to avoid marriage?"

Maybe for some, but … "I don't think that's your reason."

He saw her lips quirk. "You don't, huh?"

He brushed his palm along her back. "Did it have something to do with the guy who gave you an STI?"

Now she jerked her head up and glared at him. "You can't be serious."

His hand paused. "Seems like a fair question."

She rolled her eyes. "You think I avoid relationships because a bad one ended over a decade ago?" She snorted, the sound so close to the one she made when she laughed that he had to bite back a smile.

"So, that's not the reason?"

"No! Bad relationships are supposed to end!"

She was so indignant, her delicate brows crashed together and her eyes flashed behind her thick-framed glasses. He wanted to cuddle her close and press a kiss to her forehead.

"Typical male," she muttered, shoving a wet strand of hair off her brow so hard, it landed on his shoulder. "Besides, all those things that happened in past relationships were just as much my fault. They wouldn't have been able to fool me if I hadn't lost my focus. No, I'm not against marriage because of bad relationships, mine or the ones I see in my office every day." She looked at him again. "Though, I will tell you, from what I've witnessed, the only thing worse than wishing you *were* married is wishing you *weren't*."

He resumed stroking her back. "Something you'll never have to worry about."

For a moment, the no-nonsense look in her eyes wavered. She looked as though she were going to say something in return, and the corners of her eyes and lips relaxed. He felt that relaxation stronger than if she'd stroked him with her hands.

But then she cleared her throat. "You either," she mumbled.

Before he could respond—with what, he didn't know—she flopped back down beside him. "It's not the bad relationships. It's the good."

She'd spoken so quietly, he wasn't sure he'd heard her correctly. "The good relationships?"

She nodded wordlessly.

"I'm sorry, *bonita*, I don't—"

"Good relationships don't have a chance of lasting, either."

Now on that point, he emphatically disagreed. They were forging the right kind of good relationship this second. "Charlie—"

"I don't have anyone to invite to the wedding," she blurted suddenly.

His brows crashed together. "What?" Were they changing the subject? "Charlie, neither do I—"

"My dad is dead," she said bluntly. "I haven't heard from my mom in ten years."

He shut his mouth. Inside his head, however, thoughts were screaming. What in the world had happened to Charlotte Moore?

"She left him." The words left her at barely a whisper. "Right after their twentieth wedding anniversary."

His arm tightened around her. *Oh, shit.*

"He was dead within a year. Just"—she waved a hand through the air, and then it collapsed onto his chest—"stopped caring. I'd always thought dying of a broken heart was something people with too much imagination believed in, but I watched it happen. It was terrible."

Finally, she looked up at him. Behind her glasses, her blue eyes were bleak. "Their marriage was perfect." Her eyes shifted. "Before I came along."

He stiffened. "Wait, what?"

She ducked her head, avoiding his gaze. "I could see it in pictures from the early years of their marriage. Could hear it in their voices when they talked about the good days." She sniffed, and Ryker swore to God that if she was crying, he'd hunt down that woman this second. When he was able to snag a peek at Charlie's eyes, though, they were dry. And hopeless. "He was wonderful. Such a good father. He always made me feel like he was proud of me. I've never been able to understand how she could turn her back on him." She paused. "But I know it was because of me."

"Because of you?" He sat up in bed and reached for her. "Charlie, that is in no way true."

She sat up as well and dodged his hands. "She told me herself."

His hands paused in midair between them. "Your mother told you—" He couldn't even bring himself to finish the thought.

She did it for him. "That my diagnosis had been the beginning of the end for them. That I ruined everything."

He gritted his teeth. "Did she say those exact words?"

"Oh, yes." She tapped a finger against her temple. "I have an excellent memory."

Ryker lowered his hands slowly to his lap, flexing them into and out of fists. "Where is your mother now?" They were going to have a talk. A loud one.

Charlotte's breathed laugh was bitter. "No idea."

He ground his teeth together and pulled in a slow breath through his nose. When he was sure he could speak again and not sound like he was spitting mad, he said, "*Bonita*, no offense, but I wouldn't call that a happy marriage. It sounds like a happy marriage and your mother couldn't possibly coexist."

She shook her head. "But they had coexisted. Before I put my touch on their relationship. I've already ruined one marriage." She pulled her knees up and wrapped her arms around them, effectively blocking her nudity from view. "The divorce rate among marriages in which one partner has Asperger's is seventy-five to eighty percent. Did you know that?"

He swallowed hard. "No, I didn't."

"I'm a walking marriage curse." She propped her chin on her upraised knees.

Damn, that statistic did have some bite. It felt like his gut had bottomed out. Placing a palm on her back, he stroked gently up and down. "Charlie, that won't be true for us." He wouldn't let it be. "What are the variables in those marriages? I'm betting missed diagnosis is one of them. Also, there's emotion.

Something we're working very hard to make sure won't affect our marriage."

She turned her head, her cheek against her knees now, and examined him through her glasses. "I suppose that's true."

Had that been a glimmer of hope in her tone? He studiously kept stroking her back in the same, measured movements, lest he betray his own flare of hope.

Suddenly, she sat up, dropping her knees. "Anyway," she continued, her tone entirely different now, "through my profession, I've learned that bad marriages are more common than good ones. In my own experiences, I've learned I'm liable to get too involved and forget what's really important. And from my parents, I learned that even good relationships don't stand a chance." She shrugged against him. "I'd say that's plenty of reasons to prefer our type of relationship."

Yep, that had been hope. It was still there, hiding behind her carefully clipped words. Ryker had to clear his throat before he could speak again. "Fair enough."

"So." She looked up at him. "Now that I've sufficiently ruined the mood, can we not have to talk about things like this ever again?"

Ever again? That heavy feeling rushed back with a vengeance. "Is that what you want?"

Her blue eyes cleared. "Yes. You have no idea."

He pressed his lips together, holding a sigh in just in time. What was his deal? All she was really asking for was a halt to an overemotional conversation. No emotion: that was what he wanted, too. What on earth was compelling him to push for this? "Then, of course." The words tasted bitter as he spoke them. He shoved his thoughts aside. "And who says you killed the mood?"

She snorted. As she leaned back against the pillows, her breasts bobbed, drawing his gaze like a lightning rod in the middle of a summer squall. Reaching over her head, she stretched, a lazy, sensual noise tumbling past her kiss-bruised lips. And just like that, he didn't have to pretend she hadn't stabbed the mood about thirty times. It came roaring back.

She squeaked as he rolled, quickly pinning her beneath him. Shoving her knees apart with his own, he settled his hips between her spread legs. Her eyes widened as his hard dick nudged right at the entrance to her sex.

"Oh, my," she breathed, her hands landing on his biceps and squeezing.

"I think it's definitely time for talking to be over." He rotated his hips, and as the head of his cock dragged over her clitoris, her eyelids fluttered. "Wouldn't you say?"

"Yes," she blurted. "I say that."

He bit back a grin. "Now..." He pulled back his hips, fitted himself right where he needed to be, and slid home.

She exhaled slowly, the tiniest moan sounding as he seated himself to the hilt.

"Let's get this relationship back on track, shall we?" he asked, framing her face with his hands and digging his fingers into her remarkable hair.

"God, yes," she breathed.

They didn't talk for the rest of the night.

Just the way they both needed it.

Chapter Eleven

A week and a half. It had been only ten days since Ryker moved in with Charlotte, and he was ready to tear his hair out.

"Missing out on the fun part of Netflix and chill." He jabbed the pause button on the remote, freezing an episode of the new *Queer Eye* in its tracks. He'd already watched the entire season two times anyway. A third time was just desperate.

Leaning forward, he propped his elbows on his knees and buried his face in his upraised hands. Damn it, he *was* desperate. Swear to God, this morning when he'd headed out for a morning run a few minutes after Charlie left for work, he'd paused beside Roger's desk. For company.

Roger's horror-widened eyes stopped him in his tracks. And just in case Ryker hadn't gotten the hint, Roger's clipped, dismissive, "Enjoy your run, sir," certainly erased any ambiguity.

They were not going to be friends. Right.

No job. No one to talk to. A quickly dwindling on-demand menu.

He'd promised himself he wasn't going to be a kept man, yet here he was. He needed a pastime. Stat.

Part of the reason he had no savings was because he'd constantly donated any surplus income to the local foster care system. Maybe he could volunteer there?

He reached for his phone. Hell, it was something. Though, in his gut, he knew it would be a bad idea. He didn't even know if the system accepted volunteers. Lord knew he'd never seen any when he was a foster child. Even if they did give him something to do, how would he explain to Charlie the ten to fifteen kids he brought home every day to live with them? Was his heart even strong enough to work with those kids and then leave them at the end of the day in the system that had broken him down as a child?

He paused, his phone in his hand and resting against his knee.

Shit.

Maybe he should just call Gage. Cassidy and he both had busy work schedules. They might need a nanny for Sasha. Or, *manny*.

This lost feeling was not what he'd expected when he'd dreamed of an emotionless marriage.

At least he had the nights. Charlie would barely put her keys down before their hands were all over each other. They fucked until they collapsed into sleep on their respective sides of her big bed. Sometimes they remembered to eat supper instead of each other.

This morning when Charlie's alarm had gone off, she'd been spooning him, her bare breasts branding his back. Their arms and legs intertwined. Her hand wrapped around his morning wood. A smile tipped his lips.

Damn fine way to wake up. Before she'd jerked away from him with a gasp and gone through her morning routine without meeting his eyes once. As though they'd had a torrid orgy complete with acrobats instead of waking up cuddling.

This was what you wanted, remember?

He growled, dropping his phone. Okay. More *Queer Eye* it was. Because he needed something to drown out how pitiful he was being.

As he reached for the remote, the sound of a key fitting into the front door froze him to the spot.

Charlie was home? Three hours early? He was grinning before he could catch himself. Shoving up from the couch, he made his way toward the front door. Maybe he could greet her with his mouth between her legs.

Yeah, that'd start their night off right.

The door opened before he could get to it. He stumbled to a stop as a small blond woman carrying a caddy full of bottles in one hand entered the apartment.

Not Charlie. Not even close.

"Um, who are you?" The woman was a little small to be a burglar. No way she would have made it past we're-not-pals Roger.

With a gasp, she spun around. Her eyes widened. She dropped her caddy, and a bottle bounced out and rolled across the floor, a label reading Pine-Sol flashing with every rotation.

Ah, a cleaning lady.

And great, thinking about going down on Charlie had given him a hard-on. He clasped his hands in front of his groin. Maybe she hadn't noticed that detail yet.

She started screaming.

"Shit." He flinched. He'd hold his hands up to demonstrate he meant no harm, but they were definitely busy right now. Instead, he took a step back. "Hey, it's okay."

The screaming continued, only now, the woman fumbled in the pocket of her apron. Her hand emerged clutching pepper spray; he no longer had a hard-on problem.

He crossed his arms over his face and took another step back. "Wait! I'm Charlotte's fiancé!"

The screaming cut off abruptly.

He slowly lowered his arms, watching her the entire time to see if she was just trying to trick him into vulnerability.

Nope, she was staring at him as though he were a creature she couldn't identify but had decided she didn't like, her nose wrinkled and brows drawn together. "Fiancé?"

She still held the pepper spray.

"Yes." He swallowed. "I'm Ryker Martinez." Should he extend a hand for her to shake?

She humphed. "Miss Moore has never mentioned a fiancé."

No shit. "It's recent."

She raised an eyebrow.

Judging me. He knew that gut-hollowing feeling intimately. Did she not think he was good enough for Charlotte? He was familiar with that feeling, too.

This is some bullshit. He straightened, dropping his hands to his sides. "Sorry for the surprise. I didn't know she had a cleaning lady."

"You didn't know your fiancée had a cleaning lady?" She smirked.

All right. He was more than ready for her to leave. "You know what?" His smile felt tight. "Thank you so much for coming all the way out here, but," he gestured around the apartment, "I've actually already cleaned."

It had been something to do. After his shower this morning, he'd found some Lemon Pledge and Clorox Wipes under the kitchen sink. The apartment gleamed, and it'd felt good to accomplish something. Anything.

He straightened, an idea forming. "As a matter of fact, we're not going to need someone to clean the apartment anymore."

She had no reaction for several seconds, but then her jaw dropped a bit. "What?"

"I can clean the place in my spare time." This was brilliant, actually. Finally, he could contribute around here. And cleaning took time. Time he wouldn't have to sit around and ponder how things weren't going the way he wished.

"You're firing me?" She narrowed her eyes.

Uh oh. Damn it, he'd really thought he'd seen the last of that scorned look when he left the agency. "Oh, I wouldn't say that. We just don't need a maid anymore. It's nothing that you've done."

"You can't fire me." She planted her fists on her hips. "How do I even know you're who you say you are?"

With a sigh, he pinched the bridge of his nose. He'd turned this into a mess. "Okay. Yes, okay. Go ahead and do your thing." Path of least resistance. Always.

Besides, there was no rule that said he couldn't still clean a little every day to fill the time. But what was he supposed to do while someone cleaned the apartment with him here? Did he just sit here and, what...watch her?

Was this how rich people lived?

There was a commotion at the door. "Oh, God, please tell me that's not the gardener," he muttered beneath his breath.

The door swung open, and Charlie burst into the apartment, her bun slightly askew and her keys clutched in a fist she placed over her chest.

Something loosened in his own chest at the sight of her.

Her blue eyes were wild as they scanned the space, finding him in a moment. She stepped toward him. "Ryker!" she gasped. "Erin is coming to—"

The cleaning lady cleared her throat.

Charlie blinked at the small, belligerent woman standing beside Ryker and straightened, her fisted hand falling to her side. "Oh, drat. She's already here." She shook her head as her gaze slowly traveled back toward him. "I'm so sorry. I tried to call, and when I didn't get an answer, I hurried over. I can't believe I forgot to tell you this morning."

Well, bonita, you were too busy fleeing the scene of the cuddle-crime to remember small, pesky details.

She reached out to him, and he had to lock his knees to keep from stepping into the offered touch. "I hope she didn't startle you," she whispered.

A rough, disbelieving laugh broke the silence. He and Charlie turned toward the now-incensed maid. "Startle him?" Erin sniffed.

Charlie frowned. "Is everything okay?"

Compared to what? "Yes," Ryker blurted, leaping in before Erin could. No need for her to divulge everything that had happened right before Charlie arrived. He tried to smile, but it felt a little shaky. "Of course everything is okay."

Erin snorted. "No, it's not." She jabbed a thumb his direction over her shoulder. "He tried to fire me."

Oh damn. This was going to be ugly. Well, uglier. Was he even allowed to fire her? Probably not.

Charlie's lips parted. She looked at him again. "You what?"

And that answered that question. "Look, I know I should have talked to you first. It's just, I can clean the house. Not a problem. We don't need to pay anyone else to do it."

Her eyebrows shot up. "I don't think I like that."

He ground his teeth as the bottom fell out of his stomach. She was going to do this here? In front of a hostile witness?

"I told him he couldn't fire me," Erin said, drawing Charlie's gaze.

Something flashed in Charlie's eyes as she turned back toward the maid. "You told him he couldn't fire you?"

"That's right." Erin lifted her chin.

A muscle ticked in the delicate line of her jaw. "Is that true, Ryker?" she asked without looking away from Erin.

He swallowed. What was he supposed to answer here? Was he still in trouble? Or was Erin? This had slipped out of his usual area of expertise, and he just wanted to keep the peace. Make as little waves as possible. "Yes?" After all, there was no denying it at this point.

"I see," Charlie said quietly. "Well." With the fist still holding the keys, Charlie pushed the front door wider open. "I know I don't like that." She stepped to the side. Behind her, sunlight shone off the marble floor leading to the elevator. "Erin, your services are terminated. Effective immediately."

Wait, what?

"Wait," Erin said. "What?"

Charlie's glare burned hot, even through her glasses. "For insubordination. Please collect your cleaning items and leave. Now."

She was…taking his side?

Fuck. That was hot. Was this how she looked in a courtroom? A curl tumbled across her forehead, and his heart thudded.

"You can't be serious." Erin looked at Charlie for a moment, then cast a glance at Ryker before looking back at Charlie. "This has to be a mistake."

"It's not." Charlie raised an eyebrow, her glare intimidating.

Erin swooped down, grabbed her caddy and snatched the errant bottle of Pine-Sol, muttering beneath her breath the entire time as she stalked out the door Charlie held open for her. As soon as she was through it, Charlie closed it behind her. Hard. The sound echoed through the entire apartment.

Wow. His fiancée stood there, her breathing a little heavy, the red highlights in her hair making an appearance in the light from the chandelier.

She looks like my avenging angel.

A slow grin spread his lips. "That was amazing." He took a step toward her. "You're amazing."

Charlie looked at her wristwatch and sighed. "Drat."

Ryker halted.

"I'm going to have to work late to make up for this." She sighed and met his gaze again. "Don't wait up for me, okay?"

Turning back toward the door, she hesitated with her hand on the knob. "And, maybe sleep in your room tonight?"

His head was spinning, his thoughts still wrapped up in what she'd just done for him. His chest, however, seemed to have caught up with the sudden change—with the dismissal in her tone. "My room?"

She wasn't looking at him anymore. "I just—" She cleared her throat. "Need some rest. I'm a little tired."

"My room," he said again like a perfect idiot.

"Yes."

He pulled in a slow breath, his heartbeat thumping in his temples hard enough it forecasted a headache.

So much for avenging angel. She'd just been keeping order in her house, hadn't she? And he'd snatched onto it like a pathetic, drowning soul and turned it into something it hadn't been. Son of a bitch. He rubbed a hand over his sternum, but it didn't help. "Sure." He took a step back. "Whatever you say."

Fuck. His temper was slipping, right along with his cool.

She turned around, her gaze landing on him as she tilted her head, and her lips parted.

"Have fun at work. I'll see you in the morning." He spit out words, cutting off whatever it was she had been about to say, then turned so he couldn't see her anymore and started down the hall. "I guess."

"Ryker—"

He got to his room and slammed the door behind him, collapsing back onto it with a thud.

Shit.

Goddamn it.

He stared up at the ceiling and tried to calm his breathing. "Don't freak out. Don't you dare do it." He'd gone through all this before. "It doesn't matter."

So she'd totally emasculated him in front of the maid. Then dismissed him. After a week and a half of keeping him firmly in his place.

"It doesn't matter."

It sucked, yes. But it wasn't anything he hadn't already lived through. And the truth was, there was nothing he wouldn't do to make sure this marriage worked out.

Damn it, though. This was all so much harder than he'd thought it would be.

"It doesn't matter."

His heart was thundering. Sweat broke out all over his back. This pep talk wasn't working.

He jerked away from the door, lurching toward the bed. Snatching a pillow, he lobbed it toward the door with all his might. It barely made a sound before falling to the floor.

Collapsing to the mattress, he hunched over and covered his face.

He'd lived through hell. He could walk through flames now without getting burnt. So, why did his entire soul feel scorched?

And it didn't matter how many times he tried to convince himself otherwise. That look Charlie gave him when Erin said he'd tried to fire her…

He released a shaky breath.

It mattered.

***

There was a soft *thud* on the other side of Ryker's door, and then the squeak of protesting mattress springs.

She'd messed up. She wasn't sure what she'd done that was so bad, but one thing was clear: she had messed up horribly.

Oh, dear. She didn't know what to do.

Her heart was still racing after hearing Erin had disrespected Ryker. The nerve! Half of her wanted to race right after the woman and yank at her blond ponytail. It was an urge she'd never suffered from in her life, and she didn't really know how to combat the strength of it as it coursed through her, tightening her muscles until they simply awaited a command to act. It had taken all her focus to calmly fire the woman.

In her office, she'd be able to breathe easily again. Work on eliminating the rage.

Yet while she'd been distracted, she must have said or done something to Ryker that hurt him.

Of course she had. If there were a way to screw up a relationship, she would find it.

You don't have a relationship.

She released a breath. True. She didn't. She had a partnership. And, somehow, she had to repair whatever she'd just destroyed so their partnership could continue without issue.

With a sigh, she dropped the doorknob. *Might as well find out how I failed him now.* There was no way she'd be able to focus at the office, thinking about him being angry. She had trouble focusing at work these days anyway.

This was not going to be fun.

She plodded down the hallway and hesitated only for a moment before she raised her fist and knocked once at his door. "Ryker?"

There was heavy silence on the other side. Drat. She'd messed up so badly he didn't even want to speak with her?

"Um." She leaned forward until her forehead brushed the door. "Can we talk? Please?"

Before she could catch her breath, the door flew inward. Ryker's heat washed over her as she straightened.

Their gazes met, and the strange, cold look in his eyes made her reach for him.

"What do you want, *querida?*"

Her hand froze in midair. She lowered it back to her side, hoping she did so surreptitiously enough that he hadn't even noticed she'd tried to touch him in the first place.

He sounded so tired. And *querida?* He hadn't called her that since the day they met.

She licked her lips. "Are—are you mad at me?"

A muscle ticked in his jaw, and he glared at a spot over her shoulder.

"I see." Her fingers trembled, and she curled them into her palms. "Tell me what I did. I don't know— I just"—she took a step toward him—"don't understand what happened."

He sighed and seemed to deflate before her eyes. "Charlotte, our feelings don't matter, remember? It's fine. Just go to work."

"What? No." She shook her head. "It is not fine, Ryker. Not at all. This has to work. We have to be able to make it work."

His glare snapped toward her now, and she immediately wanted to call back the words. She'd just made it sound like she only cared about their agreement, hadn't she? "That's not what I meant—"

He raised his chin, a look of pure challenge flashing through his eyes. "Okay. You want to know what pissed me off? Fine."

She swallowed hard, the quiet fury in his voice so strong that she took a step backward. This was going to be bad.

"Maybe it's the fact that you gave me a brushing down in front of your maid."

Her eyes widened. "What? No—"

"Maybe," he said louder, "it's that you've turned me into a kept man who just sits around the house all day waiting for you to come home, like a miserable dog. No, wait." He laughed bitterly. "I know what it is."

"Ryker, maybe we should—"

"It's that I'm no different from one of your other service people. Send me to my room." He flung an arm through the air. "Keep me in my place." His other arm swept out. "Except—"

His voice cracked, and she froze.

"I'm so low that I'm the servant your other servants disdain. Roger, Erin—is there anyone else I should be bracing for who will look down their noses at me for daring to step a toe out of the line I should be staying behind?"

Oh. Dear. God.

Her servant? Was that how he saw himself?

Was that how she treated him?

She was going to be sick.

His harried breathing was the only sound in the room as all of his strength seemed to seep out of him at once. He regretted it. Everything he'd just said. The dejected slant of his eyes made that perfectly clear.

But thank God he had said what he had.

How in the world was she going to fix this? Was it even possible?

She cleared her throat. Sliding past him, she entered his room, quickly scanning the area until she spotted it: his duffel bag.

Without a word, she walked over to it and picked it up. Turning back around, she found Ryker gazing at the floor.

"Are you kicking me out now?"

She gripped the bag in front of her, both hands knotting in the strap. "Do you want to leave now?"

Silence descended on the room.

He didn't say yes.

Of course, he hadn't said *no* either.

Pulling in a slow breath, she crossed to his side once more, where she took his hand, coaching herself fiercely to keep from gripping it too hard.

She tugged him out into the hall and began to lead him toward the master bedroom. Was it a good sign that he followed without argument? God, she hoped so.

In the room, she dropped his duffel bag beside the dresser before turning toward the bed. As soon as they stood beside it, she pulled at his hand until he silently sat down on the edge of the mattress. He blinked up at her, his normally brown eyes almost black. Using only her fingertips, she pushed gently at his shoulder until he reclined, his curls a sharp contrast to the pillowcase.

She walked around the bed and then crawled up beside him, lying close to him but not allowing any part of herself to touch him. She couldn't be distracted when she said this.

"I could have very easily clawed Erin's eyes out when I saw how she treated you."

In her peripheral vision, she saw him turn his head toward her.

"What she did—what she said." She shook her head. She wasn't making sense. "When I told you I didn't think I liked what you'd done," she whispered toward the dark ceiling, "it was because I don't like the thought of you having to clean the apartment. Not because you didn't have every right to fire someone who works in your home."

The sound of his breaths rasped over her skin. She turned her head as well, meeting his gaze. The warm brown was beginning to return.

Her brows drew together. "You," she said, enunciating carefully, "are not a servant. And no one is allowed to treat you like one. Especially not me."

He blinked slowly.

Her throat became tight. "I'm not trying to make you a kept man. You just—" She had to clear her throat. "You deserve so much better than me. I was only trying to make life with me as pleasant for you as possible so you wouldn't leave, and—"

Ryker's sudden frown was fierce. "What did you just say?" he asked.

She looked back toward the ceiling. "You're so much better than all of this. I thought, if I made your life easy—" She shrugged. "Waking up like we did this morning"—her eyes slid closed—"was difficult for me. I didn't send you to your room to put you in your place. I did it so I could remember mine."

He swallowed loudly. Then, his head rested against her chest, right over her heartbeat.

Her eyes sprang open, and she placed a cautious hand on his hair. "Ryker?"

"We're quite the pair." His voice rumbled through her sternum.

She could barely breathe through the hope. "We are?"

"I don't think I'm good enough for you. Every damn day."

She gasped. "What? How could you—" His looks. His ease with people.

He raised his head, his warm brown eyes capturing her gaze. "I could say the same to you, *bonita*."

She sifted her fingers through his hair. Not *querida* anymore. She felt fifty pounds lighter. "Will you tell me what I did to make you feel like"—she could barely even say the word—"a servant?" She needed to know. So she would never do it again.

He pulled in an incredibly slow breath, held it for a moment, then released it, all his muscles relaxing against her. "Well, I misunderstood what you were saying in front of Erin, but, honestly?" His gaze slipped away from hers. "Other than that, you didn't do anything. I—" He breathed a laugh that sounded self-deprecating. "I think this fight was actually my mistake."

Her head kicked back. "Your mistake?"

"Maybe I was"—he scrubbed a hand down his face and glanced away—"projecting?" With a groan, he collapsed back to the bed beside her. "Ugh, how pathetic."

"Wait a minute." She placed her hand over his, and he turned his head, meeting her gaze. "Projecting what, exactly?"

He twisted his lips, and a ruddiness she'd never seen outside of a sexual situation stained his cheeks. "If I expect people to walk roughshod over me, it hurts less when it happens." He shrugged. "It's just part of survival for me. And it always works." His smile was abashed. "Except for when I thought you'd done it." He looked away. "It hurt like hell." Those final words had been a barely audible whisper.

Her own cheeks felt hot. "I'm so sorry," she said. Maybe she could just keep saying it. "I told you I was bad at this. I—"

His strained laugh echoed through the room. "Charlie, it's all a moot point anyway. I didn't have any right to be hurt. We agreed to keep all emotions out of this relationship, remember?"

"Didn't have the right?" She flailed upright, forcing him to sit up, too, or take a chin to the head. "An emotion-free marriage doesn't mean I get to treat you like an inferior and then expect you to just take it! And, heaven help you if you try that business on me."

Finally, his gaze met hers once again. His eyes were lighter than normal. Or maybe she was just imagining that. She shifted, an alarming lump rising in her throat.

Speaking of inappropriate emotion.

Blowing out a breath, she looked down at the bedspread. "Do I want to know what Roger said or did?"

He breathed another tight laugh. "Probably something I blew out of proportion."

Not likely. "Right. So, his Christmas bonus will be delivered in pennies this year." And be much, much smaller than it should be.

This time, Ryker's chuckle was free of all strain, and her shoulders finally loosened. She turned to face him, smiled softly, and nodded toward the dresser. "I'll have drawers cleared out for you by tomorrow morning."

For a moment, he looked as though he was going to protest, but then he just nodded.

He was gazing at her softly. She found herself leaning toward him, her fingers itching to touch him in any way she could.

Too much. It was all too much.

She jerked back. Making a big show of it, she glanced at her wristwatch again. "And now, I really do have to go."

She didn't really have to go. She could work from home if she wanted to. She could even just put it off until she went to the office tomorrow. But her brain kept working over what had just happened between them, and it was starting to have an effect on an organ a little farther down. The same organ that had sped up this morning when she'd awoken to find herself wrapped around her convenient fiancé.

He swallowed audibly, but what looked like a little flare of relief lit his eyes. Was he feeling the heavy emotions, too? This had been a necessary conversation, but, goodness, the aftermath was a bit of a mess.

It was definitely time to retreat. "I'll try not to wake you when I get back, okay?"

He nodded. "Okay," he said softly, rubbing a hand over his face roughly enough that his stubble made a rasping sound.

"Okay. Right." She slid from the bed, her knees wobbling for a second before accepting her weight. She wasn't imagining it; things had gotten awkward again. She backed toward the door, flaring her fingers in a quick wave. "Good night." It was only four in the afternoon. "I mean—"

"Good night, Charlie," he whispered.

She smiled tightly, then spun around and bolted out the bedroom door.

She nearly raced down the hall, abandoning the quiet sounds of him moving around the bedroom they now shared.

She could hardly breathe.

Four days. They had four days until the wedding, and the past hour felt like both a giant step forward for them and about five steps backward for her carefully guarded plan.

Their year hadn't even started yet. If this relationship was going to start ducking around some of her carefully crafted walls, she needed to toughen up.

Or she'd never survive it.

Chapter Twelve

The pastor of the Vegas Wedding Chapel kept talking, despite the fact that Ryker had not heard a word she'd said since asking him if he wanted a religious ceremony, and, if he did, "like, how religious?"

He'd grunted something. Not quite sure what he'd agreed to, but it was entirely possible there would be snakes involved now while he and Charlie said their I do's.

Charlotte's simple golden wedding band burned a hole in the inside pocket of his suit jacket. He just wanted to slide it on her finger. More than anything in the world. Get this thing started for real before she could change her mind.

The past four days had been constant torture as he waited for her to come to her senses and either realize she was agreeing to a dead end compared to what most women wanted or that, after Erin was fired, they'd crossed the emotional line they'd both agreed they would stay behind.

And yet, neither of those things had happened. They'd made it here today. And Charlie was in the back room slipping into a wedding dress at this very moment.

Almost there. She's almost mine.

Keys jangled in his pocket, and he realized he was restlessly jiggling his leg. He placed a palm over it and gave the pastor his best client smile.

Her words stuttered and tapered off, just as he'd intended. "Thank you so much for your help," he said smoothly. "I think that's all we need. I'll see you at the altar, okay?"

The pastor blinked a couple of times, as though she couldn't decide whether to be offended that he wasn't hanging onto her every pre-wedding admonition. She opened her mouth, and he braced himself.

"Ryker!"

He spun around. Behind him, he heard the pastor huff off, but all he could focus on was the two—no, make that *three*—people hustling in his direction.

"Oh, thank God," he breathed, something in his chest loosening.

Gage Adams's towering height would be visible across the Strip, much less a tiny wedding chapel. He wore a baby carrier on his front from which Ryker's goddaughter, Sasha, waved grubby fists and gave him a two-toothed grin.

Cassidy rushed over, Gage on her heels, and wrapped her arms around him. Her hair tickled his nose, which was the only reason his eyes stung. "Jesus," she muttered, pulling back and staring up at his face. "You look pale as a ghost."

"Naw," Gage said, slapping his shoulder with a huge palm. "That's just excitement, right bro?"

If excitement felt like he was about to throw up. "Yes. It's excitement."

Like always, Ryker's gaze traveled back to Sasha. "Let me hold her?"

Sasha let out an ear-piercing squeal and reached for Ryker, and, swear to God, his heart melted on the spot.

"Hell yeah, you can hold her," Gage said, reaching for the buckles of the baby carrier. "Thought we were going to be late because she fought this thing like a warrior in the parking lot. I think she hates it."

"She does hate it," Cassidy said, reaching for Sasha and pulling her free.

The six-month-old wore a onesie with the Triforce from *Zelda* on the front and a headband with a bow on her completely bald head. As soon as Cassidy handed her to him, he held her against his shoulder, and she cooed up at him, a thin line of drool leaking out of the corner of her mouth. One of those tiny fists found his mouth, and she forced something between his teeth. He dutifully chewed, and she clapped enthusiastically. "A Cheerio?" Ryker swallowed. "Thank you, *pequeño ángel*."

"Uh, when's the last time we gave her Cheerios?" Gage asked Cassidy.

"I've never given her Cheerios."

They both turned to look at Ryker. Cassidy looked like she was about to burst out laughing; Gage looked like he was about to apologize. Sasha now used her empty hand to tug on Ryker's bottom lip, her tiny, razor blade baby nails digging in for all they were worth.

"Well, whatever it was," Ryker told her around her fingers, "it was delicious."

She gurgled as if to say, "Of course it was."

"Where's the bride?" Cassidy asked.

Ryker nodded toward the right. "In the bride's room." Alone. Unlike him at the moment. He'd never been more grateful to see some friendly faces in his life.

"Good," Cassidy said, "because we want to talk to you."

Damn it. He knew it had been a bad idea to confide the convenience part of his marriage to Cassidy and Gage. Sasha tugged at Ryker's hair, and he would have given anything in that moment to just ignore Cassidy and pay attention to the baby. He patted Sasha's back.

"Oh?"

Gage placed his hand on Cassidy's shoulder, and the fiery redhead snapped her lips closed as though she were holding in a whole string of opinions. "We just want to make sure this is what you really want. That's all."

Ryker stiffened. Gage held out his hands. "No offense intended, Ryker. You know that."

He did know that. Gage, and now Cassidy by default, were the only two names on his friends' list. *Well, not anymore.*

He definitely counted Charlotte among his friends. In fact, the past two weeks, and especially the past few days, had settled her firmly at the top of the list.

At that, all his tension evaporated, along with his nerves. "You have no idea how badly I want this," he said softly, rocking side to side as Sasha rested her cheek against his shoulder. "Just wait until you meet her. She's perfect for me."

Cassidy pinched her mouth together but then sighed. "I don't know, Gage. He looks serious."

Ryker rolled his eyes. "I am serious."

"All right, all right," Gage said. "Don't know how you do that every time, by the way." Gage nodded toward Sasha.

Ryker looked down to find the little girl sleeping against his chest. Already, a tiny puddle of baby drool started at his shoulder and dripped slowly onto his lapel. Ryker grinned. "Damn, she's cute."

"Shit." Gage reached out and tried to wipe the baby drool away with a swipe of his hand but only managed to smear it. "I'm so sorry. Freckles, we got a diaper wipe anywhere?"

Cassidy started rooting around in the massive bag that hung off her shoulder.

"Naw, don't worry about it," Ryker said. "Seriously."

Cassidy pulled a case of what had to be wipes from the bag. "But, your wedding suit—"

Ryker shrugged and kept swaying. Charlie would probably be too distracted to notice, and she was the only one who mattered. She'd been quiet all morning as they'd gotten ready in her apartment—*their* apartment. He shook his head. Remembering the *their* part still took some getting used to.

"Excuse me, Mr. Martinez."

They all turned toward the doors to the small room where the ceremony would take place. The man who had taken his and Charlotte's ninety-nine dollar wedding fee and ensured they had an official license stood next to the open doors. "We're ready for you now."

Cassidy reached for her daughter. "Showtime, big guy."

For a moment, Ryker tightened his arm around the tiny little girl, but it was stupid for a grown man to seek strength from an infant, so he handed her over. As he watched Cassidy carry Sasha toward the chapel, Gage leaned in. "Last chance. We got a close parking spot. I can have you out of here in thirty seconds. Tops."

Gritting his teeth, Ryker glared at him. Gage immediately held up both hands. "Okay, okay."

Just wait until they meet her. They'd see how perfect she was. He rolled his shoulders and smoothed a hand down the front of his jacket, making sure it fell perfectly, which was silly, really, given the drool stain. His shoes thudded along the tile floor as he approached the room where he would marry Charlotte.

Ivy covered every available surface as he walked down the aisle. Gage, Cassidy, and Sasha were the only people on his side. He cast a glance at Charlotte's empty side of the room and swallowed thickly.

Last day she ever has to be alone. At least, as far as he was concerned it was. After today, he had a year to convince her to play this thing for keeps.

He planted his feet where the preacher indicated and smoothed his jacket once more. He'd dressed up more formally when he'd met Charlie for the first time, and not wearing a tux to his own wedding felt odd. But Charlie had insisted.

He didn't know what she was wearing today, only that it wasn't a traditional bridal gown. She'd carried a simple, unmarked garment bag down to the car this morning. He suspected that avoiding a tux and gown had been an attempt to casualize the wedding and thus their relationship.

Over the speakers, a tinny version of the bridal march began to play, and he straightened. The attendant heaved the doors open, propping first one and then the other before stepping out of the way and nodding toward the right.

And then Charlotte stepped into view.

Ryker's heart thudded.

Her hair was down, and she'd done something magnificent to it while she'd been sequestered in the bridal waiting room. It shone beneath the buzzing florescent lights as she stepped hesitantly into the chapel, falling in copious curls upon her shoulders and down her back. Her thickly framed glasses caught a glare, momentarily blocking those beautiful eyes of hers, but the red lipstick—oh, the red lipstick had made a return.

Her dress was simple, which was why the devastating effect it had on him made no logical sense. It was a white, knee-length sheath with a lace overlay. It may have already even been something she had in her closet. But against her dark hair and those red highlights that only appeared beneath the light...

Ryker shuffled his feet wider, and something filled his chest with such speed he wondered if he'd burst a lung. He wanted to jut his chin toward Gage—*Do you understand why I want this now?*—but that would require taking his eyes off his bride, and that simply wasn't something he was prepared to do.

Charlotte walked down the aisle alone, the bouquet of red roses the chapel had provided as part of their "package" matching her lips perfectly. As soon as the glare left her glasses, their gazes clasped each other.

Any remnants of nerves vanished as he took the strength he so desperately needed straight from its best source: his future partner.

Charlotte arrived directly across from him, and the recording of the bridal march cut off mid-note, but Ryker barely noticed the silence in its wake.

"Hey," he whispered, feeling a grin stretch his lips.

Her cheeks were slightly flushed, and she dipped her head, glancing at him almost shyly from above her glasses. "Hey."

"Dearly beloved," began the preacher.

Ryker reached for her, and she met him halfway, shifting her bouquet and sliding her free hand into his. He squeezed her fingers, already counting down the minutes until he would get to kiss her. Claim a bit of that lipstick for himself as a badge of honor.

Damn, I can't believe this is real life.

***

I'm getting married. Dear God, she never thought she'd do this.

So, why did it feel so right?

Of course, that could have something to do with how good it felt to just look at this man she was joining herself to legally as the preacher droned on.

Ryker's navy-blue suit, which bore a new, mysterious stain on the shoulder, caressed his frame in much the same way she had learned to in the past two weeks, hugging all of her favorite parts and showcasing them so that she couldn't help but catalogue a list of what she was going to kiss tonight in order of importance.

Item one: his chest. Items two and three: those thighs.

She'd turned into an absolute lecher in an alarmingly short amount of time. She no longer worried which side of the fifty-fifty divide she'd fall on concerning sex. She was one hundred percent on the sex side when it came to Ryker. Had even joined his once-a-day-isn't-enough way of thinking. When they'd had sex lately, though, she'd begun to feel things. Emotions. It was worrisome. *Maybe he won't affect me so greatly in a few months.*

One could hope, at least.

When Ryker's rumbly, slightly accented voice broke through her haze of thoughts, she nearly jumped. His accent was barely noticeable today. In fact, it had diminished every day they'd been together. Perhaps an indication of how at ease they were with each other?

That was certainly a benefit of this arrangement she hadn't anticipated. She'd been sure a marriage of convenience would be awkward. Stilted. Had depended on it, as a matter of fact.

Instead, what she'd found was...

A friend.

He squeezed her fingers again as he gazed intently into her eyes and vowed to love, honor, and keep her for as long as they both should live.

Or twelve months. Whichever comes first. She nearly winced at the thought, not liking the reminder of their expiration date as much as she had when they'd first agreed on it two weeks ago.

Which was a major problem.

But, when the preacher shifted her attention to Charlotte and began coaching her through the recitation of her own side of the vows, Charlotte found it difficult to remember why it was such a problem.

Think about it later.

Next she knew, Ryker was slipping one of the matching gold bands they'd purchased last week on her finger. "With this ring, I thee wed." His voice was so soft, she could barely hear it.

It was as though he focused on each word, internalizing it. Goose bumps skittered across her breasts.

It was the same earnest voice he used when he whispered promises of what he was going to do to her while they were in bed together. He always kept those promises.

She swallowed hard and slid his wedding band from the wrapping around her roses. "With this ring, I thee wed." Her voice cracked, and she felt her cheeks heat but focused on slipping the ring on his finger.

And then, it was done.

"I now pronounce you husband and wife." The preacher beamed. Turning to Ryker, she said, "You may kiss your bride."

He muttered something that sounded like, "Finally," and then he took one giant step toward her, filling her senses as he wrapped his arms around her body.

Her bouquet was crushed between them, but she didn't care as she tipped her face up, already anticipating his lips upon hers.

Her toes left the floor, and his fingers tangled in the length of her hair as he slanted his lips over hers. She sighed against his lips, every coil of tension within her chest loosening as she inhaled his scent and absorbed the strength of his muscles flexing against her body.

He, apparently, took her sigh as an indication to deepen the kiss, and before she knew it, he was kissing her, in front of a pastor and their three guests, just as he kissed her every night when he was inside her in their bed, or on their kitchen island, or the couch, or...

Thought shattered as her body began to respond, her nipples pebbling within the strict confines of her size-reducing bra. As her breasts swelled, she wondered if she would be able to breathe if he continued, but air was something she was more than willing to sacrifice to the cause as her toes curled in her sensible pumps.

He was stroking his tongue in and out of her mouth in an approximation of what had become second nature with their sexes, when a clearing throat broke through the haze of lust.

With a soft groan dripping with regret, Ryker ended the kiss by nibbling on her bottom lip and slowly lowering her back to her toes. Her eyes fluttered as she opened them, and she could barely see through a thin layer of steam on the inside of her lenses, but Ryker's eyes were bright, his cheeks slightly ruddy. His lips, larger than normal from their bruising kiss, tipped up at the corners—a promise of what would come when they really were alone.

Pulling in a slow breath, he stepped back from her. She swayed without his body providing balance, and the bouquet that had been crushed between them hit the floor with a thud.

"Oh!" Her cheeks burned.

Ryker bent over and swooped up her bouquet, handing it to her while he surreptitiously rearranged the front of his jacket with the other hand. Her eyes widened. *He's hiding an erection.* The things she could do with that.

She shook her head, trying to clear the cobwebs.

"Well," the preacher said, clearing her throat again. "Congratulations, you two." She nodded toward the now-open chapel doors, and the attendant waved them over. "They'll have a wedding certificate waiting for you at the cash register, and a date of when you can expect your official license in the mail."

Ryker gripped her fingers in a soft squeeze, then tucked her hand in the crook of his elbow before escorting her down the aisle toward the exit. Cheeks still burning, she cast a glance at Ryker's friends. The redheaded woman holding a sleeping baby was grinning, but the man beside her was staring at them.

She swallowed hard. Was that disapproval wrinkling his forehead?

Ryker had told him the truth, then. Surely, she wasn't…embarrassed that Ryker's friend knew she'd had to bribe him with hundreds of thousands of dollars to marry her.

Yes, I'm definitely embarrassed.

At the register, the attendant handed an eight-by-ten envelope to Ryker and began talking, but Charlotte was too focused on their guests—Ryker's guests, really—standing right behind them.

When Ryker turned them around, they were immediately and simultaneously engulfed by his friend.

"Congratulations, you two." His voice boomed. He towered over both of them. How was it possible that a human being could be this big? The giant pulled back and gave them the smile his wife had been giving them earlier. Charlotte didn't know whether to trust it or not.

"Thanks, Gage," Ryker said, clapping the enormous man on his shoulder. "*Bonita*," Ryker turned toward her, "this is my best friend and his wife, Cassidy." He held out his arms, and Charlotte's hand slid from the crook of his elbow. "And this"— Cassidy handed Ryker the baby, who was just starting to wake with fitful little mewls—"is Sasha."

No sooner was the baby in Ryker's arms than she calmed, fluttering sleepy eyes and curling into the broad chest Charlotte herself often found solace in. Ryker gazed down at Sasha with a clear look of pure adoration on his face, then turned toward Charlotte again, grinning broadly. "She's pretty great, huh?"

Something pinged in Charlotte's chest. As though her hand moved of its own accord, it raised and spread over the baby's tiny back. Shallow breaths raised and lowered Sasha's gently curved spine against her palm. "Yes, she is."

Looking back up at Ryker, she found the glint in his eyes had changed. Deepened. Their gazes locked; her heart pinged again.

"Well, welcome to the family."

Charlotte jerked, the magnetic hold between her and her new husband severing in a second. She turned to the right and Cassidy was there, grinning at her with that same goofy grin only a person in the honeymoon phase of her own marriage would give to a new bride.

Charlotte schooled her lips into a smile. *The family?* She flicked a curious glance toward Ryker and then looked at Cassidy again. "Oh, I didn't know Ryker had a sister." Why wouldn't he have told her that? And why did it hurt that he hadn't?

Cassidy snorted. "No way."

Instinctually, she stiffened, but another look at Cassidy's face and she was pretty sure she wasn't being teased. Charlotte forced her shoulders to relax.

"No," Cassidy continued, "none of us are really related to Ryker." She grinned again. "Well, except you now." She jerked her chin toward Gage. "Ryker and Gage grew up together, so they're close as family. I just force my awesomeness on Ryker."

Now, it was Charlotte who was looking at Gage as though he were under a microscope. If they'd grown up together, it had to have been in the system. And here he was, married and with a baby, looking happier than she'd ever seen Ryker look.

Hmmm.

Gage rolled his shoulders and gave her an uneasy version of his earlier smile. *Knows I've put two and two together, does he?*

Gage reached out a massive hand and patted her shoulder awkwardly. "Welcome to the family," he said, much softer than his wife had.

Charlotte flicked a quick glance toward her husband, the unease in her gut steepening. She'd thought they were in the same boat here: the "alone" boat. She had no family and friends; he had no family and friends.

Except, here his pseudo family of friends stood. She hadn't felt this out of place since that night she'd asked Ryker to marry her two weeks ago.

Ryker was still smiling down at the tiny little girl curled against his chest, but when he looked up at Charlotte, his smile faded. His gaze seemed to sharpen as he looked at her; just what was her face revealing? She was usually much better about hiding that part of her, but in only two weeks, Ryker had edged past some of her more stalwart defenses.

He gave the baby a pat on the back, then handed her back to her mother. "If you don't mind…" He wrapped a warm hand around hers. "I'm eager to get my wife alone."

Charlotte wanted to tilt her head to the side. He wasn't telling the truth, at least, not in the way she was used to. His tone implied he wanted to get to the wedding night, but that wasn't the tone he used with her. He wanted to get her alone, though, that much was true. For what purpose was a mystery.

"Sure thing," Cassidy said, settling the baby on her hip. "But we have to get together soon." She turned toward Charlotte. "I can't wait to get to know you better. Take care of our guy, okay?"

He doesn't need me to take care of him. He has you guys. She smiled tightly. "Of course."

Ryker's fingers tightened around hers. "Okay, we're leaving now." The lascivious pretense in his tone had vanished. His friends must have heard it, too, because Gage's eyes widened slightly, and Cassidy's lips parted.

In the next second, Ryker was tugging her toward the exit.

"Oh, bye!" Charlotte tossed over her shoulder, nearly tripping in the process.

The glare of the Vegas sun off black pavement momentarily blinded her, and she had to rely solely on Ryker's guidance for a few steps. She blinked her vision clear to find Ryker gazing at her with his brows drawn together.

"Is everything okay?" she asked.

Now, his brows rose. Wordlessly, he unlocked the passenger door of her Cadillac and handed her in. When the door shut behind her, she watched Ryker stalk around the hood of the car to the driver's side. And there was no other way to describe it than *stalk*. Usually, the man glided, poise and suave seeping from every good-looking pore. Now, however, he looked as though he were going to war.

He sank into the driver's seat, closed the door, and cranked the engine, but they didn't go anywhere. Instead, he turned toward her. "Okay, what happened?"

"What...happened?" she repeated.

"In there."

She felt her forehead wrinkle.

He reached across the center console and snagged her hand, weaving their fingers together and giving hers a squeeze. "Your big, beautiful brain told you something, and you shut down. So, what was it?"

Oh. So, she had been right. Her defenses no longer seemed to work around this man. That was...disconcerting.

Considering she'd just entered into a legally binding, emotionless agreement with him.

She tugged her fingers, trying to reclaim them, but he held fast. "It was nothing. Really. Nothing that you need to worry about."

"Charlie," he said softly, his tone admonishing, "we don't lie to each other. Ever. And we're not going to start."

His quiet, deep voice traveled straight through her body all the way to her toes. "I'm not lying. It really is nothing that needs to concern you. We have a non-emotional agreement, remember?"

For a half second, Charlotte could have sworn she saw hurt flash through Ryker's eyes. But when she blinked, it was gone.

"We do have an agreement. But we're still friends. In fact, I'd say we're friends first, wouldn't you? So," he ducked down until she was forced to meet his gaze, "what happened?"

She sighed. Fine, if he wanted to go there, she would get it over and done with. "You said you were alone in the world. You're clearly not. It threw me for a loop, but now I'm over it."

I'll never be over it. What? Where had that come from? She was slipping. Hard. And no amount of mental scrambling seemed to be getting her back on even footing.

It was dead quiet in the car for several seconds, and Ryker's brow furrowed. Immediately, Charlotte wished she could take her rushed words back and choose to stick to her guns instead. Now he was going to think she was growing emotional, or even worse, attached.

Suddenly, his brow relaxed. His lips muttered a silent *Ah*. "Gage and Cassidy," he said, as though those two names were the solution to a riddle she'd posed.

"And Sasha," she supplied, like an idiot, instead of keeping quiet or even shaking her head and changing the subject.

Ryker tugged on her hand. She futilely tugged back, but her heart wasn't in it, so she gave up after one attempt and watched as he drew her fingers slowly to his lips. His eyes were grave as he pressed her fingertips with a soft kiss. Then he cradled her hand between both of his and placed their jumbled hands in his lap. "About a year and a half ago, you'd have been right. Gage was my family. My only family." He shrugged. "Now he has Cassidy. And together they have Sasha. And I—"

Have no one.

The words echoed as loudly in the still car as if he'd spoken them.

Good heavens, to have gone from having someone who understood you—who grew up in your same horrible conditions and had your back—and then to lose them to someone else.

Well, it was the entire reason she'd wanted the type of marriage she had with Ryker. "That had to be a very painful transition."

A muscle ticked in his jaw. "It has been. But he's so happy, what kind of friend would I be to begrudge him that?" He smiled, but it was crooked and halfhearted. "And Sasha is a nice bonus. She's not mine any more than her parents are, but I get to borrow her now and then."

That's why he wants children. She nearly sucked in a breath. It made sense. Someone who belonged to you for an indefinite amount of time. If one was lucky, that indefinite amount of time equated to forever.

What a lovely idea.

She jolted, her hand jerking within his tangle of fingers. And, of course, he noticed. He gave her a reassuring squeeze, but she didn't miss that analyzing glance of his.

Unfortunately, that the direction of her thoughts had turned toward children seemed to have been obvious, because he didn't question her.

Or maybe that was fortunate. Because what would she have said if he'd asked? That just now the idea of them having children sounded great?

She almost snorted. What a disaster. What a reason to panic.

"Well, you're not alone anymore," she blurted into the silence. Immediately, she squeezed her eyes shut. Panic always did this to her! Popping her eyes open, she tried to think of something to say that would take them back to safe ground. A way of apologizing for being inappropriate given their understanding without making the situation worse, something she managed to do all of the time.

But when her eyes opened, Ryker's expression froze her to the spot. His brow was furrowed once more, but it had a completely different, desperate, feel to it this time. His lips seemed almost tight, as though he were not only pressing them together but also biting them from the inside.

That was an action she personally knew very well. She did it whenever she was trying to keep herself from speaking. Whenever the words bursting from the tip of her tongue would reveal too much.

He cleared his throat and looked down at their intertwined hands. "You're not alone anymore either," he said so softly she had to lean forward to catch it.

Oh, dear.

Hearing that felt wonderful. No wonder he'd looked so odd. Heaven only knew what her own expression was doing right now without her permission, but the oddest feeling, almost of tears waiting to express themselves, clogged her throat.

Safe. I need to get back to safe!

With her free hand, she reached out and snagged his perfectly knotted tie. He followed her tug eagerly.

Their lips had just crashed together when a wild "Woo hoo!" from outside the car made them spring apart.

Charlotte peered through the windshield to spy two tourists with massive beverage containers hanging from their necks by cords standing only feet away from the car's bumper.

"Woo hoo!" one of them screamed again, flashing a drunkenly exaggerated double thumbs up. "Congrats, guys!"

Her gaze slid sideways toward Ryker, whose lips were swollen, even though they'd only kissed for a fraction of a second before the interruption. Those lips quirked at the corners, and he raised a hand in a quick wave before turning abruptly and catching her staring at him with what had to be undisguised lust.

She was getting to know him well enough though to recognize his own lust flaring in his dilated, warm eyes.

"Hold that thought," he said in a rumble. He cranked the key in the ignition, and the Cadillac flared to life. In front of the car, the two tourists stumbled on down the sidewalk. "I'm going to get you home as quickly as I can, and then we're picking up where we started, all right, *bonita?*"

She licked her lips, detecting the slightest hint of his mint ChapStick and nearly groaning. "Oh, yes."

He pressed his lips together as he glanced her way once again, and that heated gaze of his traveled down the column of her neck and came to rest on her breasts, which felt suddenly way too confined within her bra and wedding dress as they seemed to grow beneath his regard.

He grunted. "A quickly as I can," he repeated, tearing his gaze away from her breasts with obvious effort and sliding the car into reverse before nearly peeling out of the parking spot.

Chapter Thirteen

She kept touching herself. Little flutters of her sweet fingers as she tucked a curl behind her ear or straightened her dress over her thighs. And all the while, as he drove through Vegas like a man possessed, she squirmed in her seat.

He knew he was imagining it, but he swore he could detect the sexy bite of her arousal in the air itself.

As a result, he sat perfectly still in the driver's seat, because if he moved in the slightest, it was going to be to launch himself at his bride. Thank fuck those two drunken idiots had interrupted them when they had, because the possibility of him making love to Charlie in the front seat of her Cadillac had been very real.

They were together now.

For at least the next year, he was not alone. And if Ryker had his way, he'd never be alone again.

Between his thighs, his cock was hard and throbbing with every thump of his heart. He gritted his teeth as he finally—

finally—pulled into the parking structure of their building, the jostling of the speed bumps mixing with the brush of his suit pants over the sensitive head of his dick in a catastrophic way.

He pulled into the vacant spot next to his clunker and applied the brakes a little too vehemently. Charlie swayed forward as the car lurched to a stop, catching herself with a hand to the dashboard.

"Sorry—"

But she was already out of the car. The Cadillac was still swaying on its axles, and her pumps were clacking against the parking structure pavement as she rounded the back and began making a beeline for the elevators.

"Fucking perfect for me," he muttered beneath his breath as he snatched the keys and hauled ass out of the car to catch up with her.

She stood beside the glowing elevator call button, her blue gaze eating him up as he strode her way. His erection strained the seam of his pants where it was trapped against his right thigh, and her gaze narrowed in on it.

She licked her lips.

"*Mujer*," he growled, "you can't look at me like that right now."

She blinked, but she didn't look away. He didn't even know if she'd heard him, as she gave no indication that she had.

She just shimmied a little again, shifting her weight to one foot and then back to the other, clasping her hands together in front of her and then moving them back to her sides.

Her barely contained sexual energy poured off her in waves, crawled toward him across the structure, and nearly slapped him down to his knees.

The elevator behind her dinged. Without looking away from him, she walked backward onto it as the doors opened.

She backed into the corner and lifted her chin as he followed her, pausing only to push the button for their floor before planting his open palms against the elevator walls above her head.

She bit into her bottom lip, unerringly drawing his gaze to the plump, red flesh. But when she slid her small hands onto his hips and pulled him toward her only to squirm against him when his erection met her soft belly, he had to close his eyes and block that image from view or completely lose control.

"We did it," she whispered.

Without opening his eyes, he lowered his head, burying his nose in her hair.

"We got married." Her hands tightened on his hips and then slid around to his backside.

"Oh, I'm very aware of that." His words ruffled the soft hair catching in the beginnings of his five o'clock shadow.

"Thank you."

Those whispered words finally made him open his eyes. He blinked a couple of times, then pulled away and gazed down at her. "Thank you?"

She nodded. "For doing this for me."

His laugh was strained. "Trust me, *bonita*. I'm not doing you any favors. I wouldn't want to be anywhere else right now." He shifted his weight to only one hand against the elevator wall. With the other, he tucked one shiny curl behind her ear. "You don't thank me for this. Ever."

His dreams were coming true. Right in front of him. He should be on his knees thanking her, and as soon as this elevator delivered them home, he would be.

As though sensing his need and urgency, the elevator doors opened behind him. Charlotte pushed away from the wall, but when Ryker didn't move away from her, she tipped her head back and looked at him again, her brows drawn together.

"Welcome home, Mrs. Martinez." His whispered words seemed to echo back down into his chest, making it ache.

Her lips parted, forming a delicate *O*. Before she could say anything, he smoothed his hands down her shoulders, drawing her away from the corner until he could maneuver one arm around her back.

With the other, he scooped her up behind her knees, cradling her against his chest.

She gasped and wrapped her arms around his neck as he strode out of the elevator and toward their front door. "Ryker?"

He grinned down at her. "Just carrying my bride across the threshold."

Her brows shot toward her hairline. "Oh!" Her gaze slid away from his, something he'd noticed over the past two weeks that she did when she was having trouble concentrating. The slightest tinge colored her cheeks, and, not for the first time, he wished he could cup them. Feel that heated skin against his. "You don't have to do things like this," she whispered. "They're entirely unnecessary, considering..."

His grin slid right off his face. He nearly stumbled, and played it off as an intentional stop in front of the door as he shifted Charlotte's weight to one arm so he could root around in his pocket for their keys.

Now it was he who avoided her gaze as he fit the key into the door. "A guy doesn't get married every day." He pushed the door in, braced for impact, then looked down at her in his arms. Excellent. He didn't flinch or anything. Didn't give any indication that her untimely reminder about their arrangement had hit a mark that shouldn't even exist in the first place. "We have to make sure we do this right, you know." He smiled again, but he could feel it wobble.

As she peered up at him, he could see the wheels turning behind her vivid eyes as she tried to place what emotion he was feeling.

Good luck, bonita. He didn't know what he was feeling either. Luckily, life had taught him how to be an excellent pretender. He forged iron into his smile and stepped across the threshold, kicking the door closed behind him.

The living room was dim as the light from the setting sun streamed through the wall of windows, and Ryker relaxed into the faded light as though shrugging on a blanket. It was always easier to pretend in the dark.

Like a genius, he'd managed to take the positive mood that had overwhelmed them both in the car and elevator and stomp it until it was a whimpering mess. But seduction was his game. And he and Charlie communicated best between the sheets.

No better way to get us back on even footing.

"Since you're already in my arms," he said, his accent curling through the air for the first time in a couple of days, "I should probably keep walking down the hall, yes?"

Like magic, her eyes went heavy-lidded behind her glasses. She sagged in his arms, the tips of her fingers playing with the fine hair at the base of his head. "Yes," she said, the simple word weighted with so much more than one syllable.

Ryker dropped the keys into the bowl on the entryway table, so used to the move now that he no longer had to look. Shoulders back, he walked past the guest room he'd never slept in. The slow, lazy circles of her fingers in his hair were sending tendrils of pleasure straight down his spine to curl low in his gut. By the time he walked into the bedroom they shared, he was blessedly hard again with his head—both heads, really—back in the game.

Walking toward the bed, he pulled her close, nuzzling her hair away from her ear. "What do you say we make this marriage nice and legal, hmm?"

Her breath left her in a sigh, and she tightened her arms around his neck. "That sounds…perfect."

He lowered her knees, letting her slide down his body as her toes sought the floor. Her beautiful breasts pressed into his stomach, and, with his hands cupping her shoulders, he drew her in closer, reveling in the way they plumped against him.

He smoothed his hands down her back and cupped her ass, kneading her curves with his fingers. "This dress is beautiful." His fingers moved back up her spine, tracing the line of her zipper. "But I think it would look even better on the floor."

The words were practiced. Drawn from his personal arsenal of things to say to clients. They felt bulky and tasted as fake as the wedding cake they hadn't served as he directed them toward his wife.

She wound her arms around him and slid her hands beneath his jacket. Her palms scorched through his dress shirt as she pressed them to his back.

"Less talking." Pushing to her tiptoes, she just barely reached his neck above his shirt's stiff collar. Her petal soft lips brushed against his skin. Immediately, goose bumps erupted all over his body.

His eyes slid closed. *Definitely less talking.*

As he began to lower her zipper and she skated her palms around to his front and began pushing his jacket from his shoulders, he tried to shuck his thoughts as easily as their clothes falling to the floor with the sound of soft, crushing fabric.

The damn things seemed stuck.

Less talking? She'd never asked for that before. Did that mean she noticed he was being fake? Was he trying too hard?

Obviously, he was trying too hard. He'd never had to do that with Charlie before and had been looking forward to possibly an entire lifetime of never having to try hard again.

She made a small sound of distress, and he snapped to attention to find her trying to wrestle his tie free as his hands lay like dead weight on her curvy, naked hips. Her dress was a puddle around her ankles. His jacket was nowhere to be seen.

Damn, just how long had he been inside his head? What was wrong with him?

He lips curled into his signature crooked grin, and he covered her straining fingers with his own, making quick work of his tie. It slid from the collar of his shirt with a hiss, and by the time he had it coiled around his fist, she was already slipping his buttons free and pressing wet, open-mouthed kisses to each inch of skin his opening shirt revealed.

Hell, yes. This was what he needed. At last, the turmoil of his thoughts loosened its tight grip on him. He rolled his shoulders, sending his shirt floating to the floor and the last of his tension scattering to the wind.

Keeping his tie wound around his hand, he reached for the clasp of her bra, not bothering to disguise his hungry gaze as he stared down at her plump breasts where they pressed into his stomach again.

The clasp gave way. Charlie shrugged the bra away with no ceremony, and it slid from between their pressed bodies to join her dress on the floor. With one arm curled around the small of her back, he drew her close and dragged the pointer finger of his free hand down the dark valley of her cleavage and back up again, watching with deep satisfaction as her eyes fluttered behind those glasses of hers.

His usual endearments tripped toward the end of his tongue, but he swallowed them down. He hadn't used one of his usual endearments on Charlie since the Erin fiasco, and he wasn't going to return to them.

However, on this day—their wedding day—his default *bonita* felt utterly weak in the face of the major life event they'd just celebrated together.

He needed something more.

The word that he'd battled back into the corner of his mind he never visited—that ridiculous *amor* he'd dropped when they first met—flitted to the forefront for the first time in weeks.

He nearly grimaced. Definitely not.

"Ryker?"

He blinked. Charlie was gazing up at him, her lips parted and a question in her eyes.

God damn it! He'd gone down the rabbit hole again, hadn't he? He resumed stroking her cleavage. "Yes, *amor*?"

Oh, fuck all.

Her parted lips sealed, and she stiffened slightly against him.

Before she could open those lips again and say something else that would inexplicably hurt even though it was perfectly acceptable, he needed to get nasty to get this back on track again.

And fast.

He stepped back. If he hadn't ruined this, she would do that devastating thing she did when she wasn't done touching him yet. That silent protest of—

Ah, thank God. Her brows drew together, and her lips plumped into a pout: something he knew she was unaware of doing. If she ever figured out the power that look had on him, he was in trouble.

"*Bonita*." He shoved the word through tight lips. "Do you want to play a little bit tonight?"

Now her brows crashed down. "Play? I don't..." She shook her head, wariness filtering into her eyes. "I don't understand what you—"

When he snagged her hand and began tugging her toward her side of the bed, she stopped talking and followed him. That was a good sign. When they reached the bed, he gave her fingers a squeeze before dropping them.

She still looked up at him with confusion, but she was also breathing slightly shallower than she had been moments before.

He dipped his gaze down to her breasts as they rose and fell beneath those quick breaths. Slipping the tight leash of his control a bit, he allowed himself the pleasure of reaching out and cupping one, brushing his thumb over the pebbled nipple and welcoming the ache in his stomach as it puckered even further beneath his attention.

All mine. For as long as she'd have him.

Before that errant thought could take hold and undo all the good he had planned, he smoothed his palm over the breast he held until his hand rested over her heart. He applied pressure. "Down you go," he whispered.

Her lips parted, but she didn't object as she sank down on the mattress and lay back. Over the past two weeks, she'd grown unabashed by her nudity.

The best development in the history of mankind, truly. Because Charlotte naked was the most breathtaking sight he'd ever encountered.

The new position did amazing things to her breasts, and he bit his lip as he climbed onto the bed after her. She watched silently as he swung one thigh over her hips and sank down slowly until he was straddling the hot, welcoming juncture of her thighs.

She licked her lips, her gaze devouring him from his shoulders down to where he rested against her.

"Weather okay, *mi esposa?*"

Well, hell, where had that endearment been five minutes ago? It wasn't creepy and fit the day perfectly.

"The weather is...okay." Her words were timid.

Leaning over, he braced his weight on his outstretched arms, hands planted beside those gorgeous breasts of hers. He ducked his head and brushed the tip of his nose against hers. "I'm going to make sure the weather is streams of sunshine and rainbows, *mujer*. I promise you this."

Beneath him, he felt her relax into the mattress.

"Do you trust me?" he asked.

She drew her head back as far as the pillows beneath it would allow and met his gaze. "No."

Ouch. This time, there was no preventing a wince. Well, he should have learned better by now than to ask Charlie a question he didn't know the answer to ahead of time. She was far too honest.

"Oh, drat." She shifted beneath him. "I shouldn't have said that, right?" Reaching up, she dragged a finger over a spot on his cheek. "Your dimple is extraordinarily deep at the moment. It does that when you're upset." Her hand dropped. "I think."

"Charlie." He had the overwhelming desire to sigh. "*Bonita*, you say whatever you want to me. Always, all right?"

291

She made a face at that. "I didn't mean anything by it. Honestly. I don't...trust. It's unnecessary, and—"

He straightened his expression and lowered himself enough that his chest pressed against hers. "Look at my dimple now."

She tilted her head. "There isn't one anymore."

"Exactly." *Less talking coming right up.*

He closed his lips over hers. When she sighed and wrapped her arms around his neck, he sank into her, lapping her top lip with his tongue before delving into the sweet heat of her mouth.

She arched into the kiss, her nipples sliding against his chest, and he officially forgot all the awkward.

She felt so good beneath him. Better with every day that passed as he learned what she liked and she did as well, becoming bold.

And wanton.

Still confined within his pants, his cock pressed into her soft belly as she started undulating against him, rolling her tongue into his mouth now in time with every arch of her back.

He moaned against her lips and reached behind his neck for her wrists. The silk from his tie, still wrapped around his left hand, slid against her skin as he pulled her arms free and stretched them toward the headboard.

With Herculean effort, he pulled from the kiss just as she started rocking her hips fretfully in an effort to get some sort of pressure against her sex.

Her eyes were closed. His five o'clock shadow had already left its mark on her fair skin and those kiss-bruised lips.

Madre de Dios. He was a lucky man.

"Look at me, Charlie."

Her lashes fluttered, but it was several seconds before she was able to obey. "You...stopped kissing me." There was no missing the accusation in her tone.

The first genuine smile he'd had since arriving home crossed his lips.

"*Lo siento, mi esposa.*" He ducked down and kissed her quickly, pulling back before he could get lost again.

He wrapped his tie around one of her wrists. Her eyes widened. "What—"

"Looking cloudy outside?" Slowly, he tied a knot around her delicate wrist. The sound of the silk sliding against itself was extraordinarily loud in the suddenly quiet room that was absent of even their loud breathing.

He brushed the pad of his thumb against her fluttering pulse, content to wait as long as she needed to decide what she felt about this.

"N-no."

His thumb paused. "No, what?" Already, he braced the muscles in his thighs to get off her.

"No…clouds."

He exhaled. *That's my beautiful girl.*

Pulling the tie taut, he looped it through one of the spindles in the headboard. As he wrapped the loose end around her other wrist, his gaze continuously pored over her—her face, her eyes, her body—looking for any sign that this was becoming too much.

She lifted her chin. "I said no clouds, Ryker. No need to watch me like I'm about to break."

He lifted an eyebrow. "*Su deseo es mi placer.*" There was his demanding Charlie. He slid the second knot home.

Leaning back on his haunches, he surveyed his work.

She gave an experimental tug. Her big breasts jiggled.

God, yes. He rubbed an open palm down the length of his erection. "So beautiful."

Pulling in a big breath, she peered at him through her glasses. Her cool gaze was heated. "What…do we do next?"

He rose to his knees. "Nasty, nasty things, *bonita.*"

Her eyes flashed.

On all fours over her, he pressed first a kiss to the curve of her neck. With a sigh of surrender, she canted her head to the side, affording him better access.

He licked across her collarbone. Blew a draft of air in the hollow of her throat. Above his head, her hair rustled against the pillowcase.

Dropping open mouth kisses down her chest, he paused only to cup both breasts and abrade their curves with his facial hair before continuing down the gentle slope of her belly with more tender kisses.

She was undulating again. A creak from the headboard told him she was struggling against the tie. He paused, craning his ears for any indication she was about to object.

Instead, she moaned, arching into his mouth where his lips rested just above the band to her panties.

He scraped his jaw along her sensitive skin, hooked his thumbs in her underwear, and began dragging them down her legs.

Sucking in a breath, she raised her ass, making his job even easier.

"That's the way, Charlie." The soft cotton of her panties crumpled in his hands as he drew the underwear free and cast it over the side of the bed.

Gloriously, completely naked.

Planting her heels into the mattress, she butterflied her knees open.

"God have mercy." He palmed his chest. The thundering of his heart against his palm was swift and hard.

She clutched the tie with her hands. "No more waiting, Ryker." Her words were husky. Tinged with desperation.

She was demanding him. He loved when she did that.

His hands were steady as he reached for her, covering her knees with his palms and spreading her open even more.

Between her legs, she blossomed. Pink petals opening for him, gleaming with arousal. In their midst, the shadowy, enticing opening to her pussy called to him.

He dragged his hands down the inside of her thighs, and she trembled, releasing an audible breath when his thumbs stroked along her lips.

"So very gorgeous." He stroked again.

Her knees fell to the side, hitting the mattress with a soft thud.

His lips quirked. "Something you're wanting, *esposa*?"

She canted her hips, making the dim light of their bedroom dance off of her slick, aroused sex. "Your mouth." Another undulation of her hips. "On me."

He groaned soft and low. "You're perfect."

As he lowered himself to his belly between her sprawled legs, the tide of happiness roiling through him nearly took his breath away.

Charlie was perfect. Everything she did knocked him on his ass. She was intelligent. Just his type, with her studious look that he could undo with a heated glance and some well-placed fingers.

And over the past two weeks, she'd become blunt and demanding in bed. Something he'd never known he wanted.

He nuzzled her, just above her clitoris. The headboard creaked again.

Sucking his bottom lip between his teeth, he held back a grin. This spot above her clit was his favorite: sensitive enough to drive her wild, but not enough to send her over the edge.

Releasing his lip, he looked up at her over the mound of her sex. Her head was thrown back. The delicate muscles of her arms were strained taut, and the fingers wrapped around the tie were bleached white and clenched in the silk.

He dipped his tongue out, licking her now instead of nuzzling her. She exhaled a quick breath that carried the slightest hint of a moan in it.

Keeping his eyes on the long column of her throat, he traced a circle around her clit with the tip of his tongue.

Another creak. "Ryker."

With a wicked curve of his lip, he placed his mouth against her. "Hmm?" he hummed.

Her back arched. "Oh!"

So damn responsive. He couldn't tease her anymore. One more quick nuzzle, and then he opened his mouth over her clitoris and sucked softly.

She cried out.

Between his legs, he was so hard the mattress felt bruising rather than soft against his dick. And as he flicked his tongue against her clit while sucking, he caught himself thrusting into that mattress in a bid to relieve any sort of pressure.

It wasn't working. Not even a little bit.

She started working her hips, pressing her sex to his mouth in a quick rhythm he recognized in a heartbeat as the frantic pace she set right before she came.

Already?

He couldn't have that yet. With a soft groan, he forced his mouth away.

She moaned. "No!" The headboard creaked with a vengeance.

He glanced at her wrists only to find that the silk was abrading her pretty skin. His eyes widened. "Hey, *bonita*, hey." He placed a soothing hand on her hip and squeezed.

She shook him off with a violent twist of her hips. "More." She pinned him with a no-nonsense glare. "Now."

He quirked an eyebrow. Wow. "More kisses?" He leaned down to suck her again.

"No."

His head snapped back up.

"Ryker." Her voice cracked. He loved it when it did that. "Inside me." She licked her lips. "Please."

Oh, hell yes. He should probably seduce her a little more. She deserved it. But she'd issued an invitation he was never going to have the strength to turn down.

He pushed back up to his hands and knees and prowled up her body. She watched the muscles roll in his shoulders and arms as he moved, her eyes growing even more hooded.

Reaching by memory for the drawer beside the bed, Ryker located a condom in the span of one of the throbs in his erection.

It was definitely time to take off his pants. For more than just the need to get inside her as quickly as possible. Things down there were...pinched.

He placed the condom between his teeth, sat back on his haunches over Charlie, and unzipped his pants.

The quick ricochet of her gaze from his torso to his busy fingers moved down his body like a rough caress.

She began nibbling her bottom lip, her focus laser-like. He rose up on his knees and slowed down just enough to tease her a bit more, rolling his pants down his hips achingly slowly.

Her lips parted as he eased his slacks down his thighs. When they'd gone as far as they could with him straddling her, he stopped. Her brows drew together.

"No stopping. Ryker, please."

So damn lucky. Snatching the condom from his teeth, he ducked down for a quick kiss before swinging off her and shucking his pants in record time.

The foil wrapper ripping seemed to wring a shiver from her body. The fine sheen of sweat covering her breasts caught the dim light and set them to glittering.

As if I didn't already notice them. Now she was just showing off.

He placed the condom and began rolling it down his length. The headboard creaked again as she tugged the tie.

He *tsk*ed. "No more hurting that beautiful skin." Reaching down, he brushed his fingers across one red wrist. Her fingers groped for his, and he gladly interwove their hands. "It might be time for me to untie this—"

"No!" She jumped, as though she had spoken louder than she'd intended.

Ryker paused.

"No," she said again, quieter this time. "I...I like it."

He squeezed her fingers, swallowing down a moan. He should say something. Heaven knew, she was spouting enough sexy things making him hot that this was already in the danger zone of going too quickly.

But he couldn't think of anything. His signature, cultivated suave had abandoned him.

He knelt on the mattress. As it dipped, she rolled toward him, her naked breast brushing against his thigh. He cupped it, running his thumb over her nipple, then spread out atop her. Her softness met him in all of his body's hard places.

Makes sense. On the inside, they were the opposite: her hardness meeting and filling every place he'd gone soft over the years.

What the ever-loving fuck is that thought?

She raised her knees on either side of his hips, and he slid in the slickness of her arousal right to the spot where they both most wanted him to be.

Holy hell, was he just a big softy?

She made a quiet, mewling sound and ground against him.

By rote, he slid home. Even as distracted as he'd become, the pleasure of entering Charlie was just as intense as it always was. He closed his eyes to keep her from seeing them roll back in his head.

So snug. So his.

He pressed his forehead against hers and reached for her hands, twining their fingers once more. He drew back his hips, and, when he thrust for the first time, she met him more than halfway, a moan catching in her throat.

Damn, if he was soft, he was safe with Charlie. Despite his worries, despite his projection, she'd never walked all over him. He suspected she never would. This woman hid nothing. From him or anybody. She always said what she was thinking. Even though she'd just said she didn't trust him, he...

He trusted her.

She pressed her breasts into his chest, leaned up, and nibbled his chin. "Faster, Ryker. It feels so good."

With a groan, he buried his face in her neck, held onto her hands with all his might, and gave her faster.

Trust her? God, are you insane? He didn't trust. Anyone. Ever. Completely understood where Charlie had been coming from.

But somehow, Charlie had become an exception.

She was undulating beneath him. Her every breath rang in his ear, sending tendrils of pleasure skating down his spine. Each of his thrusts was so deep, he couldn't imagine being more joined to her.

Perfect for him in bed. Someone he trusted. His opposite in all the best ways: she made him better. She saw his insecurities, and not only did she believe they were unfounded, she was starting to make him believe the same thing. And—if he flattered himself—he was good for her, too. How common was that? Even in the best of relationships?

Jesus—what if Charlie was the one person he could be in a real relationship with? What if…what if they could have more?

Shit. They'd just entered into a carefully manufactured relationship with an indefinite expiration date and an explicitly stated lack of "realness."

He growled, loudly. Started thrusting harder.

Shut the fuck up.

Stop thinking. He had to stop thinking.

This was what he wanted. Not the fairy tale that didn't exist.

He deepened the angle of his thrusts, and the most exquisite pressure hit the one spot on his dick that always made him lose control: that small triangle on the underside right beneath the head. Stars lit behind his tightly closed eyes, and he threw himself headlong into the pleasure, focusing on that spot and thrusting again and again.

Finally, *finally*, his thoughts quieted.

"Thank God," he muttered, his lips brushing against her pulse point.

"Yes, Ryker." She threw her head back. "Oh! I'm so close."

Yes! He picked up the pace, knowing exactly how to grind against her to take her that final distance to the edge.

Oh, shit. His hips jerked.

She wasn't the only one who was close.

Without any other warning than that, the end of his cock practically shot off.

"Fuck!" He turned his face and shouted into the pillow as he completely lost control.

No. No, no, no. This wasn't happening. He wasn't coming before his wife the very first time he took her to bed. He wasn't losing his professionalism. His cool.

His heart?

His back bowed as the greatest pleasure he'd ever experienced grabbed hold of his backbone and yanked with all its might. "Charlie," he groaned.

And then her name just kept tumbling from his lips as, with absolutely no finesse, he thrust into his powerful orgasm, firmly leaving Charlie behind in the dust.

The pleasure vanished as quickly as it had arrived, leaving behind only an asinine, amateur twitching deep in the muscles of his thighs.

He lay atop Charlie, blinking into the pillowcase, praying with all he had within him that he was having a nightmare. Anything other than the reality of realizing he'd possibly shot himself in the foot with this carefully crafted relationship that would never go further than this. And then immediately fucking up in the one department where they were allowed to mesh.

"R-Ryker?"

Ah, hell. He had to face her.

No, he had to fix this.

Chapter Fourteen

He'd stopped moving. Abruptly.

Well, that wasn't exactly true. Her brows drew together; the shaking she was feeling was Ryker's massive body, boneless atop hers.

He was…shivering?

"Ryker? Are you…?"

"Shit." He stiffened atop her. And that was when she was able to feel that he was no longer stiff inside of her.

"Charlie, I'm so fucking sorry." He pulled back, straightening his arms. She could see his face now but not his eyes. They were downcast. He reached down, wrapped a hand around the base of the condom and pulled out of her.

The condom was heavy at the tip with…

Her eyes shot wide. He'd orgasmed.

Her body still tingled all over, with certain parts—the tips of her nipples, her throbbing clit—tingling more than others. She was perched right on the edge of pleasure; her body, apparently, had not yet caught up to the fact that they weren't getting an orgasm tonight.

Drat!

She really, really wanted to orgasm.

He moved so quickly, he was a blur in her passion-addled gaze.

"What—?"

He knelt between her spread knees and slid two fingers deep, deep inside her body.

"Oh!" Her back bowed. With one simple touch, he'd shoved her right to the edge again. "Oh my."

"That's it, *bonita*." He eased a third finger inside her. With his other hand, he thrummed her clitoris.

She gasped, her eyes cinching closed. Her rasping breaths thundered in the quiet of the room, her breasts moving with the rapid fall and rise of her chest. She reached for them, wanting to touch them—anything to help send her over this cliff at last.

But her wrists drew her up short. Ryker's tie held her fast. She wrapped her fingers around the silk, tugged, and moaned while trying to chase her pleasure with hectic thrusts of her hips.

"*Dios*, you are so beautiful." His voice edged on rough. The mere sound of it traveled along her body like the touch she had longed to give herself.

He angled his fingers, finding a spot inside her that lit her up like a lantern. She sucked in a breath, writhing against the sheets. The headboard creaked ominously as she yanked, trying to find some kind of purchase.

Liquid heat replaced the rough scrape of his thumb across her clit. Her head snapped up; her eyes wrenched open.

His dark, curly hair tumbled across his forehead. Only his eyes were visible. The rest of his face was buried between her thighs. He licked her again, then did that devastating thing with his mouth that involved hot suction and just the right amount of pressure—

"Ryker!" She couldn't look at him anymore. Giving herself up to it all, she sprang into paradise. With a creak and a snap, her hands were suddenly free. They shot down, the silk tie dragging across her nipples on the way. Her fingers dove into his hair, and she held onto him with all her might as she undulated to his mouth. He groaned, the reverberations traveling through her clit like a vibrator. He matched her every movement with a searing thrust of his fingers, bringing her orgasm spiraling to new heights. And new heights again.

She tossed her head back, crying out as the pleasure grew so intense it bordered on pain. She stiffened, no longer able to move, and just knotted her fingers in his soft, thick hair. There was no other option than to ride it out.

Her body jerked involuntarily as she finally started coming back down again. Every lap of his tongue pulled another shudder from her until, at last, she couldn't take it anymore. She went from pulling his head toward her to pushing it away. He resisted for only a moment before drawing back.

Their gazes connected over the length of her wrung-out body. His expression was something she'd never seen before. His eyes were thunderous, but he couldn't possibly be angry. *Right?*

He breathed heavily through his nose. His lips gleamed.

"Ryker?"

As though his name on her lips prodded him into action, he shot upright on his knees. Her gaze was automatically drawn to the part of him that remained moving long after he'd stilled, bouncing a couple of times before coming to rest at a soft, upward angle.

Her lips parted. "You're…hard again?"

He leaned over her, brushing a curl from her forehead. "Let me have you again, Charlie. God, please let me have you."

"But—" It'd been mere minutes! Was a man supposed to be able to orgasm and then go again moments later?

His brows drew together as he gazed down at her, and this time, there was no mistaking his expression. He ached.

For me.

The ache flashing in his eyes set up a sympathetic residence between her legs. It appeared her body was up to logic-defying deeds as well. "Ryker." She reached for him. Wrapping her fingers around his hardness, she squeezed.

His head fell forward, hanging from between his stiffened shoulders. His groan shook his entire body.

When she gently tugged him forward, however, his head shot up again. His gaze met hers in a wordless question. In answer, she notched the head of his cock at her entrance, then squeezed one more time before releasing him.

His eyes slid closed. He muttered inaudibly. When she dragged her fingernails up the ridges of his abdomen, he seemed to helplessly thrust forward. They both bit off a moan as he slid home, stretching her already sensitive sex in the most delicious ways.

He gave her no quarter, not pausing for even a moment after he seated himself to the hilt as was his usual tactic. Instead, he braced himself on outstretched arms above her and began thrusting into her at a teeth-clashing pace.

It was perfect.

Her breath caught as she met him on his next thrust with a robust one of her own. Their bodies slammed together, and Ryker, in the first demonstration of complete abandon she'd ever seen from him, clenched his teeth together in a near grimace and shouted through them.

Something overwhelming shot up through her from where he pounded into her, zinging through her stomach, arching through her heart. It expanded, filling her just as completely as he was with his body.

On the next thrust, she cried out, quickly cupping both breasts with her hands and furiously strumming her nipples with her thumbs.

So good. It all felt so good.

Ryker made a desperate noise, and her eyes opened to find him staring fixedly at her hands and what they were doing to her own body. When she stroked her own nipples again, his pupils flared. "That's it, Charlie. Harder for me, *mi esposa*." He pulled in a ragged breath. "Pinch them."

Without question, she obeyed him. His rough groan was nearly as pleasurable as the fissure of pain that shot through her as she tightened her fingers more and more.

"Oh!" Her eyes widened. "This is going to make me—"

He growled. "Fuck yes." He thrust more quickly. "Come apart for me, Charlie. Do it."

As though she were no longer in control of her own body, she immediately orgasmed. Violently.

A scream tore up her throat.

A stream of broken Spanish mixed with it.

She choked back a stream of her own words, not even sure what was brewing, but it was completely out of her control.

His perfectly measured thrusts lost their finesse. Then, with a roar, he completely stiffened. Knowing he was coming, too, sent fingers of pleasure shooting throughout her entire body. She dug her fingertips into his bulging, shuddering biceps, clutching at him. Needing grounding of some kind.

There was nothing that could ground her in this perfect storm.

"Charlie. Oh, God."

With a shaky breath, she opened her eyes. Short puffs of breath were leaving his lips at irregular intervals. Sweat gleamed on his forehead, and his hair was damp. He stopped thrusting, but his body still shivered with fine tremors. His eyes were wide and unfocused.

She uncurled her fingers and smoothed them up his arms, which seemed to snap him out of whatever daze he was in.

With a grunt, he pulled out of her and fell to his back beside her. "Holy hell," he groaned.

With her own trembling hand, she reached up and shoved a few tendrils of hair out of her eyes. She startled when the end of the tie tickled her nose. When had she forgotten she'd been tied up at one point? She was finding it difficult to catch her breath.

Ryker groped beside him, found her hand with his, and clasped it tightly. "Please tell me I wasn't too rough."

She turned her head to the side, meeting his gaze. "Definitely not," she said firmly. Everything about that had been perfect.

His eyes moved, his gaze traveling to her hair, and his lips parted. "Oh, Jesus." He reached out and plucked something from her curls, then held it out for her to see.

It was a splinter.

What? She craned her neck back and looked at the headboard. "Oh, my goodness."

"You broke the bed."

"I...broke the bed." The spindle that the tie had been looped around was torn in two, gaping outward with two jagged, splintered ends thrust into the night. She held up her hands. The tie, still bound to both of her wrists, hung between them, swinging just above her breasts.

Ryker made a noise. "Charlie!"

Next she knew, he was jerking upright, his fingers wrapped around both of her wrists as delicately as if he were handling spun sugar. She hissed in a breath when he pressed a finger against the angry red stripe traversing one wrist.

He began jerking at the knot almost frantically, his fingers fumbling. "I can't believe you didn't say anything!"

She frowned. "About what?"

He glared at her as he freed one wrist and went to work on the other. "About being hurt!"

She shook her head. "It doesn't hurt."

Raising an eyebrow, he touched the red welt again. She sucked in a breath. "Well, okay, it does hurt when you do that."

"Charlotte Martinez."

They both paused. Slowly, they raised their heads and their gazes met. The feelings were too much, and she wasn't able to hold his gaze for long, but before she broke to focus on a point over his shoulder, she spied a soft smile on his lips.

One she felt curling her own lips.

Charlotte Martinez.

They were married. She was married.

And if the past two hours were any indication of what married life was going to be like, she shouldn't have been avoiding it all these years.

Ryker clucked his tongue. "Damn."

She looked at him again only to find him gazing down. She, too, looked at his lap. "Oh."

Their condom had surpassed maximum capacity.

"Oh," she said again.

Goodness. They had used it twice. Through two of his orgasms, the evidence of which had spilled over the edge and smeared across his pubic bone. She reached between her legs and felt the sticky evidence of more than just her own arousal. She pulled up her hand and held it in a shaft of light. Her fingers gleamed. She bit back another *Oh*.

He swore beneath his breath and placed a hand over her knee. "We can fix this, Charlotte. I promise you."

She stared at her fingers and said nothing for a moment.

It wasn't the first time they'd been unsafe. That night he'd moved into the apartment, they'd completely forgotten a condom. She hadn't remembered until she'd started her period the next night. Since it hadn't been an issue, she hadn't thought about it any further.

"I—" She flexed her fingers. "I'm only a week into my cycle." Way too early for a baby.

His fingers squeezed her leg. "There's still a chance." His words were so quiet, there was no way she could get any hint of emotion from them. Something he'd done intentionally? "Do you want me to call your pharmacist?"

She swallowed. Did she? Did she want him to do that? A quick flash of Sasha's little face, with rosy cheeks and bright eyes as she snuggled against Ryker's shoulder, flitted through her mind. "I… Can we…? I can do it tomorrow. We can talk about it tomorrow."

Those are two different things, Charlotte. Which one was it?

His fingers paused mid-squeeze. "Okay."

Was he speaking carefully? Again, his voice was too soft for her to tell.

"I'm going to take a shower." He leaned over and softly kissed her shoulder. "Get cleaned up." He looked up at her, his lips still brushing her skin. "Care to join me?"

She blinked several times, but she still couldn't look away from her slick fingers. "Uh. I think no, actually."

He inhaled slowly. "Charlie…*amor*, are you all right?"

It was the second time he'd called her *amor* tonight. Why didn't it bother her? It might even do the opposite.

"I'm just tired." It wasn't a lie. It wasn't the whole truth either, but at least she had still never lied to him. That was important to her.

He made a soothing noise. "Of course you are." Slipping his hand behind the fall of her hair, he massaged the muscles she hadn't even known were tight at the base of her neck. "It's been a big day." With one final squeeze to her neck, he slid from the bed.

The massive muscles of his thighs locked and released as he shifted his weight. Her glistening fingers were forgotten.

"I'll only be a moment, *bonita*." He turned and began to walk toward the bathroom.

The perfect globes of his backside shifted beneath luscious, tawny skin. Now, not only were her fingers forgotten, but she was having trouble remembering her name.

It's Martinez.

The corners of her lips curled again as the sound of water hitting tile drifted out from the bathroom.

In the distance, the tinny sound of a ringing phone barely made it to the bedroom. It was only at the second ring that she remembered she had a landline and that people used it now. Well, person. Roger.

Her legs resisted working and even wobbled once she stood. A twinge between her thighs made her hold back a wince. When the phone rang a third time, she forced an awkward jog, nearly bouncing from wall to wall as she moved down the hallway. She picked up the phone at the tail end of the fourth ring.

"Hello?"

"Good evening, Miss Moore."

"Good evening. Actually, it's Mrs. Martinez now." Something bubbled in her chest. The first time she'd introduced herself by her new name. She'd liked it so much, she forgot to be terse with him after whatever he'd done to Ryker a few days ago.

There was a pause on the other end. "Congratulations, Mrs. Martinez."

"Thank you." She fiddled with her wedding band, discovering that she could rotate it with her thumb. "What can I do for you, Roger?"

"You've had a delivery, ma'am. I'm sending someone up with it now."

She stiffened and looked down at her naked body. Her naked, well-used body with red patches all over it from Ryker's rough jaw and rougher hands. "Yes, thank you," she squeaked.

She returned the phone to its cradle hard enough that it echoed a small protest ring. How long did she have to slip into a robe? Anything—

Knock, knock, knock.

She froze. "Um, who is it?" *Please let me have been loud enough to hear through the door.*

"Delivery, ma'am."

She sagged against the wall, but her mind raced. "Can you just leave it there?" *Because, you see, I'm obscenely naked and can't answer the door right now.* "I'll get it later."

There was a brief, muffled shuffle on the other side of the door, and then nothing. She craned up on her tiptoes and was barely able to peer through the peephole. She was just in time to see the uniformed back of someone enter the elevator, and then the metal doors slid closed.

With a quick inhalation, Charlotte eased the door open and slid her arm out, groping blindly for a package. Her fingertips encountered it, and she attempted to drag it through the door, but it was surprisingly heavy. She got it on the second try. Pulling it across the threshold, she just barely kept herself from slamming the door, closing it with a gentle *click* instead.

The package was rectangular and covered in glossy silver and white wrapping paper. A card was taped to the front and read *Congratulations* in blocky, masculine script.

A wedding present.

Charlotte sank to the floor eagerly, crossing her legs and reaching for the gift. When was the last time someone had given her a present? It was so many years ago, she couldn't remember it now, that was for certain.

She went straight for that pretty paper first, ripping into it with less decorum than she should. The box beneath the paper was blue and stamped with Tiffany & Co. She pulled off the lid.

A crystal platter.

That was…anticlimactic.

She laid the box lid aside and rifled through the torn wrapping paper, searching for the card. Now that she looked at it closer, she recognized the writing on the front right away. It was the handwriting of Ben Miller.

"Congratulations," the card read. "Our apologies that we could not make the ceremony. We wish you all possible luck and happiness in your marriage. Sincerely, Miller, Smith, and Lee."

Miller, Smith, and Lee. He'd signed the card in an exact replica of the letterhead of their firm. As though they were first-nameless entities. The powers that be.

And they were.

She closed the card with a hard swallow. When had she gotten so far off track? Smiling at her new last name. Playing naughty games in bed. With her husband of convenience whom she was only married to as a means to an end. A way to get her name nestled between Miller and Lee on that letterhead.

Was she…oh, goodness. She was feeling things for him. Losing her grip.

She'd been honest with Ryker: her past failed relationships had no bearing on her desire to avoid relationships now. But they had taught her that she didn't do well when her emotions got involved with another person. Her focus slipped. Goals changed.

This goal could not change.

She wouldn't let it.

The shower shut off with a squeak. Automatically, her head turned toward the sound. Ryker was in the bathroom now. Beautifully naked and dripping with water. And, he always looked at her like she was...

Someone.

Her chest panged. Her feet ached to walk down that hallway. Her arms longed for the feel of his warm skin.

Instead, she wrapped her arms around herself, the soft crinkle of the crumpled card shocking her back to reality.

One year.

Three hundred sixty-five days.

No. Not a problem. She'd just throw herself into her work. With every ounce of her soul. She could do this. She could.

Could she?

Chapter Fifteen

Charlotte flipped closed the file for Mr. Grabow's divorce case and shoved it away from her across the desk. Her other hand rubbed a slow circle across her stomach. She flicked a glance at the clock.

Drat.

Mr. Grabow would be here in about fifteen minutes to go over the latest developments, and her stomach was still off.

What had she eaten to deserve this?

Her wedding band caught a gleam of light as she reached for her now-cold cup of coffee, the only thing she'd been able to stomach for two days. When she took a sip, even that set her stomach to roiling.

Her swallow of coffee landed in her gut with all the grace of an acid-covered anvil. Her throat worked as she swallowed again. And again.

Nope. It wasn't going to stay down.

She lurched to her feet. Her desk chair rolled back and hit the wall with a clash.

Bathroom. It was just down the hall. Fifty feet away at most.

She made it two feet.

Snatching the trash can beside her desk, she hit the floor on her knees just in time to heave up half a cup of coffee into its tinny depths.

When all the coffee had been tossed up, her stomach kept convulsing for several seconds until it finally released its death grip on her entire body.

She sucked in a hacking breath and shoved a shaky hand across her lips as she settled to the floor on her bottom. Her upper lip curling, she weakly shoved the trash can far enough away that she couldn't see into it anymore.

Two knocks on the door was all the warning she got.

She jerked around as the door flew open, dashing her fingers under her eyes to eliminate any sign of wetness. Whatever good that did. She was still sitting on the floor in the middle of her office. It was more than obvious to anyone with half a brain that something was going on.

"Um...Mrs. Martinez?"

Her shoulders sagged. Just her assistant, Mark. Thank goodness. Still, she attempted to straighten her blouse with a swift tug before turning back to him. "Yes, Mr. Williams?"

Her attempts at decorum were immediately wasted as she struggled to her feet only to sway on her sensible heels.

"Whoa!" Suddenly, Mark was there, a firm grip on her elbow. "Are you okay, Charlotte?"

She held her breath until the world stopped spinning, then lifted her chin. "Just fine, thank you." She tried to push the trash can back to its spot beside the desk with her foot but missed and nearly stumbled into Mark.

Of course, now that she'd drawn attention to it, Mark glanced at the trash can.

Just perfect.

His fingers tightened against her elbow. "You got sick?"

How horrifying.

Mark's eyes widened. "Again?"

She tipped her head to the side. "Again?" Sure, she'd been nauseous the past couple of days, but—

"That's the third time this week, Charlotte."

She frowned. It was? Granted, she'd been incredibly busy lately, but being sick that many times was not something a woman forgot. Was it? She cleared her throat. "Third time?"

Mark nodded. "Twice yesterday. Once today." His face suddenly cleared, and then he was grinning. "Oh my God."

Her brows drew together. She looked around the office but noticed nothing in particular that would draw such a response. "What? What is it?"

"When were you going to tell me?" He shook her elbow, and she groaned as another bout of nausea passed through her in a wave. "Oh shit, I'm so sorry. Here, have a seat." He led her to the nearby armchair and eased her down into it with uncharacteristic focus.

What in the world was going on here?

"Mark—Mr. Williams…"

"I can't believe it. This is great! And today of all days."

Her patience snapped. "Enough, Mark."

Her assistant sat in the armchair next to hers. "I was just on my way to tell you Mr. Grabow canceled his appointment today. He's staying with his wife—"

"What?" she exclaimed. Oh, Mr. Grabow. When was he going to learn?

"—and Smith's secretary told me they're naming partner today."

Her mouth went dry. She straightened in her seat, nausea and Mr. Grabow's errors in judgment completely forgotten.

"They're going to…" She bit her bottom lip and managed to just contain a smile. "Today?"

Mark nodded. "Today."

When he smiled, she couldn't keep hers in check anymore. Her cheeks started to sting.

I should call Ryker. Let him know.

Her smile slipped. Drat. She'd been doing that a lot lately. Thinking of him first whenever something happened. Wanting him to know about it. Wanting his opinion on it. Turning into even more of a workaholic than normal had only kept her emotions in check for a couple of weeks.

If that.

Now, she feared she was learning to rely on him. Depend on him. Want him in ways that were not acceptable given their agreement and her goals.

Her goals. That may be achieved as soon as this afternoon.

She breathed a laugh, immediately caught a whiff of her breath, and grimaced. She definitely needed to go rinse her mouth out in the bathroom. And take care of that trash can. She got to her feet. "That's great news." She took a step toward the door, hoping Mark would take the hint that she wanted him to go now.

"That's not the only good news, though." He winked at her.

She drew her head back. "Did you just wink at me?"

He laughed. "Not like that, Charlotte. We both know Ryker would kick my ass the next time he met you for lunch if I did."

Huh. He would?

"So, are you going to tell everyone you're pregnant before or after you get partner?"

Her thoughts ground to a halt.

Mark's gaze scanned her expression and he chuckled. "Didn't think I would figure it out? I have three sisters, remember?"

She watched his lips moving, but a dull roar had built up in her ears and was slowly gaining in volume. What had he said? "P-pregnant?"

Mark was no longer smiling. "Okay, Mrs. Martinez, I think you should sit down. You're white as a ghost."

He took a step toward her. She took a corresponding step back. "Pregnant," she said again.

Mark held up both hands. "You're really worrying me here."

She raised a finger in the air. She just needed a moment, and he wouldn't stop talking. Blessedly, he caught the hint, and

Charlotte made a wide turn back toward her desk. Her steps were uneasy as she crossed the office. Once she could peer at the desk calendar mat covering most of her desktop, she counted the days backward.

Two weeks. Her period was two weeks late. How had she missed something like that?

You know exactly how. By throwing herself into work so hard that when she went home every night to a man who was more a temptation than the apple had been to Eve she would have a distraction. Something to keep her from tumbling headlong into a gigantic mistake, like falling for her husband.

They'd never talked about going to the pharmacist the day after their little accident. Or any day the rest of that week. She'd avoided the topic. The timing was off, and that next morning, the quietest little voice had asked her, *Would it be that bad if it happened?*

Her stomach gave another ominous lurch. Today they were naming partner. While people had been dropping by her office more frequently since her marriage, and someone had even invited her and Ryker to join them for dinner in a couple of weeks, she'd seen what happened to women who took time off for maternity leave, even at a law firm.

Maybe especially at a law firm, among people who knew exactly what the law required and exactly how to skirt it so they weren't in violation. The very people who had wanted her to be more relatable would lose their patience with an extended leave and all the inherent messiness that came along with becoming a mother.

She cleared her throat. Maybe this wasn't so bad. They could name partner today, and news of her pregnancy could come out after. Hard to take back something like partner. She glanced at Mark. "How did you—. When did you know?"

He took a moment to answer. "Honestly, there have been rumors for the past week that you're pregnant, but I didn't believe them. You're so career-oriented, I would have placed bets on you saving motherhood for many years down the road, if you went on that journey at all."

She covered her mouth with her hand.

Mark took a hasty step forward. "Are you going to be sick again?"

She made it to the trash can just in time, snatching it to her chest and even managing to turn away from her audience while her empty stomach rebelled.

"Um, I think you're supposed to eat pretty regularly to keep that from happening," Mark said from behind her as her dry heaves abated. "Do you want me to get you some crackers or something?"

"Stop…talking." She gasped into the foul trash can, trying to catch her breath. Her ribs and back ached, unused to being abused in such a way.

Then, as quickly as the nausea had come on, it vanished. She felt one hundred percent better. And ravenous. Shoving a strand of hair from her eyes, she wiped her chin with her palm just in case and turned back around to face Mark. "You know I hate gossip."

He nodded. "I know."

"Besides, this could be food poisoning."

He raised an eyebrow and was quiet for several seconds before he said, "Sure it could be." He jerked a thumb over his shoulder. "Do you want me to call Ryker for you——?"

Oh God. "No!"

Mark froze. That eyebrow he'd raised hiked even higher.

"I'm going to…take lunch now." She straightened her blouse and tucked the trash can against her side. She couldn't leave it here and ask Mark to contact the cleaning service. That would only fuel the rumors. "I'll be back in an hour—wait, two hours." She'd have to stop by the pharmacy, then head home. She couldn't take a pregnancy test in a public restroom.

"All right."

Had he spoken cautiously? Drat, she couldn't deal with this right now. On the biggest day of her life. Potentially.

She fumbled for her purse and shoved the strap over her shoulder. Then, with the trash can in tow, she strode out of her office. She didn't know if she was actually feeling the eyes of everybody in the law firm follow her out, because she refused to look and verify, but she imagined the hot beads of their gazes on her back as she left.

As soon as the large glass and brass doors of the firm closed behind her, she gulped huge lungfuls of the Vegas afternoon air. The temptation to lean back against the doors and try to calm her thundering heart was almost too great to resist, but she forced herself to keep walking toward her Cadillac.

The cinderblock-enclosed dumpsters were only a few feet away from her car. She slipped through the large, metal gates, which squealed loudly enough to give her a heart attack. Luckily, when she scanned the parking lot, she found it empty. She ditched the trash can in the nearest dumpster and left the enclosure as quickly as she could.

She'd just pick up a new trash can at the pharmacy. Two birds, one stone.

As she settled behind the wheel of her car, her hands were shaking. She placed one of them over her lower abdomen. Something foreign and warm traveled up from that spot, filling her chest.

Pregnant.

Dear God.

Cranking the car over, she drove with more than the usual caution toward the nearest Rite-Aid. Did she want the test to turn out negative—or positive?

And what would this do to her carefully crafted marriage?

Chapter Sixteen

Ryker drummed his fingers against the armrest of the couch.

He was so fucking bored. He hadn't yet heard back from the foster system after reaching out to volunteer, and Cassidy didn't need a manny. The apartment was already spotless thanks to his cleaning it just yesterday, and he'd switched to twice-a-day runs to fill the time.

Who would have guessed two months ago when he was longing for the end of his gigolo days with all his heart that being unemployed would be a completely soul-sucking experience?

For about the twentieth time in the past hour, he glanced at the watch on his wrist. It'd only been five minutes since he'd last looked at it.

Was this his life now? Watching every minute that passed until his wife came home?

Because, face it, that was what he was doing.

He missed Charlie. Badly.

He scrubbed a hand down his face and groaned.

Outside the front door of their apartment, the elevator dinged. He perked up like Pavlov's damn dogs.

Stop that shit. It was barely lunchtime. Since the run-in with Erin the cleaning lady, Charlie never came home early. And lately, she'd been arriving home later and later. Almost as though she were avoiding him. Though, the time they'd had together over the past couple of months had been magical. They seemed to grow closer each and every day, and he wasn't just imagining it. The increasing closeness wasn't just on his side.

Keys jingled outside the door.

He straightened.

Holy hell, she was home. Quickly, he scanned the living room. *Find something to do, man. Look busy.* He shoved his fingers through his hair. No time to check his appearance.

Why did his chest hurt so badly? No, not hurt. It felt pretty damn good, actually. He placed a palm over his heart and rubbed an experimental circle. Yes…that was a good feeling.

The door opened, and he jerked his hand away from his chest. Charlie stood framed in the open door, and the heart he'd just been rubbing thumped extra hard.

Traitorous organ.

He pushed to his feet. "Hey, you're home."

She stepped into the apartment and closed the door, but she didn't move any farther. "Oh. So are you." She closed her eyes. "I mean, of course you are." She opened her eyes again. "I don't know why I didn't expect that."

The good feelings vanished. He was walking across the apartment in the next second. "Charlotte, what's wrong?"

Her eyes widened as he walked toward her. He only noticed she carried a white plastic bag when she quickly ducked it behind her back.

He stumbled. She was hiding something from him? She didn't do that. Not ever. It'd been a long time since he'd felt panic. Not at this level. Probably not since high school. He'd forgotten that it had a taste. Like bitter pennies in the back of his throat.

He didn't even remember crossing the rest of the distance between him and his wife. He was just suddenly right in front of her. From this close, he could see a gleam in her blue eyes that not even her glasses could hide. Her already light skin was sickly pale. He caught the quick flash of a white piece of candy in her mouth as she shoved it from one side to the other with her tongue. It smelled minty.

He cupped her shoulders with both hands, drawing soft, soothing circles against her clavicle with his thumbs. "Oh, *amor*, are you sick?" Some of the panic abated, but a new, overwhelming need to take care of her replaced it.

She blinked and swayed toward him, drawing in an unsteady, audible breath.

He clucked his tongue and pulled her into his body, wrapping his arms around her in a tight band and tucking her head against his chest. "I've got you." Pressing a kiss to the top of her head, he reached for the bag that hung listlessly from her clenched fingers. "Here, give me your medicine. I'll put you to bed, then get you some water, okay?"

She stiffened in his arms. As soon as his fingers touched her hand, she jerked away from him. "Wait."

His arms fell to his sides. "Charlie?" Some of that alarm was returning.

She jostled the bag as she passed it to her other hand, and through the thin, white plastic, he caught sight of a rectangular box covered in pink. The words *First Response* blared through the thin barrier as loudly as if they had been shouted.

Ryker rocked on his feet. "That's a—" He pointed to the bag. His finger shook. "Is that a…pregnancy test?"

Her fingers shook, too, as she raised a hand to her throat. She jerked a nod.

They stared at each other for several moments, neither of them saying a word.

Something drastic was happening inside of him. The pressure built and built, starting in his gut. It then moved to his chest, and he nearly rocked on his feet again. Finally, the pressure settled behind his eyes.

Dios. Was he going to cry? "Charlie—" He reached for her, needing to touch her. Hold her. Kiss her. Take her to bed. Coddle her.

Just...hold her.

Before his fingers found purchase, however, she sidestepped them. "It might be nothing." Her gaze was no longer connecting with his. Her posture was stiff.

He drew up short, his hands hanging in midair between them. Quickly, he straightened again, his instinct to cover his momentary flash of vulnerability. But then he looked at her closely and spied her quivering chin.

She was going to cry. Dear God. This had to be what it felt like to get gutted.

He took a cautious step toward her. "*Bonita*, are you okay?"

She raised her chin. Stared at a spot over his shoulder. Then her face crumpled.

"Oh, no." He brushed a curl from her forehead, and the tiniest tear he'd ever seen spilled over the edge of her lush eyelashes, tracking down her cheek. "No, no, no." Unable to stand it anymore, he wrapped her in his arms again.

He crooned to her in Spanish, not really paying attention to what he was saying. What he said didn't matter. Only she did.

He rocked them slowly back and forth, praying the soft, continuous flow of his words had some sort of calming effect.

Abruptly, she straightened. Shoving a hand beneath first one eye and then the other, she stepped back. He had to fight every urge in the book to keep from reaching out for her again.

"I should just take the test." She sniffed.

He nodded so quickly, his neck ached. "Okay. Yes. Yes, that's a great idea."

Slow down. Just slow the fuck down. He was babbling. His hands were still shaking.

She looked as lost as he felt. That test…man, on the other side of it could wait a whole different life.

The life of his dreams.

She began walking down the hall, and he stood for a moment, staring at her back. What was he supposed to do right now? Everything within him wanted to follow after her. To huddle outside the bathroom door.

But everything about Charlie's body language right now screamed *give me space.*

So, he waited until she disappeared into the bedroom. Until he heard the quiet click of the bathroom door. He settled for huddling outside the bedroom door.

Leaning back against the wall of the hallway, he crossed his arms over his chest. How long did a pregnancy test take?

He glanced at his watch and began bouncing his leg. The change in his pocket jiggled.

Another glance at his watch.

Damn. Ten seconds had passed. He could have sworn it'd been at least two minutes.

He shoved from the wall and began pacing back and forth in front of the bedroom door.

Don't think about it. Don't think about it. Don't—

A baby. They could be having a baby. Would it look like her? Have that amazing, curly hair and eyes so blue he'd be a goner as soon as he saw them?

Or would it look like him? Have his skin tone and dark eyes. He breathed a laugh. Hell, he had curly hair, too. The kid was bound to get it, one way or the other.

That's cool. Ryker could show him how to make it work. Or show *her* if it was a girl. God, a tiny little girl. With pigtails of tight, springy hair.

He stopped pacing and started grinning. Fuck. She'd have him wrapped around her finger as soon as he laid eyes on her.

The bathroom door opened.

He spun around.

Charlie stood stock still, a hand over her stomach.

He swallowed hard, his gaze narrowing in on that hand. It appeared protective. His gaze shot back to her pale face. "It was positive, wasn't it?" His words were barely a whisper.

For a moment, she didn't move. Then she nodded.

He made an unidentifiable sound—half shout, half sob—that would horrify him under normal circumstances. But he was too busy racing across the bedroom to think about it. He was grinning so broadly, his entire face stung.

Right before he reached her, however, she held up a hand.

He glanced at her face again and skidded to a stop. He tilted his head. She...didn't look happy. "Charlie?"

She closed her eyes. "How could I have let this happen?"

His head jerked back as though she'd slapped him. "Wh-what?"

Pinching the bridge of her nose, she released a shaky breath. "They're announcing partner today." She shook her head. "How could I let this happen!"

He tried to laugh, but instead, he only made a quieter version of the odd sound he'd made moments before. "Charlie, you didn't let anything happen. It just did. And—" He had to work hard to keep his voice level. "It's a good thing."

Her hand fell to her side. "I can't do this right now."

"No, Charlie—" He took a step toward her.

"I just can't. Any second now, they could be making the announcement, and—"

Charlotte's cell phone chimed from the living room where she'd left her purse. Her eyes shot wide. "Oh, my goodness."

She took off like a rocket, dodging around him as though he weren't even in the room. He blinked at the space where she'd just been, trying to come to terms with the fact she'd just devastated him. How was he supposed to even walk out of this room when it felt like he weighed a thousand pounds?

But move he did. On limbs made of wood, he made his way down the hallway toward Charlotte's form as it huddled over her purse, her movements frantic as she searched for her cell.

She jerked upright and scanned her phone. She gasped. "Oh." She looked up at him. "It's time." She glanced around the living room as though looking for something. "I have to get there right away."

Jerking her purse onto her shoulder, she snagged her keys from the bowl beside the door and wrapped her fingers around the doorknob.

He watched her move as though having an out-of-body experience.

Suddenly, she paused, then slowly turned back toward him. Her gaze didn't quite meet his. "Ryker?"

Move. Say something. Open your damn mouth! "Yes?" His voice sounded as though it'd been dragged over a cheese grater.

Her gaze dropped to the floor. "Maybe we should…spend some time apart."

He sucked in a breath.

Her keys jingled. "I'm having a hard time focusing right now, and… If I make partner, I have to be my best."

Why did it feel like a knife was twisting in his chest? "You can't be your best with me?" He was his best with her.

She turned back toward the door. "Not the best partner. No."

He swallowed. "I see."

Her phone chimed again, and she jumped. "I'm sorry. I really have to go."

He nodded, which was stupid since she wasn't even facing him.

When she closed the door behind her, he stared at it. He didn't know how long—five seconds, thirty minutes. But he hardly breathed the entire time.

What had just happened?

He recognized this feeling. It was the one he'd gotten each and every time he'd moved foster homes growing up.

Rejection.

Damn her for making him feel it again. He'd worked so very hard to make sure their relationship was rejection-proof. For that matter, she'd worked so hard, too.

So, what the hell?

You slipped. That's what the hell, man.

He gritted his teeth. Damn it, he had slipped. Had allowed himself to start feeling things for Charlotte Moore. He'd broken the rules. Not only the rules they'd set in their relationship, but also the rules he'd set for himself his entire life:

Emotion equals bad news. Every time. No exceptions.

He straightened. But she'd broken the rules, too. Time apart? Fuck that. They'd agreed to at least a year, and that was before their situation had changed. They were going to be parents. He'd die before he allowed his kid to go through even a fraction of what he'd gone through himself.

He was going to be a father.

His shoulders rolled back. A father. The most important job of his life.

He wasn't going to fuck it up. And he wouldn't let Charlie fuck it up either.

He snatched his keys from the bowl.

Charlotte was upset. This hadn't been her plan. It was a big day. Objectively, he could understand everything she'd done just now.

Objectively. Which was the only consideration that mattered. Subjectivity could eat a bag of dicks.

As he stormed from the apartment and toward his beat-up car, intent on hashing this out with Charlotte, he had to acknowledge that at least one good thing had come from all of this.

He was firmly back on track.

He and his baby's mother didn't love each other. Just as it should be.

They would, however, be on the same team. He just had to reach Charlotte's logical side once more.

Which was her dominant side, anyway.

Piece of cake.

Chapter Seventeen

She dashed yet another stream of tears from her cheek as she huddled over the steering wheel.

What in the world was wrong with her? She hadn't been able to stop crying since she left the apartment.

Spend some time apart.

Even now, the words speared through her in a feeling she hadn't had since her father died. But that had been grief.

How could she be feeling grief over spending time away from Ryker? It made no sense. This was a marriage of convenience. It had stopped being convenient. End of story. In fact, when she made partner this afternoon, she wouldn't need the marriage anymore at all.

I might not need it, but I may want it.

She lurched to a hard stop in the parking lot of the firm.

No. Oh, no. That couldn't possibly be true. Want a marriage? How could she? After all her careful planning.

How did someone betray themselves?

She grabbed her purse and got out of the car, smoothing a hand down her blouse to make sure everything was in place.

This was not an issue. She'd been working hard enough lately to prove to the partners that a pregnancy would not interfere with her work. She was an exemplary lawyer.

Repeat: not an issue.

With a nod, she hurried into the office, butterflies tossing and turning in her stomach. As she strode through the opulent lobby, she could already hear the strains of a celebration emerging from the office area.

She picked up her pace. Had they announced partner already? She placed a hand over her stomach and turned the corner.

Several clerks stood around, chatting and holding flutes of champagne. Chip Wesson huddled with Miller, Smith, and Lee under a big sign reading *Congratulations*. The men were shaking hands and smiling at each other.

Charlotte ground to a stop and simply stared. Oh, God. *Please don't let this mean what I think it means.*

There was a flurry of movement to her right, and when she lethargically turned her head, Mark was at her side. "Charlotte," he said breathlessly. "There you are. Did you get my texts?"

"Texts?" she asked in an odd voice she didn't recognize. "I got one text. Telling me to get here in a hurry."

He leaned in. "I sent you another one. Asking you to call me."

Ah. She swallowed. He'd been trying to protect her from this exact scenario. "So you could tell me Wesson made partner."

He winced. "God, Charlotte, I'm so sorry. I didn't want you to walk into what might feel like an ambush. I really tried to warn you—I'm just…so sorry."

"Nothing to be sorry about." Did her voice really sound that tinny? Or was something up with her hearing? "Wesson is an excellent lawyer. He deserves this."

"Is there anything I can do for you? Anything you need?"

She shook her head. "Don't be silly." She turned her head back toward the front of the room. Back toward the person who had won her dream. "I should go congratulate him."

"Oh, Charlotte, everyone would understand if you didn't."

No they wouldn't. No one ever understood anything she did. Well, maybe Ryker did. But she'd just asked for time apart, so that was a moot point. Her forced smile felt wobbly. "Get Mr. Grabow on the phone for me, would you? I want to speak with him as soon as possible about his latest decision. Make sure it's what he wants."

Mark paused, but eventually nodded. "Of course. Ma'am."

She didn't even watch him walk away, instead focusing on Wesson and the necessary steps she would need to take in order to cross the room to him.

She'd done hard things before. Surely, she could do this. Taking a deep breath, she began walking. Conversations petered out around her as she passed, and she could feel the sting of a hundred eyes' laser focus.

When she arrived in front of Miller, Smith, Lee, and Wesson, it took several seconds for the four men to notice her, but when they did, all four turned to her at once. She knew she wasn't imagining that the sudden silence in the wake of their conversation was awkward.

"Chip." Charlotte thrust her hand forward. "Congratulations are in order. You certainly deserve this."

Slowly, Wesson took her hand and gave it a measured pump. "Thank you, Charlotte. I appreciate that."

"Yes." She dropped his hand. "Well." Straightening her blouse once more, she smiled. "Back to work for me. Have a client waiting on the phone. Enjoy your celebration." She nodded toward Miller, Smith, and Lee. "Sirs."

They nodded back, varying degrees of stiff smiles on all their faces.

When she turned around again, several people nearby whipped back toward their small circles of colleagues, as though they didn't want to be caught staring and eavesdropping.

Which was fine. They could eavesdrop. She had conducted herself with class. *Not that it will earn me any points.*

Her eyes began ominously stinging once more. Oh, goodness, was she going to cry again? Right here in front of everybody? Quickly, she cleared her throat and started walking toward her office. She'd just stop in at the restroom on the way and take a moment to compose herself.

She could see Mark speaking on the phone at his desk outside her office. He must already have Mr. Grabow on the line. She would have to hurry.

Ducking into the bathroom, she turned and quickly flipped the lock on the door. It wasn't a private restroom, but right now, she couldn't bring herself to care. A quick scan of the open stall doors showed that the restroom was completely vacant; Charlotte finally allowed herself to loosen the knot at the top of her spine.

Her head fell forward, and she caught herself with two outstretched arms planted on the bathroom vanity. She let her head loll and closed her eyes.

Gone. Her dream was gone.

She released a shaky breath and blinked. Several tears dropped into the sink, leaving small puddles against the porcelain.

There was the sound of several more drops hitting the tile at her feet. She frowned. Surely she wasn't crying that much. When she pushed away from the bathroom vanity, she looked down.

She tilted her head.

The drops were red.

She made a soft sound in the back of her throat. Several seconds passed, then her eyes widened.

The drops are red.

"Oh, my goodness."

She spun on her heels and charged into a stall, slamming the door closed. Her fingers fumbled with the metal lock, and it took three tries for her to click it over. She ripped the blouse from the waistband of her trousers, but the button and zipper of her pants proved as difficult as the lock.

"Come on," she muttered as she tugged. Her breathing carried the faintest hint of the tears she hadn't quite kicked yet.

Finally, the zipper gave way, and she shoved her pants and underwear down her thighs.

Her panties were swimming in blood.

"No, no, no, no, no." She reached for toilet paper, but her pants had become saturated as well.

"Oh, my God." *I'm losing the baby.* "No, please." She shoved the tissue to her mouth, but it did nothing to muffle a cry.

Ryker. She wanted—no, she needed Ryker. Her cell was in her office. "Hold on, baby. Just hold on, okay?"

She wrestled her pants back into place. There was an ever-growing stain crawling down the thighs of her trousers, and she swayed in place.

This couldn't be happening. Anything but this.

The stall door banged against the wall with a clash, and she stumbled into the bathroom door, flipping the lock with numb fingers, then prying it open.

Mark was standing ten feet away, talking to someone she would recognize blindfolded.

Ryker is here.

How? Why?

A sharp pain shot through her womb, and she doubled over with a gasp. The two men turned toward her.

Mark was smiling. Then he looked down. "Oh my God."

She reached out a shaking hand. "R-Ryker?" *I need you. Oh, God, how I need you.*

The blood drained from his face. "Charlie!" He took off in a sprint, arms pumping, and was in front of her faster than should have been humanly possible. "*Amor.*" He scooped her up in his arms. "Oh, Jesus." Spinning with her in his arms, he faced a motionless Mark. "Call the fucking hospital. Tell them we're on our way."

He blinked.

"Now, damn it!"

Mark lurched into motion, colliding with his desk, his hand smacking against the phone as he snatched it toward him.

Another pain shot through her, and she moaned, shoving her face against Ryker's neck. "It's okay, *amor*. It's okay." He started walking toward the exit. "I've got you."

The clerks celebrating Wesson's promotion parted around them like the Dead Sea. Smith took a step toward them. "Oh my God, Charlotte. Are you okay?"

Ryker just kept moving toward the door like a man possessed. Once he got there, he kicked it open and turned them sideways to ease her through the threshold.

She twisted her fingers in his shirt and gritted her teeth. "It hurts."

A desperate sound echoed through his chest. "Shh, *mi amor*." His palm smoothed over her back as he carried her to his car. "I know it does."

She didn't know how he got the car door open with her in his arms, but suddenly, he was settling her gently into the passenger seat. He strapped the seat belt around her, then raced around the hood to the driver's side.

They left the parking lot with a squeal of rubber.

The pain just kept coming. Between her legs, she could feel herself bleeding more and more. The stain on the front of her pants continued to grow.

She groped blindly over the center console, and his hand was over hers in a second. His fingers squeezed almost to the point of pain. "I'm here, Charlie."

"The baby," she said through tight lips. "I'm losing—"

Another squeeze of her fingers. "Shh, don't say that. *Amor*, we're only a couple of minutes from the hospital, okay?"

She cranked her eyes closed and nodded her head.

Minutes later, the car shuddered to a stop. Charlotte opened her eyes to find Ryker had double parked behind an ambulance. He was already running around the car.

When he wrenched open her door, she said, "Ryker, the car—"

"Fuck the car," he muttered, unbuckling her. "Okay, *bonita*, put your arms around my neck."

She could tell he was trying to be gentle when he eased her from the car and back into his arms, but even that slight jostling made her moan into his shirt.

"I'm so sorry," he said into her hair. "Almost there."

The ER doors opened with an automatic whoosh. The security guard stood up from his desk.

"Help," Ryker nearly shouted. "She needs help. Please." His voice cracked.

"Over here, sir."

She was jostled again as Ryker changed course. Next she knew, she was being laid down. His warmth vanished. She groped for him. "No. Ryker."

"Shh, I'm not going anywhere."

"Sir, it's family onl—"

"I'm her fucking husband!"

"I understand," came the soothing, professional response.

They began to move. The squeaking of wheels followed them, and the florescent lights in the ceiling flashed in her eyes over and over again.

"How far along is she?"

"Um…six weeks? We only just found out today." His voice cracked again. "Please, can you tell me if she'll be all right?"

"We'll let you know what's going on as soon as we can, sir."

The gurney stopped. The nurse pulled a curtain around them.

Things moved even more quickly. She was undressed. Someone drew several vials of blood. A doctor came in and talked in hushed tones to the nurses, then Ryker.

All the while, she writhed, a hand over her womb and tears streaming down her cheeks into her hair.

Then, suddenly, they were alone.

Ryker leaned over her, smoothing her hair away from her forehead. She reached for him, and he wrapped his hand around hers. She tugged him closer. "Ryker."

"Anything, *amor*. Ask me for anything, and I'll give it to you."

She shook her head. No, he wasn't understanding. "About what I said earlier—"

"Shhh." He pressed a kiss to her hair. Nuzzled her neck. Wove their fingers together. "You don't have to say anything about that."

But she did. She had to. Because— "I want this baby." She sobbed. "So badly."

She felt him stiffen against her. His own shuddering breath sounded near her ear, and then he seemed to deflate. "Me, too," he whispered.

"I'm sorry," she blubbered. "I'm so sorr—"

"Mr. and Mrs. Martinez?"

They both turned. An impossibly young doctor in blue scrubs stood near the curtain, a massive piece of equipment by her side.

Ryker scrubbed a hand down his face and sat up, keeping her hand firmly tucked in his other one. "Uh, yeah. That's us."

"We're going to do a sonogram." She nodded toward the machine. "Check for the baby's heartbeat. Okay?"

Charlotte tightened her hand around Ryker's.

He looked down at her. "I'm not going anywhere, *amor*. I promise."

A nurse helped Charlotte into the stirrups as the doctor calmly explained what the sonogram would entail, as though it were perfectly routine.

And it probably was. Yet an entire life hung in the balance.

The doctor clicked the machine on and took up her position between Charlotte's feet. "Okay, you'll feel some pressure."

She felt nothing as she focused with all her heart on the screen of the machine. There were several loud, static whoops, and then the tiniest, gummy-bear shape appeared on the screen.

Ryker sucked in a breath. "Is that—?"

"That's the baby, yes," the doctor said brusquely. She frowned at the screen, then pushed several buttons.

Even before the doctor turned back to them, Charlotte knew.

"I'm sorry, Mr. and Mrs. Martinez. There is no heartbeat."

Chapter Eighteen

Ryker plodded down the hall, a cup of the swill they passed off as coffee clutched in one hand.

The picture from the sonogram burned a hole in his back pocket. He didn't know what had possessed him to ask for a printout of that tiny, indistinguishable blob, but the doctor had asked no questions as she'd handed it over.

Charlotte had finally fallen asleep after being poked and prodded the whole day. The nurses had encouraged him to go get something to eat.

As though he had any appetite. Or any inclination to be away from his wife's side.

He looked down the hall and spied Charlotte's doctor ducking into the room she'd been admitted to. He ditched the coffee in the nearest trash can and picked up his pace. Maybe the lab results had come back.

harlotte was just waking up as Ryker entered the room. Her blue, foggy gaze clapped onto him as strongly as if she'd touched him, and he rushed to her side, reaching for her hand.

They faced the doctor together.

"Mrs. Martinez, something came to light in one of your blood tests that you need to be aware of."

Charlotte pushed herself upright, and Ryker rushed to prop a pillow behind her back. "All right."

The doctor frowned. Ryker felt a corresponding pang in his gut.

"I'm afraid you have Antiphospholipid syndrome."

He tightened his grip on Charlotte's hand, but she merely shook her head. "What is that?"

The doctor pulled a chair up to Charlotte's bed and settled into it, and Ryker tasted pennies.

"It's an autoimmune disease. It means you may have issues with blood clots, among other things. We've already ordered you a prescription for blood thinners."

"Okay," Charlotte said slowly.

There was more to this. Ryker could sense it. "What other things?" he bit out.

"I'm sorry?" the doctor said, turning his way.

"You said 'blood clots, among other things.' What are the other things?"

The doctor turned back to Charlotte. When she reached out toward her patient, placing a palm over the hand Ryker didn't hold, he knew their lives were about to change.

"Charlotte, I'm sorry to say that one of the complications of Antiphospholipid syndrome is that you may never be able to carry a baby to term."

Ryker's eyes slid closed. *Oh, Charlie.*

When he opened his eyes again, Charlotte was staring at the doctor without blinking, no trace of emotion on her face.

The doctor looked at Ryker and fidgeted with the stethoscope hanging around her neck before glancing back at Charlotte. "Mrs. Martinez, did you hear what I said?"

"I'd like to be alone, please." Charlotte's words were hollow. A mere echo of her normal tone of voice.

The doctor looked at Ryker again. "Do either of you have any questions? I'm more than happy to—"

"Alone." Charlie said firmly. "Please."

The doctor swallowed harshly. "Of course." She turned back to him. "I'll be making my rounds in a couple of hours. We can talk more then."

He must have nodded at her, because she left, but he had no memory of moving. He only started tracking again when Charlotte tugged her hand from his.

She looked up at him, her eyes stark. "I think you should go."

His brows drew together. "What? Charlie, of course I'm not going anywhere—"

"Now, Ryker. You need to leave."

He knelt down beside her bed. He wanted to reach for her hand again, but something in her posture warned him away from it. "Charlotte, this is terrible news, yes, but I don't think you should be by yourself. Let me stay—"

"Do you know the divorce rate for couples who lose a child to miscarriage?"

Ryker froze. *Lose a child.* The words were a slap.

That's exactly what had happened to them. They'd lost a child. Ah, God. He could barely swallow past the lump in his throat. "Charlie, I don't care what the rate—"

"Twenty percent higher than normal divorce rates. And divorce is three times more likely in couples unable to have children."

"Charlotte, damn it—"

"All you wanted from a marriage was children." He could barely hear her, she spoke so softly. "I can't give them to you."

He felt the blood drain from his face. "The doctor said you *may* not be able to carry a baby to—"

"When are you going to get it!" Her head snapped his way. Her eyes flashed. "We are doomed, Ryker. All the odds are stacked against us, and we don't even have a real marriage." She hit her fist against the mattress. "The outcome of this is no mystery. We are doomed." She enunciated every word.

He shook his head. This was a mistake. Yes, he wanted children. But, he wasn't sure he didn't want Charlotte more. "*Amor.*" He reached out to cup her cheeks.

She gasped so loudly it was nearly a cry and wrenched her head back. "Don't touch my face!"

Her shout echoed through the room.

Something within him detonated. "Fine!" He shot to his feet and shoved a hand through his hair. "You want to push me away? Great. This is me going." He jabbed a finger her direction. "I swear to God, woman, I was here for the thick of it. And I would have stayed for it all. But I can't fight you. Not when you're so bound and determined to send me packing. To keep me at a distance. I can't do this relationship alone."

She pursed her lips. "We don't have a relationship."

He swayed. Shook his head. "You're right." He laughed without humor. "You're always right. Congratulations on that. At least you have that to keep you warm at night."

A muscle ticked in the delicate line of her jaw. "Please leave."

He jutted his chin. "My pleasure." Snatching his jacket from the back of the chair, he shoved his arms through it and left her hospital room without another word.

As he stormed toward the exit sign, their nurse spotted him. "Mr. Martinez?"

He ignored her and kept walking.

Outside, it was already night, and the cold, desert air slapped his cheeks. He flipped up the collar of his jacket and ducked behind its cover. He'd moved his car to the main parking lot several hours ago but had been so distracted at the time that now he had to search for it before locating it beneath one of the light poles.

He collapsed into the driver's seat and slammed the door. His breaths ricocheted around the car for several seconds.

"Fuck!" He beat his fist against the steering wheel. There was an ominous crack in his hand, and Ryker shook it out, not caring if he'd broken it.

When he collapsed back into the seat, there was a tiny crinkle from his back pocket. His breaths still billowing, Ryker eased the sonogram still frame from the back of his jeans and slowly raised it to the halo of light streaming through the windshield from the streetlamp.

He could barely make it out in the dark, but he saw enough to be able to trace the tiny white shape of his baby with his thumb.

He clenched his teeth.

How was it possible to miss someone you'd never even met? And how was it that walking away from Charlotte hurt just as much?

I lost them both in one day.

Ah, God. How was he supposed to survive this?

He'd never gotten to meet the baby, but he'd loved it. Those precious few hours when it was his—God, he loved that child.

And the way he'd felt when Charlotte had asked for time apart earlier today: completely gutted and empty. Missing part of himself.

Oh, no. There was only one explanation for that.

He loved Charlotte, too.

All that work he'd put into making sure loving her was never going to happen, and here he sat. A shell of himself, longing for his wife with all his heart.

This was hard. This was too hard. His clenched teeth couldn't keep his chin from wobbling.

Slowly, he leaned forward and propped his forehead against the steering wheel.

And then he let the sobs come.

They started as a small trembling in his shoulders, but within minutes, they were shaking his entire body. He couldn't catch his breath. They just kept coming. Coming. Coming.

A brisk knock on his window; he shot upright with a gasp.

The ER nurse stood outside his car. "Mr. Martinez!"

He fumbled for the window crank, his brow furrowed. "Yes?"

"Sir, come quickly. It's your wife."

Chapter Nineteen

Oh, God, what had she done? She struggled to get out of the bed.

"Mrs. Martinez, you have to calm down." The nurse gripped her shoulders and tried to force her to lie flat.

"No! Don't touch me!"

"Okay, she's going hysterical. Have we found the husband yet?"

"Angela went to check for him outside, but she hasn't come back."

The nurse was still touching her, and her grip was so strong it hurt. Charlotte slapped at the nurse's hands.

"I think we need to sedate her."

"Yeah, okay. Keep her as calm as you can while I get the syringe."

"No!" Charlotte shoved the nurse away. She had to get to Ryker. Catch him before he left. Before he was gone. "Please."

"We need some help in here!"

Suddenly, hands were all over her. Pushing her. Holding her down. One of the orderlies reached for her IV tube, a syringe in his other hand.

Oh, God, if they sedated her, it would be too late. She'd never get to Ryker. "No, stop!" She was screaming now, but they just ignored her as though she didn't have a voice. "Ryker!"

"What the hell is going on in here?"

Charlotte's gaze snapped to the door, drawn by the voice she would always recognize.

Her husband stood in the door of her hospital room, both hands braced on the frame, muscles bulging in his arms. He took in the scene, and his face grew thunderous.

He stormed her direction. "Get your hands off her! She's on the spectrum. Stop!"

One of the nurses holding her down immediately backed off. Another gentled her grip. "She's autistic?"

Ryker shouldered a nurse in his way aside. "Asperger's," he muttered negligently.

At last, Charlotte was released. She scrambled upright, shoving her hair from her face and drinking in the sight of Ryker like she'd never thought to see him again.

And she hadn't.

He came back.

The orderly lowered the syringe, and Ryker eased past him and crouched beside her bed. His gaze roved her face, and he fisted his hands in the sheet, but he didn't touch her. "Charlie, baby, it's okay. Shhh."

She reached for him with both hands, a sob ripping from her mouth.

His face crumbled. "Oh, *mujer*." He launched to his feet and crawled into bed with her, his enormous frame making it creak.

She buried her face in his chest and his arms came around her in a tight band. "Don't go," she cried. "Don't go. Please, don't go."

His hand paused in the middle of stroking her back for a moment. "*Mi amor*, I'm here."

She shook her head. He wasn't understanding. "I don't want you to leave. I don't want time apart. I don't want just twelve months. I don't want a divorce." She sobbed anew. "Ryker, I just want you."

He pulled back, and she fisted her fingers in his shirt, giving a sharp tug, but he wasn't leaving the bed. He was looking down at her through red-rimmed eyes. "What did you say?"

Slowly, she cupped his cheek. His two-day beard scraped her skin, and when he turned his face into her palm, his lips brushing her skin, a zing shot through her. "Ryker, if this had been one of my cases, the outcome would have caught me completely by surprise."

His brows drew together. "*Amor,* I don't understand."

She didn't either. But, for once, she didn't care. "None of the statistics are in our favor. We were both so sure of our decision. When we put this on paper, it was clear. Romance was not a possibility and never would be."

He pulled her closer, his open hand a warm brand against the small of her back. "I feel like I'm hearing a *but* in there."

She pulled in a deep breath and held it for a moment before releasing it. "*But* I don't care about that. I don't care how risky all of this is on paper. I fell in love with you anyway. Against all odds. Against all our hard-limit decisions."

His expression was carefully neutral. "Love."

It's too late. She'd pushed him away, and everything had gone horribly wrong.

Her gaze dropped to his throat. "I know it's not fair for me to say this to you now. You want children, and I—" She swallowed a sob and shook her head. She couldn't think about that right now. About how his dream and her dream had never been so far apart after all. About how her arms would never hold her child. Their child. "So, I understand we're over, but—"

His eyes snapped up. "Charlotte—"

"Do you think that, if today had gone differently…" she met his gaze and used all her willpower to make sure she held it. No matter what he answered, it was going to hurt, but she couldn't keep from asking, "Could you have loved me someday, too?"

He tucked a strand of hair behind her ear. "*Mi esposa bonita.* The only reason you married me was because you wanted to make partner."

Partner. Oh, goodness, the partner decision felt a hundred years removed from her. How could it have only been hours before?

"Yes," she whispered.

"And right now that's not a possibility." His gaze wandered away from hers. "Does that…does that change how you feel about me?"

"No!" If she never thought of the word *partner* again, she wouldn't even notice. She cupped his face with both her hands now. "Of course it doesn't."

He released a breath. "Well, right now, in this tiny fragment of time, children aren't possible for us either."

Her gut twisted. Sobs that she'd hoped had gone dormant suddenly reared their heads. Oh, God. "Our baby." She closed her eyes. "Ryker, our baby."

"Shh." She was bound in his arms again, her face pressed against his chest, her arms around his neck. He rocked her back and forth. "I know, *amor.*" His voice cracked. "I know. But Charlie?" He pulled back just a fraction and gazed down at her. She was captivated by his eyes. By the tears that swam in them. "Charlie, if we never have children," he said gravely, "it will never change the way I feel about you."

She swallowed. "The way you feel about me?"

He leaned down and pressed his forehead to hers. "This has been the hardest day of my life."

She shuddered. Tears slipped down her cheeks.

"But," he cleared his throat, "when I thought we were in it together, my head was just above water. I knew that this bad day and any other bad day we came across wasn't going to break me, no matter how badly it hurt."

He pressed his lips to her forehead, and they trembled slightly as he continued to talk. "And then, I didn't have you. We weren't together. And I knew I would never be okay again."

It was exactly how she'd felt. She would have never been able to put it into words. She pulled in a shaky breath. "Ryker?" Please let this mean what she thought it meant.

He gazed down at her, his eyes wet. "Charlotte Martinez, I fell in love with you, too. I knew it the moment I sat in that car alone, facing a future without you by my side. Our child is gone, and it guts me. But without you?" He swallowed, and a tear trailed down his cheek, making her eyes widen. "I can't do that, *amor.*"

She released her breath. Was this really happening? "You...love me?"

He nodded slowly, his hair brushing against hers. "With all my heart."

That heart he spoke of beat steadily against hers where they were pressed together.

Leaning up, she pressed a soft kiss to his lips. He sighed against her mouth and cradled her against him.

"Damn, Charlie," he whispered against her lips. "I thought I was never going to see you again."

Another soft kiss. "I know. I thought the same thing. As soon as you left, I knew I'd made a horrible mistake."

He pulled back. "Charlotte Moore made a mistake?" He shook his head "That can't possibly be right."

She raised her eyebrows. "Excuse me, but my name is Charlotte Martinez."

His eyes flashed. His gaze dipped to her lips. "So it is," he whispered. "So it is."

She looked down at the collar of his shirt. "I've grown kind of attached to that name, you know."

"Have you?"

She nodded. "I think…I may want to keep it."

He cleared his throat. "For how long?"

She shrugged with one shoulder. "Maybe forever?"

"Forever," he repeated. He closed his eyes and placed his hand over hers, pinning it against his chest more firmly. "It won't be long enough." He opened his eyes again. Stroked the back of her hand with his thumb. "But it's a start."

When she looked around the room, it was to find that all the medical personnel had left at some point. Not that she would have cared if fifty people witnessed what had just happened.

"Come here, *amor*." Ryker scooted down on the bed and held his arms open.

She lay beside him and curled over his chest, placing her ear right over that heartbeat of his. He dragged a blanket up and over them and tucked it around her.

"Sleep, baby," he whispered in her ear. "Because in the morning, we have big plans to make."

She closed her eyes. The weight of the day covered them both like its own blanket, but beneath that weight, she felt their combined strength. Knew that it meant they wouldn't be crushed.

Today had changed her. Forever. She would never pass a day where she didn't think about their baby; she knew this instinctively. Even now, her tears began to soak Ryker's shirt.

He simply tightened his arms around her, his own tears dampening her hair.

It would be a long time before they would be able to smile without feeling a twinge of guilt. Without remembering what they'd lost.

But they would smile. They would remember. And they would live happily ever after among whatever mess life brought their way.

Together.

Epilogue

Ten Years Later

"Ryker!" She shut the door to their apartment behind her and dropped her keys into the bowl.

"In the kitchen, *amor*!"

A grin nearly split her cheeks as she rushed across the living room. He was going to flip when she told him. And when he flipped, it always meant good things for her.

Good and naughty things.

She swung into the kitchen, ready to race into her husband's arms and whisper the good news in his ear, but the sight that greeted her made her skid to a stop.

Their kids sat around the marble island, and her heart nearly lunged out of her chest to get to them.

Nathaniel, their oldest, rocked back and forth on his stool, his sound-canceling headphones securely in place as he nibbled on apple slices. He was only twelve, but Charlotte swore every day she came home that he looked more and more like a man and less like a little boy, and it very nearly broke her heart every time. She wanted to throw her arms around him, but any kind of touch was a big no-no for Nathaniel, so she settled for walking into his line of vision.

He noticed her right away and lowered his apple slice. A wobbly smile spread his lips, and she swallowed hard. Since they'd adopted him nine years earlier, he hadn't said more than a handful of words.

But that smile. Goodness, that smile made her want to give him the world.

"Hi, Mama!"

She turned toward their middle child. "Hi, baby." She reached over the island and cupped Ray's cheek in her palm, using her thumb to wipe a stray smear of peanut butter from the corner of his mouth. "Good snack?" she asked.

"Yes. It is my favorite snack. I love apples and peanut butter." His words were slightly clipped, but he was verbose as ever, with a bigger vocabulary than most children who were six years old.

"I know, sweet boy. I know."

"Aunt Cassidy came over with another video game today." Ray, so named because he was always grinning so broadly—their ray of sunshine—meticulously dipped another apple slice in his dollop of peanut butter. "Daddy let me play it all day. I beat it on the hardest level!"

"You did?"

Ray was incredibly gifted with coding already, something Cassidy was over the moon about. She doted on her nephew, spending extra time playing coding games with him and, of course, teaching him the wonders of gaming.

"Yes, I did."

"That's great, baby. Maybe you can show me all the trophies you won later."

He nodded his head and shoved his apple into his mouth, the dimple Charlotte adored—the one he first flashed at her the day they brought him home as a three-year-old toddler—making an appearance on his cheek.

There was a squeal to her right, and Charlotte at last turned to the subject of today's good news.

Their youngest. Well, not quite *theirs* yet, but that was about to change. Baby Chloe sat in her high chair waving her tiny fists around and staring at Charlotte while Ryker tried to get a spoonful of something mushy and green into her mouth.

"I know Mama's home, *mija*," Ryker said, trying to get the spoon past her fists again. "You still have to eat." He glanced over his shoulder at her, and even though his face was covered in several blobs of that same green substance, his looks caught her straight in the chest, just as they always did.

His gaze roved her from head to foot, his pupils dilating as he looked her over. "Not that I can blame you. I want Mama as soon as she comes home, too."

Hearing that would never get old. Every day when she came home from work—the law firm focused on adoption law that she'd opened herself ten years ago after leaving Miller, Wesson, and Lee—Ryker welcomed her home, and she immediately wondered how she'd ever thought to live life without the joy he continuously provided her. She bit her bottom lip and pressed her tongue against the back of her teeth. So many things she wanted to say. Too many things she wanted to say. She settled for, "I missed you."

A slow, sexy grin curled his lips. "Then come here and show me how much."

She walked to his side, wiped a blob of baby food from its dangerously close proximity to his mouth, and sealed her lips over his.

He groaned softly and teased the tip of his tongue across the seam of her lips.

Before she could get carried away, she pulled back.

"Hey," he said, gazing at her through hooded eyes. "I wasn't done yet."

"We got a court date."

He continued to stare at her for several seconds, and then he blinked. "We got a court date?"

She nodded.

He shot upright in his seat. "We got a court date?" he asked again, this time louder.

She breathed a laugh. "The judge called this afternoon." She'd answered the call at her firm herself, having a gut feeling that it was going to be one she wanted to hear. "Our adoption day is scheduled for five weeks from now."

Ryker raised a shaky hand to his face and scrubbed it across his jaw. His eyes filled.

She stepped toward him. "Are you okay?"

He jerked a nod. "Just need a second."

She cupped his cheek. God, she loved this man. This was the exact same reaction he'd had when she brought this news home for both Nathaniel and Ray. Ryker Martinez loved his children with a fierceness that made her wild for him.

"She's really going to be ours?" he asked, his voice rough.

Chloe's process had been harder than both of their first two children's combined. All three of their children came from the foster care system, but Nathaniel's birth parents had surrendered him to a fire station as an infant and forfeited their rights without a fight. Ray's birth parents had loved him with all their hearts and met all his needs as a child on the spectrum, but when they'd died in a car accident one winter, no one in the immediate family had wanted to take on a disabled child, and he'd become theirs in less than a year.

Chloe's birth parents—Well, Charlotte couldn't think of Chloe's birth parents without losing her cool. Suffice it to say, they'd finally been declared unfit and their rights taken from them.

After a long, strenuous, and heartbreaking two years spent in and out of a courtroom.

"She's really going to be ours," Charlotte whispered, her own voice cracking a little.

Ryker reached for Chloe, who squealed in delight as her daddy lifted her from her highchair and tucked her against his chest. He held his other arm out toward Charlotte. "Come here, *amor*. I want to hold my girls."

She cuddled into her husband's chest and wrapped her arm around Chloe's small, warm back. "You can hold us forever if you want."

He pressed a kiss first to Chloe's soft curls, then to Charlotte's head. "That sounds perfect to me."

About the Author

Micah Persell holds a bachelor's degree in English and a double master's degree in literature and English pedagogy. She is an award-winning and Amazon-bestselling author of 11 romances, a pet addict, wife, mommy, classical musician, and bibliophile. She lives with her brood in Southern California where she plays in the local symphony, teaches, and writes. She loves connecting with readers. You can find her at *www.micahpersell.com*, on Facebook at *www.facebook.com/MicahPersell*, and on Twitter @MicahPersell.

Other Titles by Micah Persell

Standalone Erotic Romance
Uncharted Waters

Erotic Romance Trilogy
Hard Work
Stiff Competition
Binding Law

Paranormal Romance Series Operation: Middle of the Garden
Of Eternal Life
Of the Knowledge of Good and Evil
Of Consuming Fire
Of Alliance and Rebellion
Of Blind Fate

Historical Romance
Emma: The Wild and Wanton Edition by Jane Austen and Micah Persell
Persuasion: The Wild and Wanton Edition by Jane Austen and Micah Persell

Acknowledgements

A thank-you first to Tara and Julie, formerly of Crimson Romance. It has been a dream working with you both on this trilogy. Tara, your ideas for this book when it was in development were spot-on. And, Julie, you know how I feel about you. You do your thing so well. I know the future holds amazing things for you both.

A thank you as well to Sandy and Heidi for the help with my Spanish. Any mistakes are, of course, my own.

Thank you to Lyn, *Binding Law*'s sensitivity reader, for helping bring Charlotte to life.

Stephanie, I so appreciate your eye for detail, and that you stuck with me through the whole trilogy, even amid a huge publishing shake-up.

And, finally, a thank you to this book, for being done at last. You were my constant companion through three other books' edits, a complicated pregnancy, childbirth, and the ensuing all-nighters. I love you, but I'm kicking you out now. Time to fly.

Bibliography

Avvo. "20 Percent of Marriages End within First 5 Years."

Https://Www.avvo.com/Legal-Guides/Ugc/Marriage-

Divorce-Statistics, 12 Apr. 2010.

Banschick, Mark. "73 Percent Third Marriage Divorce Rate."

Https://Www.psychologytoday.com/Us/Blog/the-

Intelligent-Divorce/201202/the-High-Failure-Rate-

Second-and-Third-Marriages, 6 Feb. 2012.

Brix, Lisa. "Divorce Rate 3 Times Higher in Couples

Experiencing Infertility."

Http://Sciencenordic.com/Childless-Couples-Have-

More-Divorces, 11 Feb. 2014.

Fuller, Matt, director. *Autism in Love*. CG Entertainment,

2015.

Partner Support. "50 Percent of NT-AS Marriages Are

Celibate." Http://Www.aspergerpartner.com/Intimacy-

and-Romance-in-Nt-as-Relations.html, 25 Mar. 2017.

Roberson, Kenneth. "Sex and Asperger's Syndrome." *Kenneth Roberson, Ph.D.*, 2 June 2016, www.kennethrobersonphd.com/sex-aspergers-syndrome/.

Robison, John Elder. *Look Me in the Eye: My Life with Asperger's*. Ebury, 2009.

Stanford, Ashley. "80 Percent Divorce Rate for Marriage in Which One Partner Has Asperger's." Https://Books.google.com/Books?Id=NyGJHa2atDUC&Pg=PA42&Lpg=PA42&Dq=Asperger+Divorce+Rates&Source=Bl&Ots=njwuM0KmKs&Sig=9COFSnAC4uEyDm27M_ugA2KHU0I&Hl=En&Sa=X&Ei=30NYUqXTB-IyigLcwYHoBg&Ved=0CE4Q6AEwBQ#v=Onepage&q=Asperger%20divorce%20rates&f=False, 2003.

Trunk, Penelope. "What It's like to Have Sex with Someone with Asperger's." *Penelope Trunk*, 18 Nov. 2010, blog.penelopetrunk.com/2010/11/18/what-its-like-to-

have-sex-with-someone-with-aspergers/.

University of Michigan. "22 Percent Higher Divorce Rate in

Couples Who Experience Miscarriage."

Https://Www.uofmhealth.org/News/1535couples-

More-Likely-to-Break-up-after-Pre, 5 Apr. 2010.

Made in the USA
Las Vegas, NV
13 May 2022